NOW THE TRUTH

M A COMLEY

JEAMEL PUBLISHING LIMITED

New York Times and USA Today bestselling author M A Comley
Published by Jeamel Publishing limited
Copyright © 2020 M A Comley
Digital Edition, License Notes

This is a work of fiction. Names, characters, places and incidents are a product of the author's imagination or are used fictitiously, and any resemblance to actual persons living or dead, business establishments, events or locales is entirely coincidental.

ALSO BY M A COMLEY

Irrational Justice (a 10,000 word short story)

Seeking Justice (a 15,000 word novella)

Caring For Justice (a 24,000 word novella)

Savage Justice (a 17,000 word novella Featuring THE UNICORN)

Clever Deception (co-written by Linda S Prather)

Tragic Deception (co-written by Linda S Prather)

Sinful Deception (co-written by Linda S Prather)

Forever Watching You (DI Miranda Carr thriller)

Wrong Place (DI Sally Parker thriller #1)

No Hiding Place (DI Sally Parker thriller #2)

Cold Case (DI Sally Parker thriller#3)

Deadly Encounter (DI Sally Parker thriller #4)

Lost Innocence (DI Sally Parker thriller #5)

Goodbye, My Precious Child (DI Sally Parker #6)

Web of Deceit (DI Sally Parker Novella with Tara Lyons)

The Missing Children (DI Kayli Bright #1)

Killer On The Run (DI Kayli Bright #2)

Hidden Agenda (DI Kayli Bright #3)

Murderous Betrayal (Kayli Bright #4)

Dying Breath (Kayli Bright #5)

Taken (Kayli Bright #6 coming March 2020)

The Hostage Takers (DI Kayli Bright Novella)

No Right to Kill (DI Sara Ramsey #1)

Killer Blow (DI Sara Ramsey #2)

The Dead Can't Speak (DI Sara Ramsey #3)

Deluded (DI Sara Ramsey #4)

The Murder Pact (DI Sara Ramsey #5)

Twisted Revenge (DI Sara Ramsey #6)

The Lies She Told (DI Sara Ramsey #7)

For The Love Of… (DI Sara Ramsey #8) coming July 2020

Run For Your Life (DI Sara Ramsey #9) Coming August 2020

I Know The Truth (A psychological thriller)

The Caller (co-written with Tara Lyons)

Evil In Disguise – a novel based on True events

Deadly Act (Hero series novella)

Torn Apart (Hero series #1)

End Result (Hero series #2)

In Plain Sight (Hero Series #3)

Double Jeopardy (Hero Series #4)

Criminal Actions (Hero Series #5)

Regrets Mean Nothing (Hero #6)

Sole Intention (Intention series #1)

Grave Intention (Intention series #2)

Devious Intention (Intention #3)

Merry Widow (A Lorne Simpkins short story)

It's A Dog's Life (A Lorne Simpkins short story)

A Time To Heal (A Sweet Romance)

A Time For Change (A Sweet Romance)

High Spirits

The Temptation series (Romantic Suspense/New Adult Novellas)

Past Temptation

Lost Temptation

Cozy Mystery Series

Murder at the Wedding

Murder at the Hotel

Murder by the Sea

Tempting Christa (A billionaire romantic suspense co-authored by Tracie Delaney #1)

Avenging Christa (A billionaire romantic suspense co-authored by Tracie Delaney #2)

ACKNOWLEDGMENTS

Thank you as always to my rock, Jean, I'd be lost without
you in my life.

Special thanks as always go to @studioenp for their superb cover
design expertise.

My heartfelt thanks go to my wonderful editor Emmy Ellis, my
proofreaders Joseph, Barbara and Jacqueline for spotting all the
lingering nits.

Thank you also to my amazing ARC group who help to keep me sane
during this process.

To Mary, gone, but never forgotten. I hope you found the peace you
were searching for my dear friend.

PROLOGUE

Thankfully, she landed on her feet with a heavy thud, relieved to be back on solid ground. In the distance, the mighty roar of an explosion followed by plumes of orange-and-grey smoke filled the air over the mountains.

That was her cue to get out of there. To distance herself before she was discovered.

She tore off her backpack and tried to gather the billowing fabric in the gusty wind as it hampered her efforts. Her task completed, she bolted for the trees ahead. Running as fast as her tired, shaking legs would carry her. Her chest hurting, her heart pounding and her fear intensifying with each frantic step.

Why had she done it?

After years of living through that hell, a cruel existence, what had made her finally crack?

She paused to catch her breath, her body trembling out of control as the realisation and shock set in.

Don't stop! I need to get as far away from here as possible. If the truth ever comes out...my life as I know it will end...

*L*ucy left the house just before seven that evening. It was April, a nippy chill in the evening air, but not so bad as to warrant her spoiling her beautiful outfit by covering it with a coat. She'd spent a small fortune on the sparkly sequinned top; it would be a shame if no one saw it. She had agreed to meet Trisha in town as she lived a few miles on the other side. It would be silly for Trisha to come all the way over here to pick her up, even though Trisha had tried to insist. Trisha was her one and only good friend, the person she could rely on most in this world.

She had no one else.

Her stilettos clacked against the pavement. It sounded like a radio prop they likely used back in the sixties. She imagined a man standing near a microphone, bashing two coconut shells together, and chuckled.

It was good hearing herself laugh. She hadn't done very much of that over the years, not really. Life hadn't been as kind to her as it had to others. One constant, who helped to keep her spirits up, was Trisha. Some would call her a tad nutty, but Lucy loved her wayward wit. It was what made her stand out from the crowd.

The neon lights of the wine bar beamed ahead of her. Not far now, thank goodness, as her feet had begun hurting nearly half a mile back.

What was she thinking, wearing high heels when she intended to walk over a mile into town? It wasn't the brightest idea she'd had recently.

Trisha was standing by the door, waiting for her. She jumped up and down with excitement. "God, I thought you weren't coming. I was about to ring you." She kissed her on both cheeks and squeezed her tightly.

"Am I late? I left my watch at home and had no idea of the time."

Trisha shook her head in disgust. "Ideal way to keep track of the time...not. What are you like? I don't suppose it occurred to you to look at your phone? Still, let's not let it spoil our evening. We've got a lot of making up to do." She hooked her arm through Lucy's and steered her towards the busy bar.

"I'm sorry. Have you been waiting long?" she shouted above the noise of the other punters chatting and the music playing in the background.

"Forget about it, it's done and dusted, and you're here now. What do you want to drink?"

"I'm not sure what I fancy. What are you having?"

"Prosecco. Want the same?"

"Go on then, you've twisted my arm."

They stayed together at the bar until Trisha was served and then they headed towards the tables. They managed to find a small one right at the back. Not ideal, but it would do for now.

"You're looking good, Lucy. What's your secret?"

Lucy chuckled. "You're nuts. I've done nothing different, not lately." She ran a hand down the length of her blonde hair. It had taken her a while to get used to the new colour. Now she felt a natural blonde, if that made sense.

Trisha beamed at her. "You're amazing...just saying."

"You're pretty spectacular yourself. How's work?"

"Do we have to discuss it? My tyrant of a boss has been expecting me to put in the hours lately for very little compensation."

"What? No overtime pay?"

"Yep, keeps saying the business is suffering and we all have to be prepared to make sacrifices or face losing our jobs."

"What a cheeky shit! I hope you told him where to get off with that notion."

"I did, after a few nights of working an extra hour or two. It's about time he stopped taking me for granted. I love working at the gallery, but if he wants to extend the hours, he needs to step up and do the extra hours himself."

"Too right. He should be the one to forfeit his evenings for no pay, not you. I can't believe the audacity of the man, he's so inconsiderate. Have you thought about moving on?"

"I've thought about it, but not really looked into it. I can't say I've had a lot of spare time recently. Anyway, who wants to talk about my boring work? We're here to have some fun. It's been at least a month since I've seen you in the flesh. What's been happening in your exciting world?"

Lucy's eyes widened. "Are you kidding me? Exciting world? That'll be the day. I've been working my butt off as usual, rarely go out because I can't afford to. My salary just covers the rent and barely anything else."

Trisha raised a hand to stop her. "There's a solution to that. I've told you countless times to move in with me."

"And I love you for suggesting it. I just think living on top of each other could jeopardise our friendship."

"What a bunch of crap, as if we'd allow that to happen. Honestly, my house is your house, especially after what you've been through." Trisha had the decency to lower her voice when she mentioned the last part.

Lucy subconsciously ran a hand over her hair again. It was a constant reminder of her past. "We'll see. Money is super tight, and it would be an ideal solution. Let me think about it, all right?"

"Take all the time in the world, love. The offer is there for you. How's your job going? It's taken you a while to settle in, hasn't it?"

"Yeah, this is the fifth job I've had since…you know, but I feel good about this one. Working at the travel agent's appears to suit me, and the money is better than the other jobs I've had. At least I have the funds to feed myself properly these days—nothing else, mind." She laughed, trying to brush off how poor she felt.

Trisha's smile faded. "I'm worried about you. Please come and live with me? You're wasting away. I see the proof. You might think you're disguising it well by wearing a baggy top, young lady."

Lucy's cheeks warmed under her friend's scrutiny. "I'm fine. I wanted to shed a few pounds to feel better about myself. I'm at a good weight now."

"I could always slice off a few of my pounds and attach them to your thighs. Promise me you won't lose any more weight?"

She rolled her eyes and sipped her drink. "I promise. Enough about me. What about that new fella of yours? I want to know all the gossip, the ins and outs."

Trisha chuckled. "Really? All the bedroom secrets? You'd be surprised what that man can do with a loo brush."

"Oh my! No, spare me the details, please."

"Your face is a picture. As if I'd allow someone near me with one of those. I was winding you up."

"Oh dear, gullible me. The trouble is, I never know when you're telling the truth or pulling my leg."

"After all these years, that's very disappointing." Trisha wagged her finger.

"I know. Silly me. I need to nip to the loo, the prosecco has gone right through me. You stay here, guard the table with your life."

Trisha nodded, and Lucy set off. She weaved her way through the bustling crowd, which had increased considerably since they'd arrived, to the ladies' toilet situated halfway through the wine bar. "Ouch!" She slapped a man's arm. "Clumsy idiot. You just stepped on my size fives with your size tens."

"Sorry, love. I was trying to get out of your way. Want me to kiss it better for you?" He bent over and tugged at her leg.

She slapped him again. "No, thank you! Get your hands off me."

The group of friends he was with erupted into laughter.

One of the other men shouted, "Don't mind him, love, he's desperate for a date."

"Oi, Badger, no I ain't," the great oaf replied.

"*He* might be, but I'm not," she said, sweeping her mane of hair over her shoulder and continuing on her journey.

She sighed once she reached the toilet door. There was a queue. She joined the end of it and waited patiently for her chance to come. She decided to do a spot of people-watching to while away the time. Most of the women in there went to the loo, failed to wash their hands, and then messed around with either their hair or makeup before they exited the main door. She shuddered at the thought of touching the loo door after them. *And they wonder why there are so many germs around these days.*

She did her business, made a point of washing her hands with the soap provided and dried them on the paper towel from the dispenser. She took an extra one and used it on the handle of the door to protect her hands. She had standards to uphold. Lucy opened her handbag and tucked the towel inside and set off back to the table again. There was an outer door she had to go through, and a man pulled it open as she reached for it. His sapphire-blue eyes sparkled with amusement. She stepped back to allow him past.

"No, I insist, after you." He bowed and motioned for her to pass.

"Why, thank you, kind sir. I guess the art of chivalry isn't dead after all."

He tilted his head, his smile still in place, and asked, "Sorry, am I missing something?"

She pointed at the great oaf who'd flattened her foot moments earlier. "I had a run-in with him before. He stood on my foot."

"Ah." His gaze drifted down to the floor. "It's such a pretty foot, I can understand why he took a fancy to it."

They both laughed. "Thanks, I think. I'd better get back to my friend."

"That's a shame."

She frowned. "Why?"

"I was enjoying your company," he said without faltering.

Her cheeks warmed beneath his gaze. "You flatter me, sir."

"I'd like to do more than that. Would you be up to going out for a drink with me?"

"I…er…I'm not sure." *Run for the hills, you know you want to. Don't you dare accept. You could be walking into another trap.*

"Why the hesitation? Oh, sorry, do you have a boyfriend?" he asked.

"No, it's nothing like that. Maybe now isn't the right time."

He took a card from his shirt pocket and handed it to her. "Ring me if you change your mind. I'm Matthew, by the way."

She accepted the card and slipped it in her handbag without studying it. "Thanks, I'm not sure I will. But it was nice meeting you."

"Believe me, when I say this, the feeling is mutual. You're a beautiful young woman."

Again, her cheeks flared under his intense gaze. "See you around," she flung over her shoulder as she swept past him and made her way through the crowd and back to Trisha, intentionally avoiding the big oaf en route.

"Are you all right? You seem a bit flustered? I knew I should have gone with you."

Lucy took the man's card from her handbag and pushed it across the table towards Trisha. "I just got asked out on a date, I think."

"What? You think? What do you mean? A company director, oooh…sounds interesting. Point him out to me."

Lucy glanced over her shoulder but failed to see the handsome stranger. "He was on his way into the loo. I'll watch out for him."

"Some girls have all the luck. What did he actually say?"

"You're spoken for, remember? Anyway, get this…he called me *a beautiful woman*…"

"Phew, that's a bloody relief! There's nothing wrong with his eyesight then."

Lucy sniggered. "Daft mare. Then he asked me if I'd like to go for a drink with him."

"Blimey! Just like that? That kind of thing has never happened to me. How do you feel about it? Wait…what was your response first?"

"I said it wasn't the right time for me."

"What? Sweetheart..." Trisha leaned forward and lowered her voice. "It's been five years since... Come on, time is wasting if you want to start a family."

"How dare you! Bloody cheek, I'm only thirty-two."

"Ticktock, and yes, your biological clock is crying out to be serviced."

"You're warped. You do come out with some strange sayings. There's nothing wrong with my clock, I'll have you know."

"And you know that for definite, do you?"

Lucy took another sip of her drink. "No, but...bloody hell, how did we get on to the subject of my fertility?"

Trisha grinned, her front wonky tooth standing out like a beacon. Her gaze drifted behind Lucy, and she blew out a whistle. "Hot man alert. Is he the one?"

Lucy hesitated for an instant and then swivelled in her seat. Her gaze latched on to his. He smiled broadly and dipped his head as if to acknowledge her. Embarrassed, she turned back to face Trisha. "Yep. What do you think?"

"You want my honest opinion?"

"Of course."

"I think you're crazy not to take him up on his offer and even crazier for not getting him in that damn loo and ripping his clothes off. Crikey, you must be well up for it after all these years of celibacy."

"Seriously? I can't believe you would openly come out and say that."

"Why? I'm aware of a girl's needs. You're only fooling yourself if you deny your inner passions, love. How did you leave it with him?"

"He gave me his card and told me to ring him. I can't, Trisha. Unless you've experienced..."

Her friend raised her hand to stop her. "I'm mindful of what you went through, but sodding hell, Lucy, time won't wait around for you. Are you telling me you're never going to get involved with another man again? Ever?"

"Never say never, as my old mum used to say. God! I have to admit that bumping into him has ignited something I presumed would lay dormant for the rest of my days. Do I take the gamble? What if it goes belly-up, what then? Will my nerves handle it? I've been hanging on by a thread all these years, and now this." Unexpected tears filled her eyes.

Trisha left her seat and knelt on the floor in front of her. "I feel your pain, sweetheart. But there comes a time in this life…well, if you don't try, then how do you know if you'll succeed or not? Am I making any sense? Have I had too much prosecco? It feels like my tongue is tying itself into knots. Maybe I'm super-excited for you."

Lucy heaved out a breath and dared to look over her shoulder again. Matthew was staring back at her and he raised his glass in her direction while the group of friends he was with continued to chat. His attention appeared to be solely on her. In one way, she found that off-putting and, in another, the notion sent a spear of excitement shooting through her veins. *Should I give him a chance? What if…? Maybe Trisha is right. How will I know if I don't take a chance?* "I'm not sure."

Trisha sat back on her chair again. "Well, if I were in your shoes and a hunk like that was after me…it's a no-brainer."

"And if you were in my shoes five years ago, how do you think you would've handled the situation?" she snapped back. "I'm sorry, I didn't mean to say that."

"Shit! I was there for you at the end of it all, but life goes on, sweetie. It's time to put yourself out there again. You have the opportunity handed to you on a plate, take it. If it goes wrong, then…"

"It's the going wrong part that I'm struggling to get my head around. Yes, I'm attracted to him, I'd be lying if I said I wasn't…"

"Then give him a call. Sooner rather than later I'd advise, before he hooks up with someone else in the meantime."

"How do I know he's single and not one of these godawful married men out on the prowl for a mistress to bed now and again?"

Trisha sighed and shrugged. "It's better than him being gay, which most of the handsome blokes are these days."

"You're twisted. You believe a married man on the lookout for a willing mistress is okay, is that what you're telling me?"

"Okay, maybe that came out wrong. What I meant to say is, both scenarios are far from ideal. Anyway, it's all pie in the sky, you haven't got a clue what his background is. Oh, wait, give me that card."

Lucy pushed it across the table again while Trisha extracted her phone from her handbag. "What are you doing?"

"Googling the bugger. Now then, let's see what comes up."

Lucy gasped. "You can't do that. It's an invasion of his privacy."

Trisha shook her head and waved away the suggestion then angled her phone so Lucy could see the results. "Is it heck? Here you go. Wow, what do you know? He's only one of those socialites."

"A politician?" Lucy asked, confused.

"A socialite, not socialist, numpty. He goes to major social events, the type only the rich and famous people attend."

Lucy stared at Trisha, her mouth dropping open. She gulped and closed it again, sharpish. "Blimey! I'm glad I rejected him then. I'd be well out of my depth."

"Nonsense. He's the type of guy who probably has women fawning all over him. I bet he wasn't even on the lookout for a female companion when he bumped into you. Let's see what else it says about him. Oh my…"

"What? Stop bloody teasing and just tell me." She surprised herself at how eager she was to learn more about the man who had taken her breath away, who was continuing to have that effect on her, even though he was sitting on the other side of the bar.

"His father is one of the top judges in the UK."

She slumped back in her chair as if someone had just shot her with a crossbow and arrow. "Bang goes any chance of me getting involved, if that's the case."

"You what? Why should that affect your decision?"

Lucy heaved out a shuddering breath and rolled her eyes. "Think about it…"

Trisha growled. "Crap…I'm such a dunderhead at times. What was I thinking?"

"Put the phone away. Your job is done now."

"Meaning?"

"Meaning, there's no way I could ever get involved with Mr Matthew Wallender, either in this world or the next."

Trisha tutted and slotted her phone back in her bag. "I have one thing left to say on the subject."

"Go on, surprise me."

"You're wrong. The least you could do is go on one date with him and see how things turn out. After that, then you can make a proper decision, not before."

"Get you. What about gut instinct? Doesn't that factor into the equation?"

"Not really. Not when you've come into contact with him in person. It's not as if he's reached out to you online. Now that's a reason to be cautious, right there."

Several different scenarios played out in her mind during the course of the evening, the main one being whether she should take the plunge or not. She even shot Matthew a few secret glances and caught him looking her way as well. Confused, she continued her evening with Trisha and tried to force the issue out of her mind.

"So," Trisha began, her words slurring a little after downing her third glass of prosecco. "Why don't we give it a shot? You move in with me, leave that shithole of a house you rent at an ex...exnorburant price."

"You mean *exorbitant*, right?"

Trisha waved her hand in front of her, going a little cross-eyed at the same time. "Whatever. I knew what I meant, stop taking the piss out of me."

"I wasn't. Look, we should discuss this when you're sober. I wouldn't want you making any promises you'd feel awkward keeping in the cold light of day."

"You do talk a lot of twiggle."

"That would be *twaddle*."

"Yeah, that as well."

"Okay, here's the thing. If I agreed to move in with you, how would that leave things with Neil? I can't see him taking too kindly to me invading his privacy with you."

"Nonsense. Leave him to me. As long as I keep him well-serviced, then he has no need to complain. Anyway, he doesn't live with me, he has his own gaff, so most of the time it would just be the two of us. Go on, give it a trial at least."

"And what if we fall out? Where will that leave me?"

"Rentals are two a penny around our neck of the woods, but we won't fall out because I lurve you like a sister."

"And siblings rarely fall out, right?"

Trisha screwed up her nose and poked her tongue out. "All right, I hear you, neither of us know what it's like to have a sibling."

"Exactly. Let me think it over. Can we talk about the nitty-gritty, the rent?"

"What are you paying now?"

"It's horrendous—nine hundred plus the bills."

Trisha let out a low whistle. "Bloody Nora! That's absurd, no wonder you don't have any spare cash to your name. What about half that, four hundred and fifty, and half the bills? You'll be quids in, we both will. How about it?"

Lucy chewed on her lip for a few minutes, sorely tempted to say yes. "I have to nip to the loo again. Let me think about it overnight at least, and I'll ring you in a few days. I'll be right back."

"You do that. Umm…behave yourself. Don't go coming back here with yet another business card and the promise of another date. I'll get jealous if you do."

"No fear of that happening. Go easy on that stuff until I return, you hear me?"

"Afraid I'll drink your share?" Trisha laughed, raising her glass.

Lucy wound her way through the throng of customers. The noise level had risen to rowdy now that people had downed several drinks. Without realising she was doing it, she darted her eyes around, searching for Matthew. His friends were still at the table, but he was nowhere to be seen. Her heart sank a little for some unknown reason. She pushed open the ladies' and joined yet another queue, then went through the same procedure of washing her hands, drying them and taking an extra towel to open the door. She was just tucking the paper into her bag when a voice startled her.

"Hello again. We must stop meeting like this."

"Oh gosh, you scared the shit out of me. Yes, we must, especially as we always seem to bump into each other outside the ladies'. Is there anything you'd care to confess?"

His eyes sparkled with amusement, matching the broad smile that lit up his face. "I love a lady with a sense of humour. Are you sure I can't tempt you on that date?"

"Sense of humour, me? That's got to be a first. I'm still contemplating your offer. If you keep hounding me, you'll only put me off."

He held up his hands. "Hey, that's the last thing I want. I'm delighted to hear that you're thinking over my proposition. I suppose I should be grateful for that, at least. What did you find out about me?"

Her gaze dropped. *Shit! How had he figured out we were looking him up on Google? Probably because we kept glancing in his direction at the time! Amateur sleuths always mess up in the grand scheme of things.*

"I don't know what you're talking about," she said, trying to sound as natural as possible.

He winked at her. "Your secret is safe with me. It was pretty damn obvious what you two were up to. Now, if you'd come out on that date with me, I would openly tell you the truth. You shouldn't believe everything you read on Google. Sometimes it can be worse than *The Sun* for its lack of factual content, I can assure you."

"I'm sorry," she mumbled, like a caught-out teenager.

He lifted her chin with his finger, leaned forward and brushed her lips with his.

Shocked, she took a step back. "Please, don't do that."

He appeared put out by her words, as if he wasn't used to being rejected by a woman, or was she misreading the signs?

"I apologise. I didn't mean to cause you any offence. I'd better get back to my friends." He hurried out of the door before she had a chance to say anything else.

What had she done? Why had she reacted that way? She turned

around and headed back into the toilet to survey the damage. Her cheeks were redder than a stop light, and her heart fluttered wildly. That one kiss had done so much harm, and yet it had excited her beyond words. Her confusion mounted. She wanted to take flight, and yet there was a part of her desperate to remain, to see if he tried anything again. But why? Five years of solitude she'd put up with. No thoughts of ever being with anyone else, and now this. What was her body telling her? That it needed the attention? This man's attention in particular? Should she listen to it or run for shelter?

In the end, she decided to return to Trisha, keeping her gaze focused on the way ahead, trying hard not to search for Matthew during her journey. Trisha was wide-eyed as she sat down.

"What's wrong?" Lucy asked.

"Matthew came over to speak to me. He just left; I was about to come and search for you."

"Shit! What did he say?"

"That he'd done something stupid and that he was ashamed. He passed on his apology and asked for your forgiveness. Bloody hell, Luc, what did he do? Do we need to call the police? You look...well, dumfounded. Did he hurt you? Tell me he didn't, I don't want to believe that of him."

Lucy covered her face with her hands to hide the sudden tears that stung her eyes.

Trisha touched her hand and pleaded with her, "Sweetheart, tell me, don't shut me out."

In a whisper, she revealed, "He kissed me."

"Wowzer...what the fuck?"

"That's precisely how I reacted. Shit, I went over the top, I know I did."

"When a stranger kisses you, I think you're entitled to some sort of reaction."

"I can't believe he would come over here and speak with you. What's that all about?"

"He seemed mortified to me. Why don't you have it out with him?"

"What, now?"

"Now's as good a time as any. Go on, march over there and give him what for. Make sure you show him up in front of his friends."

"Tit for tat? He involved you so I should involve them? Is that truly the answer?"

"Aww...ignore me, it's the drink talking. I can't believe he kissed you. Come on, spill, what was it like?"

Lucy shook her head. "You're incorrigible." She discreetly glanced over her shoulder, only to find Matthew staring at her. Self-consciously, she turned away again. "Shit! Why me? Why did he have to pick on me?"

"I can't answer that until you describe the type of kiss he gave you."

"What difference should that make?"

"Whoa! Are you kidding me? Girl, five years of not having a man around has seriously addled your brain. Was it a full-on kiss? A peck on the cheek or the forehead? Did it involve tongues?"

"You're sick. It was a slight brush of his lips against mine..."

"And? What aren't you telling me? Holy crap! You liked it, didn't you?"

Lucy scratched the back of her neck and flicked her hair over her shoulder. "The truth? It floored me. I didn't know how to react."

"So, what did you do? Return the kiss?"

"I took a step back. He looked offended, and things went downhill from there."

"Jesus, you and I need to sit down and have a proper chat about the chase, love."

"*The Chase*? What the hell has a TV programme got to do with this?"

Trisha bashed her forehead with her clenched fist. "Shit! Why did I frigging do that? My head has had enough and is pounding as it is. Not the TV show, the chase, as in, 'courting'."

Lucy laughed. "Is that word still doing the rounds after all these years?"

"You're hopeless. I still maintain you should go over there and make a show of him. What's stopping you?"

"Doh! The fact I feel out of my depth, unsure how to react, as in, I've been wrapped up in my own little world for a long time now. I have no idea how to speak to men any more, let alone how to play the game of *chase* with one as fit as him."

Trisha pointed at her. "And there it is, you've finally admitted you're attracted to him."

"I wouldn't go as far as saying that. He's definitely sparked something within me, but at the moment, I'm unsure what that is. The truth is, I'm scared."

"Oh, sweetheart, you're bound to be. We all are when we've been out in the wilderness for so long, like you have. It's time to saddle up your horse again, love, and dive in, see where it gets you."

"You think?"

"No doubt about it. I'd give him a call tomorrow. What harm would it do to go out with him on one date? On one proviso."

Lucy frowned. "What's that?"

"That I hear all the juicy details."

They both laughed, and Lucy's gaze was pulled in Matthew's direction once again. He was staring right at her.

She rose from her chair. "I'll be right back."

"Blimey, there must be something seriously wrong with your bladder, girlfriend."

However, Lucy didn't go to the toilet. Instead, her feet carried her in the direction of Matthew and his friends. Her heart thundered against her ribs. He smiled and got out of his seat. She marched right up to him and kissed him. His friends cheered. She took a step back, and his expression was one of utter shock.

"Name the place and I'll be there."

"Here at seven, tomorrow?"

She screwed her nose up. "I fancy a change."

"All right. What about the Georgian Hotel, do you know it?"

"Yes, and no, I'm not going to a hotel with you."

He tutted. "I meant in the public bar, nothing sordid, not on our first date anyway."

"Seven o'clock on the dot. If you're late, I'll walk away, and you'll never see me again." She swivelled on her heel and walked back to her table.

"I'll be there," he called after her amongst yet more cheers from his friends.

She flopped into her chair, exhausted by the exhilaration rifling through her body. "Shit! Did I just do that? Tell me I was dreaming."

Trisha stared at her in open-mouthed disbelief. "Wow...I'm shocked."

"Appalled shocked?"

"No, just shocked. I never knew you had it in you."

Lucy took a huge gulp from her glass. "Neither did I. Bugger, what have I done?"

"I'd say you've started the adventure of a lifetime. Hang on tight, baby, I predict you're going to be in for a hell of a ride."

She swallowed hard. "Ya think? What if...?"

"No *what ifs*. I won't allow those two words to ever be mentioned again. You hear me?"

Lucy saluted her. "If you insist. Bugger! Have I really done the right thing?"

"You have. Think positive. Where are you meeting him?"

She rolled her eyes. "At the Georgian Hotel."

"Whoa! A hotel on your first date. Go get him, tiger."

"In the public bar, idiot."

"Still, it's suitably convenient if things develop nicely between you during the course of the evening."

Lucy puffed out her cheeks. *What have I done?*

2

———

"*I* insist. Come over straight from work. I'll even let you choose one of my outfits—that is if you haven't got anything suitable of your own to wear," Trisha said.

Lucy chewed on her lip in the tiny staffroom at work, grateful for her friend's thoughtfulness as she'd spent half the night awake, worrying about just that. "Okay, if you're sure it's not putting you out. What time do you get home?"

"Around six. It'll still be pushing it for you to get ready and out of my place by seven."

"It's doable, at a push."

"I've gotta fly. TTFN, lovely."

"TTFN." She was still daydreaming about the evening ahead as Shirley came into the small kitchen area, carrying a huge bunch of flowers. "Oh my, they're beautiful. Aren't you lucky? Oh no, it's not your birthday, is it?"

Shirley smiled and thrust the bouquet at Lucy's chest. "You're the lucky one, and I was about to say the same."

Lucy gasped and took the flowers, her hand shaking uncontrollably. "What? Have you spotted a card? And no, it's not my birthday, not for a few months yet. Who could they be from?"

"Stop asking damn questions and open the bloody card, I'm dying to know here." Shirley removed the card and gave it to her.

On the envelope was written: *TO THE BEAUTIFUL LADY.* She knew instantly who had sent them. No one had ever bestowed such a flattering compliment on her before. Her cheeks warmed under Shirley's gaze.

"Well?" she asked, folding her arms and impatiently tapping her foot.

"If you must know, I went out with my friend last night and met a man."

"Did you sleep with him?" Shirley said, shocked.

"No, I did not. What type of girl do you take me for?"

"Sorry, it's just that I'm bound to think that if you only met the man last night and he's already spending that amount on you. Do you have any idea how much a bunch of flowers costs to deliver these days?"

"I don't. Is it expensive?" She peered into the centre and saw there was a vase inside.

"At least seventy-five quid for something that humongous."

Lucy gasped and shook her head. "Bloody hell."

"Hey, if you've only just met him and he's sending you expensive gifts, then in my book he's a bloody keeper. I'd better get back and man the phones."

"Okay, I'll pop these down and be right with you."

"Umm…aren't you going to read what's inside?"

"Maybe, when you leave me alone."

Shirley huffed out a breath and slipped out of the room.

Lucy fumbled with the tiny envelope to reveal the card. *Looking forward to seeing you at seven this evening. Matthew. X.*

Her heart fluttered, not at the words he'd written but at the fact he'd added a kiss at the end. That was until she gasped and her heart almost ground to a halt. *How the heck does he know where I work? He doesn't even know my name, for fuck's sake, and here he is sending me flowers. What's that all about?*

She spent the rest of the afternoon distracted. Shirley needed to reprimand her several times while she was filling up the brochures as she'd placed a number of them in wrong positions on the shelves. "Shit! I'm so sorry. Not sure where my head is at today."

Shirley tutted. "I don't have to be a shit-hot detective to answer that, Lucy. Look, you're as much use around here today as a chocolate teapot. Why don't you go home early? There, I can't believe I'm saying that but I am."

"Really? You'd do that for me?"

"Like I said, I can't see me getting much work out of you this afternoon. You have to promise me that you'll be in a better frame of mind tomorrow, yes?"

"I will. I promise. Oh gosh, you're so thoughtful. I'll make this up to you, I swear I will," she babbled, slipping her handbag off the back of her chair.

"Another thing, I need to hear all the gossip in the morning as well."

"*All* of it?" Lucy chuckled and hitched on her jacket.

"Maybe not all of it. Have fun. You deserve it, hon. For as long as I've known you, I swear I've never seen you look so happy, so this guy must be doing something right."

"Thanks, Shirley. Let's say this feels right. It remains to be seen if things turn out that way or I'm talking a load of twaddle."

"PMA, love, especially where this type of situation is concerned."

"It's a long time since I've had a positive mental attitude, I must admit."

"Maybe things are on the up for you at last, eh? Now go, before I change my mind. Don't forget your flowers either."

After collecting the bouquet from the restroom, she pecked her boss on the cheek and swept out of the door. It wasn't until she was on her way to fetch her beaten-up old car that she realised she didn't have a key to Trisha's house. She rang her friend, hoping she wouldn't disturb her dealing with a posh client at the gallery.

"Hey you, what's up?"

"Trisha, I've been let off work early. Would it be all right if I dropped by your place while you're out?"

"Of course. Come by now, if you want, I'm between clients. The next one is due in half an hour."

"That's great. I'm on my way."

"See you soon."

She drove for ten minutes and pulled into the car park of the posh gallery where Trisha worked. Trisha was waiting for her by the front door and dangled her house key for Lucy.

"You're a life-saver. All right if I have a shower?"

"There's enough water if you fancy a soak in the bath."

"Hmm…I'll think about it. Hey, Matthew sent me a huge bunch of flowers today."

"What? You're one hell of a lucky lady."

"I know. Okay, I'll nip home first. Anything I can do towards your dinner?"

"That's so sweet of you. No, I want you to concentrate on yourself for a change. I'll sort myself out when I get home. I shouldn't be late. Feel free to search through my wardrobe for something suitable. Hopefully you'll find something that fits you. We used to be the same size, but you've lost so much weight recently, I'm worried now."

"Don't be, I'm sure everything will be fine. Love you lots. See you later." She skipped down the steps and raced back to her car, her adrenaline pumping around her system as if it was being carried on a tidal wave.

She stopped off at her house, collected a few things like her makeup bag and a spare towel, and then drove over to Trisha's house, where she made herself at home.

After a quick scan through Trisha's wardrobe, she decided to wear a cream slim-fitting dress which accentuated her curves beautifully. She showered and slouched around in Trisha's dressing gown until five. Then she ended up in the kitchen, preparing a few ingredients to knock up a frittata for Trisha for when she eventually got home at six. She nibbled on a slice of pepper to stave off her own hunger pangs. It was then she realised she didn't have a clue if she would be eating with Matthew later or not? He'd only mentioned taking her out for a drink, nothing more. Now she was stuck with a dilemma. Should she grab a cheese sandwich while she was grating the cheese for the frittata or not? In the end, she settled on nibbling a chunk of cheese instead.

"Hi, honey, I'm home," Trisha shouted from the front door not long after six.

"I'm in the kitchen."

Trisha rested her head against the doorframe. "You didn't?" she asked, surveying the contents of the work surface in front of Lucy.

"I did. My way of paying you back. It won't take me ten minutes to finish it off for you."

"Oh no you don't, you've done enough already by the look of things. We need to concentrate all our efforts on getting you ready. What have you found to wear?"

"I'll show you. Want me to fix you a drink first?"

"No, I've got a bottle of white in the fridge. We'll sample a glass while we're getting you ready."

"Just the one for me. The last thing I want to do is show up there already tipsy. I wouldn't want to give Matthew the wrong impression."

"Nonsense. He's smitten. There's nothing you could either say or do that would put him off, take my word for that. One thing I considered after you dropped by earlier."

"What was that?"

"These flowers. How did he know where to send them?"

Lucy inhaled then exhaled a large breath and pointed at her. "Exactly what I thought. It's put me a little on edge, I must say."

"Don't be silly. There's probably a reasonable explanation. I would definitely demand an answer early on in the evening, if I were in your shoes."

"Damn, now you've prodded my worry gene. Should I be concerned? Should I cancel this evening?"

"Don't you dare. I could always come in disguise and keep an eye on you, if that would make you feel more comfortable."

"You'd do that for me?"

Trisha flung an arm around her shoulders and pulled her close. "I'd do anything for you, if you asked me to. The secrets we've shared over the years, I'd happily risk my life for you, you know that, don't you?"

"I do. You've been an absolute diamond friend since… I'm in two minds about this date now."

"Sorry, I shouldn't have said anything."

"Hey, there's no need for you to blame yourself, I had the same thought about the flowers but discounted the notion fairly quickly all the same."

"That's it. No arguments then, I'll be there with you, just in case. We'll make up a signal for you to give me once you feel comfortable enough with him, how's that?"

"You're amazing. Let me finish off your dinner for you first."

"I can tell I'm not going to win that argument. I'll go and get some suitable clothes on while you do that then." Trisha gulped down a little of her wine and then darted out of the room, leaving Lucy to knock up her dinner for her.

Ten minutes later, she served up the frittata accompanied with a sparse side salad she'd made from the ingredients she'd found in the fridge.

"Wow, this is delicious."

"I'll leave you to it and get ready now."

"I'll be up in a mo, once I've consumed this lot."

*A*t five minutes to seven, the pair of them eventually left the house. Lucy felt a million dollars in her outfit, however, she couldn't help wondering if all her effort would have a negative effect. What if Matthew showed up wearing a casual pair of jeans? She'd feel a right numpty.

"He's right, you know, you are beautiful, especially when you put the effort in," Trisha said, slowing the car outside the hotel. "Are you ready for this?"

"I think so. It's too late to back out now."

"No, it's not. Say the word, and I'll spin this baby around and go back home."

"We're here now. Don't forget the signal to come to my rescue if things get a bit heavy in there."

"A cough and two taps on your nose. Got it! How are you feeling?"

"Nervous, excited, bewildered, all mixed up together in a confusing cocktail of emotions. Why did I ever agree to meet him?"

"Because he's a dish and wealthy if you believe everything you read on Google."

"Ha! As if any of that bothers a simple girl like me."

"Stop dwelling on things and get in there. I'll give you a breather, park the car and come in a few minutes later. He won't recognise me in this wig, will he?"

"I doubt it. It's fabulous, by the way. I can't say I've ever seen you wearing it."

"I bought it in a sale, on a whim, and it's never seen the light of day until now. Come on, you, stop stalling and get in there."

"Okay, I need to go over the plan one more time, so I don't screw up. If things are going well, you'll leave the bar and go home, yes?"

"That's right. You should know if you feel comfortable in his presence or not within thirty minutes or so. I'll watch out for your signal in the meantime. Now go in there and have the time of your life with this hunk, and yes, that's an order."

"Yes, ma'am. Thanks for everything, Trisha, you're the best friend a girl could ever have."

"I know."

"The most modest, too. I'll see you in there."

They hugged, and Lucy left the vehicle. Her ankles wobbled a little in the high heels she'd chosen as she climbed the steps to the hotel. She glanced back over her shoulder to see Trisha's car move off. She tentatively stepped through the front door and paused to see which direction the public bar was in. The receptionist smiled at her.

"Can I help you? You look lost."

"I am. Sorry, I have to meet someone in the public bar; this is my first time here."

"Take the corridor on your right, and it's down there. Have a lovely evening."

"Thank you, I'm sure I will. It's a beautiful hotel."

The receptionist nodded and went back to dealing with some paperwork.

Lucy wandered down the corridor and found the bar. She spotted him right away. He was sitting on a stool, chatting to the barman. Lucy took a couple of calming breaths and walked towards him. She was halfway across the room when he appeared to sense her presence and turned her way.

His smile lit up his face. "Wow, you look sensational." He jumped off the stool and held out his arms for a hug.

Lucy slipped into them and allowed him to kiss her cheeks—two kisses, one on each side, which sent her pulse rate through the roof. "It's lovely to see you again. I haven't overdone it, have I?"

"Not at all. You're putting me to shame." He glanced down at the crisp denim covering his legs which probably cost more than she earned in a month.

"It's always easier for a man to get dressed. You look fine to me."

"What are you drinking?"

"I'll have a medium white wine, thank you."

"Shall we sit over there?" He pointed to a table in an alcove off to the side of the expansive room.

"Works well for me."

He put the order in as she made her way across the room. He joined her, and two minutes later, Trisha walked into the bar, ordered a drink and sat at a table ten feet or so away from them.

"How was your day?" he asked, his eyes doing their usual thing of sparkling under the lights.

"Eventful. I got the flowers."

He inclined his head. "Did you like them?"

"Yes, thank you. One thing I found puzzling, though, is how you knew where to send them."

"Ah, easily explained. One of the guys I was with last night—he fancies you, by the way—told me he'd noticed you at the travel agent's. I couldn't believe my luck, and then something dawned on me…"

"Oh gosh, don't say that. How embarrassing. Umm…what dawned on you?"

"I didn't get your name. Mind if we rectify that now?"

"Sorry, you gave me your card, and I foolishly neglected to tell you last night. It's Lucy Brent."

"Ah, it has a certain ring to it. What else should I know about you, Lucy Brent? Give me one fact that no one else knows about you."

Lucy placed a finger on her cheek and paused to think for a second or two. "That's a tough one. My best friend knows everything and more about me. Here's one: I like to drink wine in the rain."

"Wow, okay. I'll have to arrange that one day, leave it with me."

"Not so fast, buster, you can't ask me a question like that and not reciprocate."

"I like pancakes for breakfast, but they have to be slathered with chocolate spread and be doused in maple syrup."

"Sounds too sweet for my tastes and too sickly. So it would be fair to say you have a sweet tooth then?"

"It would. Strange for a man, yes?"

"I think so. Where does that stem from? Have you always had one?"

"Sort of. I grew up craving sweet things. Thankfully, I've always managed to keep my weight under control."

"Do you work out at the gym?"

"In the gym, to be more accurate. I have one at home. Enough about me, what about you? I want to know everything there is to know."

"I'm a boring plain Jane, who goes to work and then straight home most days."

"That's so sad. Out of necessity or choice?"

Her gaze dropped to her drink. "Necessity really. I love my job, but the pay is abysmal."

"Can't you find anything else more suitable?"

"I wish I could, but there's nothing around. That's enough about me. Is it true what they say about you?"

"Depends what you've managed to find out."

"That you're a socialite. You attend all the best parties in town."

"True, guilty as charged, although, every now and then I prefer to have some downtime with my mates, like last night."

"During my research, I rarely saw you with a woman on your arm. May I ask why?"

He laughed and sat back. "Your research, eh? You found me interesting enough to do some digging then, I take it."

"Ugh... sorry, now that you mention it, I did sound a tad stalkerish."

"Not at all. I'm flattered that you care enough to dig into my past. Actually, I also admire you for having the gumption to do it. There are so many nutters out there roaming the streets these days. I think more girls should take a leaf out of your book."

"Phew, okay, thanks for not tearing me to shreds. You haven't answered my question, though."

"Hmm...let me think. The last thing I want to do is come across as a chauvinistic pig, not on our first date anyway."

"Go on, you're not so far."

"Thanks for the vote of confidence. Okay, here it is, the truth... women tend to bore me."

Lucy's eyes widened, and her cheeks puffed out as she tried her best to hold on to the laugh tickling her throat.

"I've shocked you with that statement, I can tell."

She eventually let out the breath and admitted, "Not really, well, maybe a little. I simply wasn't expecting those words to tumble out of your mouth."

He buried his head in his hands and chortled, then he dropped his hands to the table, looked her straight in the eye and said, "The truth is, I've never met anyone who has taken my breath away...until last night."

"Me? After two meetings, outside the toilet may I add, you can honestly say that?"

"There are some things in this life that are absolute certainties. One of them is the way both my heart and my head reacted as soon as you walked past my table."

"What? So bumping into you outside the toilet the first time wasn't a coincidence?"

"Hardly. Don't think badly of me. As the card with the flowers said, and like I told you last night, you're beautiful, you take my breath away. If anyone was to ask me to describe my perfect woman, well, it would be you, every damn inch of you."

Lucy chewed on her bottom lip. No man had ever spoken to her this way before, ever. She wasn't sure how she felt after hearing his confession either. Should she be freaked out and run or be flattered and enjoy the ride?

"What's going on in that pretty head of yours? Did I say something wrong?"

"No, not really. I suppose I'm not used to talking to an honest man…" Her mouth clammed shut—she'd said enough.

"Are you going to enlighten me as to what you mean by that? Or keep me guessing?"

"Keep you guessing." She smiled, trying not to make a big deal of the situation.

"Ah, it's going to be like that, is it? Well, I suppose one day in the future you'll trust me enough to share what's going on in that pretty little head of yours, just not right now, eh?"

"Maybe. I have a few questions I need you to answer."

"Need? Ask away, my life is an open book. Most of it can be found on the internet, but carry on."

"Personal details," she mumbled, unsure whether she should go ahead and seek out the answers, especially as this was their first date.

He raised an eyebrow and folded his arms. "Go on then, shoot, and I promise to answer your questions with complete honesty, no matter what you ask."

"Fair enough." She opened her handbag and withdrew a notebook on which she had jotted down several one-line questions during the afternoon, in between pampering herself and throwing together Trisha's meal.

"The one thing I'd truly like the answer to, is why you don't seem to have a girlfriend."

"Is it obligatory?"

"Umm…no, I suppose it isn't. What I'm getting at is, that you appear to attend all these functions without a lady on your arm."

"And? Ah, I get it, what you're really trying to ask is if I'm gay."

She stared at him, her eyes out on stalks, and blustered, "No, I wasn't saying that at all. I truly wasn't."

He laughed, and she blew out a breath.

"You're teasing me."

"Sorry, yes. I suppose I'm quite a secretive person. Hmm…I'm not even sure that description is truly accurate enough either. You might find this hard to believe, but there are some pretty bad women out there these days."

"There are?" she mocked.

"Yes, there are, and I seem to attract them with my magnetism."

"Oh my God, I've heard it all now." She chuckled and reached for her drink.

He thumbed over his shoulder and leaned in. "By the way, your friend just left without you realising. Did she do the right thing?"

Lucy swivelled in her chair to find Trisha's seat empty. Her cheeks were on fire when she turned back to face him. "I…er…we…umm…"

"You don't have to explain. Did you have some kind of code that you would share if you wanted her to rescue you?"

She placed a hand over her eyes and rested her elbow on the table. "You nailed it. I'm so bloody embarrassed."

"Why? Look at me, Lucy."

She dropped her hand and found the courage to look him in the eye.

"I'm glad you took the precaution of bringing your friend. Honestly, you can't be too careful these days, I know that better than most people."

"Meaning?"

"Meaning, I think this conversation has become too serious too soon, and I'm feeling uncomfortable."

"Heck, that wasn't my intention. If you'd rather call it a night, I wouldn't mind."

"Are you kidding me? I've been eager to see you all day." He cringed once the words had escaped.

"Let the cat out of the bag, have you?" She giggled.

"Not really. It must be obvious how I feel about you."

"What am I supposed to say to that? We only met last night."

"Don't you believe in love at first sight, Lucy? I must admit, I've always thought it was a load of codswallop and never existed...until I laid eyes on you."

Lucy stared at him, frozen in time, unable to answer. "But..."

His hand slid across the table, and his fingers entwined with hers. "Don't tell me you don't feel the same way as I do, I'd be crushed if you told me that."

"I...in case you can't tell, I'm lost for words. Yes, there's an attraction there. I wouldn't have kissed you last night in front of your friends if there wasn't."

His eyes sparkled, and he grinned. "And what a simply delectable experience that was."

"Now I sense you're mocking me."

"I swear I'm not." He released her hand, sat back again, and his gaze dropped to her notebook. "Go on then, what's next on your list?"

She closed her eyes for a moment, regretting bringing her notebook along. She opened her eyes, flipped the pad shut and placed it back in her handbag. "We don't need this. We'll see how the evening pans out and go from there, right?"

"Only if you promise to revisit those questions another time."

"I promise. Tell me about your job?"

"Only if you want to spend the rest of the evening bored senseless. IT is the most monotonous subject that ever existed."

Her eyebrows twisted into a frown. "If you think that, then why do it? You don't seem the type of man to put up with something you don't find fulfilling, or have I totally misread you?"

"No, you're right. That's the problem with working for your parents—no, that's not quite true, it's not like that at all."

"You're confusing me even more now, which is it?"

"All right, they set me up in the business years ago. At the time, it was what I wanted. Don't get me wrong, I'm good at my work and run a tight ship, however, the work neither inspires me nor blows my socks off. Is any of this making sense?"

"My heart goes out to you. I know what it's like to feel in a rut…" *Why can't I keep my big mouth shut?*

"You do? Tell me more."

"In time. We're discussing you at the moment."

"Well, that's put me in my place. I'll get the truth out of you eventually. I have ways of making people talk."

"Is that right?" She sipped her wine and then nodded for him to continue. "Go on. Did you go to university?"

"I did, and you'll never guess in a million years what I studied."

"Computers…IT…sports science or whatever it's called?"

"Nope, none of the above. Hold on to your hat—law."

"Wow, and you gave that all up to run a company that bores you? May I ask why?"

His gaze drifted behind her for a second or two. "Good question. Actually, it isn't. Do you have any notion how boring the law can be?"

"Nope, you've got me there. So why study it in the first place?"

"My father wanted me to follow in his shoes; he started out as a barrister."

"A barrister as opposed to a barista, yes?"

He chuckled. "I love your sense of humour already. Do you always make light of situations? Is that how you've survived over the years?"

His question knocked her sideways. Was he digging deep into her soul, or was she guilty of reading more into it?

"Lucy, are you all right? You've gone quiet on me. Did I overstep the mark?"

"No." Her abrupt answer appeared to stun him. She sighed. "I didn't mean to snap."

"That's okay. I shouldn't have stuck my nose in where it wasn't wanted. Have you eaten?"

"I wasn't sure if your invitation extended to dinner or not."

"You didn't answer my question."

"No, I haven't. I nibbled on a piece of pepper while I knocked up a frittata for Trisha."

"Do you live together?"

"She's asked me to move in with her, and I'm seriously considering it."

"May I ask why?"

She shrugged. "It makes sense for both of us, as money is tight. You mentioned food," she added quickly, switching the conversation around before it got bogged down again.

"Come on, I booked us a table in the restaurant."

They rose from their seats, and he collected the glasses to take with them.

"That was pretty presumptuous of you."

"Some might call it being thoughtful or eager to please a date," he countered, beaming.

The maître d' was obviously expecting them. He showed them to an intimately lit table at the rear of the large, grand restaurant.

Once seated, she leaned forward and asked, "Do you come here often?"

"Every now and again. As you can see, it's pretty quiet, which appeals to my needs."

"Do you usually bring your dates here?"

"No…well, maybe once, and that was a total disaster. The girl ended up drunk and vomited in the middle of the restaurant. Took me a while to get over the embarrassment and return, I can tell you."

"Wow, I bet. Some girls go OTT with their drinking, don't they?"

"I take it you're not one of those people?"

"Nope, can't afford it most of the time. Last night was the first time I'd been out socially with Trisha in a couple of months."

"Why? Apart from the money aspect. You can still go out socially, even when funds are low."

"You've got me on that one. Can we look at the menu? Now you've mentioned food, my tummy is complaining."

He handed her a menu and kept one for himself.

"What do you recommend?" she asked, overawed by the amount of delicious dishes on offer.

"How does steak sound to you?"

"Expensive," she replied quickly.

"This is on me. I would never expect someone else to pay, especially when I've invited them out on a date."

"In that case, yes, that would be lovely." In truth, she hadn't had the luxury of sampling a piece of steak in years, not since...

"Two fillet steaks it is then." He motioned for the waiter to take their order. Once the waiter had left, he turned his full attention on Lucy once more. "So, where were we? Ah yes, I was about to ask you what your background was."

"My work background?"

"Whichever you wish to supply. I'm fed up of talking about myself, never have liked it."

"I think your life is super-exciting compared to mine."

"I won't know unless you tell me. Let's start with your first job after you left school, or did you go on to university?"

"I didn't, again, it cost too much. My dad always used to say those with a degree had very little, or no, common sense."

He laughed. "I like the sound of your father. He's not wrong with his assessment, judging by some of the candidates I've interviewed for roles at my place. Of course, there will always be the odd exception to the rule." He smirked.

She tried to smile, but mentioning her father had cast a shadow over her.

"Hey, what's up? Did I say something wrong?"

"My fault entirely. I shouldn't have mentioned Dad."

"Why? Is there a deep, dark family secret looming there?"

Sudden tears misted her eyes, and she glanced away from him, hoping he wouldn't detect her change in mood, although she feared it was far too late for that.

"Hey, it wasn't my intention to upset you. Are you all right?"

She summoned up a weak smile and excused herself. "I think I need to powder my nose."

He rose from his chair, gentleman that he was, and nodded.

Lucy's emotions were in turmoil. She hadn't thought about her parents in a while, not really. She missed them deeply. Their death had come as a shock, one that she'd read about in a newspaper article two years before. She was riddled with guilt for cutting them out of her life. It had been a necessity, though. One of her biggest regrets to this day. She had attended their funeral heavily disguised, ensuring none of her extended family would recognise her. She'd been about to speak to a few of them during the service, to try to ease their grief, but who knew where blowing her cover would have led?

Now she had yet another dilemma to contend with, more lies she was going to be forced to keep from a man she feared she'd already lost her heart to, no matter how much she was trying to deny it. She wiped away the tears, repaired her smudged makeup the best she could and then returned to the table.

Matthew was there, watching out for her, an expression of concern covering his handsome features which only made her feel worse. He rose to his feet and pulled her chair out for her.

"I'm sorry," he mumbled behind her.

She waited until he was seated again and reached across the table for his hand. "Don't apologise, you weren't to know."

"I shouldn't have made light of something I know nothing about. Are you going to tell me what happened?"

She took a sip from her glass, which had been topped up in her absence. "My parents are no longer around."

"Damn, me and my big mouth. I can't apologise enough."

"It's forgotten about. I thought I was over it. I guess my emotions got the better of me. I should be the one apologising for spoiling the evening."

"You've done no such thing. Human emotions, and not being afraid to show them, can be an endearing feature. When you say they're no longer around, you don't mean they're dead, do you?"

She nodded slowly. "Yes. Can we not talk about it? Oh, look, I think our meals have arrived."

"I'll back off, if that's what you want. My condolences."

She smiled weakly and stared down at the food as it was placed in front of her. The smell was utterly irresistible. She was thankful her emotions hadn't put an end to her appetite. Moments earlier, she'd been relishing the prospect of eating her first steak in over five years.

Matthew paused and raised his glass. He chinked it against hers. "To the future."

"Dare I say it, to us?"

He sniggered. "I was going to say the same but didn't want to come across as either assertive or overbearing."

"You're not, anything but. Thank you for being so kind and considerate and not pushing the issue."

"One day I hope you'll trust me enough with your deepest secrets."

"Only if the deed is reciprocated. Now, if you don't mind, I'm going to tuck in as I hate letting my dinners go cold."

"Go for it," he replied, smirking.

She savoured every mouthful. It was by far the best steak she'd ever had the pleasure of eating. After placing her cutlery down, she slid the plate to the outside of the table and placed her hands over her bulging stomach. "My, I don't think I've eaten as much as that in years. I'll have to starve myself the rest of the week, the number of calories I just shoved down my throat."

"Nonsense. Do you work out?"

"I used to. I've kinda got out of the habit now. You mentioned you have a gym, yes?"

"That's right. It gets lonely, though. I'm always on the lookout for a gym buddy."

"I feel sick thinking about doing fifty star jumps and a hundred squats after eating that lot. Can we take a rain check on it?"

"I wasn't suggesting we go to the gym for a workout right now."

"Good. Do you do any sports?"

"I occasionally go rock climbing."

"Wow, really?"

"I take it you've never tried it?"

"No, I don't think I'm likely to either." She was scared of heights.

Her last experience had scared the crap out of her and put her off dealing with height issues in the future.

"You should try it. Will you give it a go with me beside you?"

"I doubt it. I can come with you, but as for being tempted, I don't think I could ever go down that route, I'm sorry."

"That's another date then. How about at the weekend?"

She covered her eyes and shook her head. "I'm sensing you're not going to take no for an answer."

"Excellent. I know just the place, not far from Bath. It's an adventure theme park. Have you ever been on a zip wire?"

"That I haven't. We go, on one condition."

"Name it."

She looked him straight in the eye and said, "That you don't stand there and force me to do things against my will."

He held his hand out for her to shake. "Deal, I promise. Once you see all those around you enjoying themselves, you'll be gasping to have a go."

"I think I'd rather stick pins in my eyes, we'll see."

"Wear leggings and trainers just in case, okay?"

"All right. Stop hassling me," she replied light-heartedly.

"Now, what shall we have for dessert?"

"I couldn't possibly eat another thing. You go ahead, though."

"Are you sure? Mum always says I have hollow legs and could eat as much as an elephant on a good day."

"Fill your boots in that case."

The waiter magically reappeared to clear their plates and took his order. Within five minutes, Matthew was tucking into a rich sticky toffee pudding. He offered her a spoonful laden with sponge and custard that proved too tempting to resist.

"Oh, my giddy aunt, that's to die for. Maybe I'll have a lighter meal next time and leave room for a pudding."

He inclined his head. "Next time? You've made my day."

"I've had fun this evening."

"Me, too. The best fun I've had with my clothes on in a long time. Jesus! Did I really say that?"

They both laughed. "I take it you meant you like to go swimming, or were you referring to something else entirely?"

"No, that's correct, one hundred percent. Phew…I got out of that one."

And that's how the next few hours shaped up. It was a relaxing evening for both of them. They laughed for most of it. It wasn't until she saw the time on the restaurant wall that she gasped, "Hell, it's eleven-thirty, I have work in the morning."

"So do I."

"Yeah, but you're the boss, you can have a snooze at your desk whenever you want. I need to concentrate, otherwise I could be booking people in to Pontins at Skeggy instead of a luxury resort in the Maldives."

"Is that likely to happen?"

"Who knows? There's always a first time. I won't tell you what I did after receiving the flowers you sent me. It was enough damage for my boss to send me home early today."

"Whoops! They were worth it, though, yes?"

"They were beautiful, and you shouldn't have."

"You're worth it."

"How do you know that?" she pushed.

"Some people shine like stars and others stick out like a nail that needs striking. I think you're the former."

"Why, thank you, kind sir. I hate to call an end to such a wonderful evening, but needs must."

"Do we truly have to say goodbye?"

Her eyes widened, and the words tripped over her tongue as they flew out of her mouth. "Yes, the time isn't right for anything else, not yet."

"There's hope for the future then?"

"I need to ring for a taxi, they'll probably be chocka at this time of night with the pubs kicking out."

"I'll drop you off."

"In your car? You've drunk as much as I have."

"My chauffeur. I'll give him a call."

Her hand darted across the table. "I couldn't put you out like that."

"You're not." He placed a finger to his lips. "Stan. Yep…we're ready to leave now…see you in five." He hung up and clicked his fingers for the bill.

"Are you sure you won't let me pay my share?" She thought she'd better offer, even though she didn't have the funds to fork out if he turned around and said okay.

"I insist, this one is on me. Why don't you bring a picnic on Saturday, how's that?"

"Deal. I love a picnic. It probably won't be up to your standard, but I'll do my best."

"I don't have standards, as such."

He paid the bill with his card, and they left the restaurant. The air outside was chilly. He slipped off his jacket and wrapped it around her shoulders. His touch and closeness affected her more than she realised. She leaned her head against his chest and devoured the smell of his cologne with its musky, woodland tones.

A limousine showed up to spoil the mood. He took her hand and led her down the steps. The chauffeur hopped out of the car, but Matthew waved his attention away. "I'll do it."

Once they were settled in the luxurious leather seats, holding hands, she felt a million dollars and somewhat special.

He kept up the conversation all the way back to Trisha's, speaking about insignificant details that went on during his working day and his life in general. She listened intently where she feared other women would have switched off. There was no two ways about it, he fascinated her.

The driver drew the car to a halt outside Trisha's. Lucy sniggered as she spotted the curtain twitch in the lounge. She knew Trisha would pounce on her as soon as she entered the house, wanting to know the ins and outs of what had gone on during their date.

Matthew exited the vehicle and held out his hand to steady her once she stepped out. He walked her to the front door. She hitched off his jacket and returned it to him with a smile of appreciation.

"Thank you for being an utter gentleman this evening."

"I'm glad you've had a nice time. You deserve to be treated like a princess, beautiful lady." He leaned in and placed the gentlest of kisses on her lips. "When can I see you again?"

"I thought we were meeting up on Saturday?"

"But it's only Thursday now. What will I do with myself tomorrow?"

"I don't know. I'm sure you'll think of something."

He kissed her again. A kiss that left her breathless. "Okay, I won't push it, you win. Shall I pick you up from here?"

"If you like. What time?"

"The earlier, the better, I want to spend the whole day with you."

"Shall we say ten o'clock?"

"Ten in the morning sounds perfect. Remember there's a dress code, definitely no high heels." His gaze dropped to her feet.

"I promise. Thank you again for such a wonderful evening."

He kissed her a third time and nuzzled her neck as he hugged her. "The pleasure was all mine."

He waited until she entered the house. The door was snatched out of her hand.

Trisha stood behind it in her PJs and dressing gown. "So, how did it go? And wow, by the way, I've never been in a limo, what's it like?"

"I'll tell you all about it over a cup of coffee and then I must think about going home."

"No way. Stay here the night. I'll put the kettle on."

She slipped off her heels and looked through the spyhole in the door to see if the car was still there. It wasn't. Her heart sank with disappointment.

Lucy wound her way through the house and into the kitchen.

Trisha drew out a chair at the table and placed a hand on her shoulder, forcing her to sit down. "Tell me. I've been on tenterhooks all evening."

"He knew you were there."

Trisha nearly dropped the mug she'd picked up. "No! How could he know that? My disguise was undetectable."

"Hardly, not if he spotted you. Don't worry, he was fine about it, totally understood and even admired us for our savvy behaviour."

"Wow, most men would've been up in arms about something like that. He definitely sounds like a keeper, that one."

"I hope so," she said in a dreamy tone. "I deserve this. All those years of misery, it feels strange to be so happy. What if he's too good to be true?"

"Stop erecting barricades before you've even had the chance to get to know him."

Lucy hugged her dear friend. "You're right. It's just…well, at the moment, everything seems too good to be true. I'm wary, that's all."

"You have a right to be, let's face it. But then, look at it another way: after all these years of loneliness, you also deserve to be bloody happy. My advice would be to go with the flow for now, what harm can it do?"

"I hear you. That's one life-changing decision out of the way. Are you prepared for the second one?"

Trisha frowned and crossed her arms. "Go on," she said hesitantly.

"I've decided to take you up on your offer and move in."

Trisha screeched, closed the distance between them, lifted Lucy off the floor and spun her around and around.

"Oh shit! You'd better put me down before I puke."

Trisha swiftly dropped her to the floor. "Oh no you don't. That's bloody marvellous news. You know what? Shame on me for not suggesting it earlier. I got the impression it would've been too soon for you."

"Don't blame yourself. I think you're probably right, the timing would have been off the mark before."

"I don't care. You've come to the right decision in the end. When do you want to move in?"

"I have to speak to my landlord first, he's bound to make me see out my notice. Maybe I can say it's a family emergency or something. Leave it with me, and I'll get back to you. I feel I'm heading in the right direction at last and I can't thank you enough for having the patience with me and for shoving me in Matthew's direction."

"You're welcome. You deserve the best after what you've been through. No one recognises that more than I do." She hooked arms with Lucy and steered her through into the lounge. "Now, I want all the juicy gossip about your date, and leave nothing out."

Lucy laughed. "So much for going home and going straight to bed, I might as well have stayed out with Matthew."

"You used that as an excuse to leave? Bloody hell, it wouldn't surprise me if he doesn't regard you as a modern-day Cinderella."

"I feel like one, I swear I do. I kept wanting to pinch myself."

"Aww…it's natural, love. One thing that's puzzling me."

"What's that?"

"I don't suppose you asked him why he's single, did you?"

"I did. Not sure I got a satisfactory answer to that particular question."

"He was cagey about it?"

"Hard to tell. I might be doing him an injustice. He brushed it aside and said there are some pretty bad women out there these days."

"Putting yourself in his position, with his wealth and status, I suppose he'd definitely attract the wrong type. How the hell would you differentiate? A bugger of a job, eh?"

Lucy nodded and exhaled a large sigh, unsure whether she should reveal what was running through her mind next or not. "Umm…I'll tell you one thing he said that absolutely took my breath away and made my heart flutter."

"Sounds intriguing. What was that?"

"He mentioned love at first sight and asked me if I believed in it."

"Whoa! Jesus, this guy definitely seems to be too good to be true. No wonder you seem a little confused, shall we say?"

"I'm not sure if *confused* is the right word, maybe *cautious*." She threw her hands up in the air. "I don't know. Let's just say the few hours I spent with him have left me with more questions than answers, I think. There I go again, unsure even if I've said the right thing."

"It's late. Why don't you sleep on it, and we'll try and make sense of it tomorrow?"

"I think that'd be the wisest plan of action."

"Dare I ask if he asked you out on another date?"

She sniggered. "He wanted to see me tomorrow. I put him off, but then he suggested we go to one of those adventure parks on Saturday. I agreed, even though it's not my type of thing. I told him I'd take a picnic along."

"Why agree if you don't fancy it?"

"Because he seemed so excited about showing me his rock-climbing skills."

"Will you have a go at it?"

She shook her head, adamant with her response. "No way, you know I have a fear of heights, going back to what happened. I'm not sure I'll ever get over that."

"You might do, in time. If he's such an expert, maybe he'll give you the courage to try it."

"Would you?"

"Not sure. It's not something I've ever had to think about really. See how the day pans out. You might feel differently about things once you're there."

"Maybe. My eyelids are drooping, do you mind if I go to bed now?"

"Not at all. Give me a shout if you need anything. I've put another clean towel on the spare bed for the morning."

"What would I do without you?"

"I'm sure you'd cope." Trisha smiled and led the way upstairs.

They hugged at the top and went their separate ways.

In bed, it took Lucy several hours to drop off to sleep as the evening's activities ran through her mind. Her final thought was questioning if all this was real.

3
_____

*a*t work the following morning, the door opened, and in walked a delivery driver carrying the largest orchid plant she'd ever laid eyes on. It was a dusky lilac colour that she instantly fell in love with.

"I wonder who that's from, as if I couldn't guess," Shirley teased once the driver had placed it on Lucy's desk.

"Oh my, isn't it stunning? One question, how the hell do I look after it?" she asked, petrified the exquisite plant would be dead by the end of the following week.

"It needs special care, I think. You'd better look it up on Google. You're so lucky. Not every man would think about sending someone he'd met a few days earlier such a thoughtful gift. That's two days on the trot."

"I know. Hard to believe, isn't it? I know that look, and no, I haven't opened my legs for him, if that was going to be your next question." She wagged a finger in her boss's direction and took the plant out into the staffroom. That's where she noticed the card sticking out of the pretty pink pot.

To the most beautiful woman I know—thank you for a magical evening.

Shirley burst into the room and swiped the card from her hand and read it. Her gaze met Lucy's, and there were tears brimming in her eyes. "Bloody hell. Some women have all the luck."

Lucy tutted and reclaimed the card. "Early days yet. I'm definitely *not* getting carried away."

"Quite right, too. Although saying that, it took my Keith over five years to buy me a bunch of flowers. Not very romantic, that one. Do you know what he bought me our first Christmas together?"

"I can't even begin to imagine."

"A set of bloody saucepans to replace the castoffs my mother had given me. Can you believe that?"

Lucy laughed so hard her stomach hurt. "I'm sorry, that's hilarious."

Shirley rolled her eyes. "You could at least pretend to show me a little sympathy. Do you want a coffee?"

"Thanks. Is it all right if I research the care of this thing?" She pointed to the plant gracing the table against the wall.

"Go for it, it's not as if we're run off our feet. I hope trade picks up soon. This year has been a dead loss so far."

Concern pulled at Lucy's brow. "We're going to be all right, though, aren't we?"

"Who knows what tomorrow will bring once Brexit kicks in?"

Lucy nodded and left the staffroom, wondering if she should consider searching for another job while she was on the internet. She hated the thought of leaving Shirley in the lurch, but these days, with all the uncertainty looming in the world right now, it was something she needed to be conscious of. Maybe she'd leave that until she got home this evening instead. It wouldn't feel right searching for a new career while her boss was paying her to do her job. Instead, she stuck to her original task and put 'how to care for an orchid' in the search box. A flood of advice filled her screen. She jotted down a few relevant details about giving the plant ample water but allowing it to dry out as opposed to letting it sit in water to maintain its good health and well-being.

"Any luck?" Shirley placed a mug of coffee beside her.

"I think so. Only time will tell, I suppose. The advice sounds a tad contradictory. I don't think they're the easiest plants to keep alive, but I'm willing to give it a shot."

"I'm sure you'll cope. Well, are you going to tell me how your date went last night? Judging by the gift, I would hazard a guess it went okay."

"It was the perfect evening. Even with Trisha loitering in the background for the first half an hour or so."

"What? Why? Were you that nervous of being alone with him? Didn't you meet in a public place?"

"Yes, we met in a public place." She twirled her mug on the desk and stared at its contents. "I haven't dated in years. She was concerned about me. As it turned out, she needn't have been. He was an absolute gentleman, and the hotel was the flawless setting which helped to make the evening go well."

"Now for my next major question: when are you seeing him again?"

"Tomorrow, although he wanted to see me sooner than that."

"Wow! I'd say he was pretty bowled over by you, if he's that keen." She smiled. "I'm thrilled for you. I don't know your background as we've never discussed it, but I've always got the impression that something bad happened in your past." She raised a hand, preventing Lucy from speaking. "I'm not asking you to divulge any secrets. All I want is for you to promise me that you won't allow whatever went on in days gone by to hinder your future with this 'perfect man'. What say you?"

"Thank you, I'm going to do my best. I'm hoping my past allows me to enjoy my future without any unforeseen hassle."

"Good girl. We've all been hurt, in one way or another, usually by a man. You're such a sweetheart, I hate the thought of you turning into a bitter old spinster."

"Bloody hell, tell it how it is, Shirley. And for the record, I've never considered myself a flipping spinster, bitter or otherwise. I'm what's commonly known as an SWF, a Single White Female.

Although, after seeing the film with the same name last week I think I should alter that. Scared the crap out of me." She smirked.

"I haven't seen it. I'll look it up."

"You might find it a little dated. I think it's around thirty years old now, and the connotations would be different for you than they were for me."

"How come?" Shirley sipped her drink.

"Because you have another half and aren't single."

"Oh, I get you, silly me. Back to you and this young man. Where are you going on this date?"

"On a picnic at one of those adventure parks. He appears to be into outdoor activities from what I can tell."

Shirley screwed her lip up. "Not my idea of a good day out. How do you feel about it?"

"I thought the same at first, now I'm quite looking forward to it. Which reminds me, I need to make a shopping list for picnic supplies. I thought I'd pop out at lunchtime to grab them, if that's all right?"

"You're nuts! What you get up to in your lunch hour is entirely up to you. Have you tried M&S's pork pies? I used to live on them for my sins around twenty years ago, but I must admit, one hasn't passed my lips in a while."

"No, I haven't. I'm quite partial to a pork pie. Do you think Matthew would appreciate me getting one?"

"I'd say it's better than turning up with a bunch of sandwiches. More inventive, shall we say. Have a look at the selection they've got."

"Aren't M&S supposed to be expensive? I'm on a limited budget, remember."

"I don't think so, not these days. Too much competition for them to keep their prices high."

"I'll have a quick look. Right, what's next on the agenda today? Do you want me to start chasing up the leads we received from last week?"

"There's no rush, this afternoon will do."

They chatted over their coffee and then got down to work. A few potential customers came in to collect some brochures, and Lucy dealt with a lady who wanted to book an all-inclusive holiday to the Dominican Republic, somewhere she was longing to go, but feared she'd never be able to afford the flight, let alone the accommodation and spending money that would need to accompany such an extravagant adventure.

*T*hat evening, Lucy drifted home exhausted. Her trip to M&S at lunchtime had resulted in a haul which took up space in three carrier bags. Had she gone over the top? She laughed at the thought. Her plans for the rest of the day would consist of preparing some of the food, easing it for the next morning. Matthew had told her he would pick her up from Trisha's at ten, therefore, she wouldn't have much time to prepare things in the morning, what with getting herself ready thrown into the mix as well.

By the time nine o'clock came around, all the food was back in the fridge, ready to go. She was pleased with her accomplishment and decided to have a long soak in the bath. She relaxed in the steaming water, no music on, and only a few flickering candles to keep her company, and her rubber duck, of course. She was totally chilled, her eyes closed, enjoying the warmth of the water and the luxury of being neck-deep in lavender bubbles.

A noise sounded outside, something she couldn't place. Was it a cat searching the bins? She doubted it, it would be the first time. Unable to distinguish what the noise was, she emptied the water, quickly dried herself and ran downstairs, her thoughts running wild, wondering if she'd locked the back door or not.

She peered out of the kitchen window and saw the bin lying on its side. She let out a relieved sigh. "It can wait until the morning. I'll be buggered if I'm going to catch my death going out there in this wind." She ran back upstairs again, threw on her PJs and dressing gown, then returned to the kitchen to collect a glass of wine from the bottle she'd treated herself to during her shopping adventure. No, she couldn't really afford it, but her finances were looking much brighter now that she'd agreed to move in with Trisha. Which reminded her, she needed to ring the landlord first thing to give him notice.

The thought of moving filled her with dread, having collected a handful of knickknacks over the years. Maybe it was time for her to be brutal and to ditch some of her belongings rather than pack them up and clutter her room at Trisha's. Perhaps she could pick up a few boxes from the corner shop in the morning, before she went to Trisha's, and got started on the packing on Sunday, unless Matthew had a better idea what to do with her time.

Everything was up in the air for now, and that was where she left it. She took her glass of wine to bed and picked up her Kindle. She had just downloaded the latest romance from one of her favourite authors, Tracie Delaney. By the time eleven o'clock came around, she had swiped through half of the heart-pounding romantic thriller and felt sad that she could no longer keep her eyes open long enough to finish it. *Draven* was a breathtakingly superb read.

She drifted off, influenced by the book, and had a dream in which she and Matthew were in the main characters' places. She woke up a few hours later, dripping in sweat, her heart rate going at a hundred miles an hour.

Gasping for a drink, she went downstairs and filled a glass with water. Her attention was drawn to the bin still lying on its side in the garden. After she rinsed the glass, she returned to bed and fell asleep. The alarm woke her at eight. She showered and put on a light touch of makeup, then pulled on a pair of leggings and a sweatshirt she hadn't worn for a few months. She looked a mess and regretted not having the spare funds to go out and buy a new outfit especially for today's trip.

Laden down with the food, she filled the boot of her car and set off for Trisha's house. She arrived with half an hour to spare. Lucy and Trisha chatted over coffee.

"Umm…can I say something?" Trisha said.

"Sure, what?"

"Your clothes, they've definitely seen better days, lovely."

"Shit! Are they that bad? I thought I might get away with it, just for today."

"Want me to see what I can find upstairs?"

"Would you?"

"Come on, we've got ten minutes."

They left their drinks and raced up the stairs to satisfy their urgent mission.

"Here, black leggings. At least these have a nice shape to them and aren't baggy on the knees."

Lucy stripped off her lower half and stepped into them. They were a snug fit but impressively transformed the shape of her legs. "Bloody hell, is that me?"

"Damn right it is. Girl, you need to take a long hard look at what you wear. Half of it doesn't do your figure any justice at all. Is that intentional on your part?"

Lucy stared at her through the mirror and nodded. "I've always felt that covering up the real me would make me feel more secure, does that make sense?"

Trisha took a step forward and wrapped her arms around Lucy. "Why haven't you said anything all these years? My heart bleeds for what has been going through your head all this time. Sharing your problems would've at least eased your anxieties, love."

"I didn't want to become more of a burden than I already have been, don't be angry with me."

"I could never be angry with you, maybe a touch annoyed, for you not having the courage to confide in me."

"It was just me. All these years I've been so wrapped up in myself, unable to express what I truly feel in case…"

"In case what, Luc? Christ, he really did a number on you, didn't he?"

Tears brimmed, and she shook her head. "Honestly, you have no idea. I kept a lot of it inside. I know now that was probably the worst thing I could've done, but I was too scared to voice the words. To seek help. That's why I did it in the end."

"Because you couldn't stand the torment any longer?"

She inhaled a shuddering breath. "Yes. No one knows how bad it was behind closed doors…" She shook her head. "No. I won't go there, not today. Today is all about me having some fun, not dwelling on my miserable past."

Trisha spun her around by the shoulders and smiled. "It certainly is. This is a totally new beginning for you in lots of ways. Don't let the past destroy the chance of any future happiness, you hear me?"

Lucy hugged her and whispered, "I love you so much. For standing by me all these years. Supporting me when I lost my parents. Well... for being you. No one could wish for a better friend in this life."

Trisha sniffed and wiped away a tear as she took a step back. "All I've ever wanted is to see that gorgeous smile light up your beautiful face. It may have taken us a few years to get there, and I'm not sure what the turning point has been this year, but hey, it's done the job and attracted a wonderful man to boot. I honestly couldn't be any happier for you. Don't let anything, or anyone, spoil your future happiness. If anyone tries, you send them my way, and I'll sort them out."

Lucy mock-saluted her. "I will. Thanks for always having my back. I can't wait until I move in here."

"Neither can I. See, that's another thing. I've been bugging you for years to camp out in the spare room, and you've always thrown the suggestion back in my face without a second thought. I'm glad you're finally seeing sense, although, I think it's too late now."

Lucy gasped. "What? Are you saying you've changed your mind?"

Trisha growled and rolled her eyes to the ceiling. "Numpty, no. I think it's too late because the way things are going, I think you'll be walking down the aisle before the year is out."

Lucy laughed so hard at that. "You're a scream. How can you say that? This is only our second date, idiot."

"You ask my other friends. I'm rarely wrong where matters of the heart are concerned. I've predicted a number of times when their boyfriends were about to propose. As if I'm some kind of love oracle."

"You are funny. Umm...do me a favour, don't go mentioning it to me if your 'oraclism' tempts you to predict my future. You'd probably scare the shit out of me, and I'd end up doing a runner."

"You wouldn't. Why? You deserve any happiness coming your way, sweetie."

"The thought of being under a man's spell again...well, no, I don't want to think about it."

Trisha tutted. "Not all men are the same. If you haven't realised that about Matthew by now, then you must have a screw loose."

Lucy swallowed down the saliva that had suddenly filled her mouth. "*He* started out the same, you know that."

"*He* is no longer around, and you need to set what you experienced with him aside and concentrate on the exciting future which lies ahead of you. You hear me?" Trisha wagged her finger.

Lucy attempted to bite it. "You can be such a bully at times."

"Yep, especially when I know I'm in the right."

"We'll see." She looked at her watch. "Shit! He'll be here soon."

Trisha crossed the room and peered out of the window. "Correction, he's already here."

"Okay, will I do now?" Lucy asked. Her arms open wide, she twirled on the spot.

Trisha rushed over to the chest of drawers in the corner and pulled out a lilac sweatshirt. "This is perfect for you, what do you think?"

"Can I?" Lucy removed her own top and replaced it with the lilac one. "I love it. Are you sure you don't mind?"

"Not at all. Now, shoo, your chariot awaits. Hang on, you might want to run a comb through your hair first."

Lucy was in full panic mode now. She ran downstairs and searched her handbag for her comb. "Damn, it's not in here. Where the hell did I put it?"

Again, Trisha came to her rescue. "Here, take mine. I don't think I have nits."

"Thanks, what would I...?"

"Do without me? Yeah, I know. Now, go, have a blast. I'll be expecting to hear all about it this evening."

"Thanks for everything, Trisha." She hugged her friend and collected the carrier bags from the kitchen.

Trisha held the door open as Matthew was getting out of the car.

"Thank God he didn't show up in that limo. I think I would've died if he had," Lucy mumbled.

"I wouldn't have. I'd be revelling in it. You need to get your priorities sorted out, love."

"Get out of here."

Matthew joined them, leaned forward to kiss her gently on the cheek and nodded hello to Trisha, then he relieved her of the bags. "Umm...I did make it clear that we were only going for the day, didn't I?"

Lucy bowed her head. "Sorry. If it's too much, I'm sure the birds will enjoy what's left of it."

"Come on, I want you to meet someone."

Lucy turned to face Trisha, her panic heightening.

Trisha patted her on the hand. "Go, you'll have a fab day."

"Are you sure you don't want to come?" she blurted out.

It was Matthew's turn to look horrified. He cleared his throat and set a smile in place. "You'd be more than welcome."

"No, you go off and enjoy yourselves. I have chores to do around here, ready for when someone moves in." Trisha grinned at Lucy.

"You're moving in?" Matthew asked.

"I am."

"Cool. Are you ready? I'll take two bags if you can carry the other one."

"Done deal. See you later, Trisha," she called over her shoulder.

She helped Matthew load the bags into the boot of the four-by-four, and then he opened the back door for her to climb in. Sitting in the front seat was another man. Her nerves racked up. She hadn't got used to being alone with Matthew yet, so how was she supposed to react in this situation, with another stranger to get used to, and so soon?

"This is my brother, Jake."

Jake swivelled in his seat to face her and held out a hand, his eyes boring into hers as she shook it.

"And you must be the luscious Lucy who has stolen my brother's heart."

"I am. Although I'm not sure about stealing your brother's heart, not after one date," she said sheepishly.

"Stop teasing her, Jake. Leave the girl alone. She's brought enough food to feed a regiment."

"Good. Mum always said that you can tell what kind of wife a girl will make by the dinner she supplies after the first date."

Lucy listened to the conversation between the two brothers but didn't have the courage to answer either of them, not that any of the questions so far had been directed at her. Having someone else in the car with them had somewhat changed the dynamics of their relationship. Lucy no longer felt at ease. If anything, she was teetering on the edge of hysteria, which was so unlike her, and she couldn't help but wonder why.

Instead of relaxing back into her seat, once her seatbelt was fixed into place, she sat forward, straining on it. *What is wrong with you?*

The drive took twenty minutes or thereabouts, and in that time she listened to the two men talking about subjects she knew nothing about, nor wanted to learn about either. Topics to do with their work that was so far over her head. Now and again, Matthew glanced up in the rear-view mirror. Every time she saw that, she smiled, but inside she was crying out to be set free from the vehicle.

The overwhelming feeling of being confined in a tight space was blowing her mind, making her reel. She inhaled and exhaled a few steadying breaths, which disappointingly did little to help.

"Matthew, sorry, can you pull over?"

Matthew frowned and stared at her through the oblong mirror. "Are you all right, Lucy?"

"No, I need some fresh air."

"Can't you wind down your window? We're almost there now."

She pressed the button in the door, eased the window down a few inches and sucked in great big gulps of cool air. The sensation initially burnt her lungs but appeared to have the desired effect in the end, as her anxiety decreased, at least to a reasonable level.

Jake peered over his shoulder, and she caught his odd expression. She found it hard to decipher, unsure whether he was concerned or annoyed.

"We're here. How are you holding up in the back?" Matthew asked.

Lucy smiled weakly. "I'm fine now. Sorry."

"No need to apologise. I should've asked if you were all right sitting in the rear of a car. I know some people get travel sick."

"Oh no, it wasn't…" She paused. Her anxiety attack had nothing to do with where she'd sat. How the heck could she explain her irrational fears to him, though, when she had trouble figuring it out herself? She was determined not to let her emotions get the better of her and tried to bury them deep within. She succeeded, too, for at least fifteen minutes, until they reached the zip wire and Matthew insisted she ride it alongside him.

"I'd rather watch you, Matthew, if it's all the same to you."

"Not scared, are you, Lucy?" Jake enquired.

"Truthfully, yes, I'm petrified. I've never been great with heights."

Matthew took her hand in his and kissed it. "You'll be with me. I would never let any harm come to you. Trust me."

She closed her eyes and exhaled deeply, aware how foolish she was coming across, but as hard as she tried, she couldn't kick the feeling of dread surging through her. He bent down and kissed her lips. It was the first time he'd kissed her properly since their first date, and she hoped it would give her the confidence to trust him. It didn't. Her legs shook uncontrollably as well as her hands. In the end, the safety guy unhitched her harness and instructed her to leave the platform.

"I'll see you at the other end," Matthew shouted, suspended from the wire, his adventure underway.

Now that she was back on terra firma, her confidence soared once more.

Jake was waiting for her. "Better now?"

"Much, thank you."

"You don't give me the impression you're the girly type at all."

"What are you trying to say? That I put on an act?"

"Simply voicing my opinion out loud. Glad to see you're not shaking so much now. May I ask where your fear of heights comes from?"

"You can ask, but whether I'd be able to explain away my years of terror in a sentence, well, that remains to be seen."

"So it stems back to your childhood then?"

"I suppose it does. I've never really thought about it. It's nice of you to be concerned, I appreciate it."

He grunted and walked on ahead.

Matthew had reached the end and strode towards them, sporting a huge grin. "That was epic, guys, you should've both given it a shot."

"Yes, why didn't you go with him, Jake?" Lucy was keen to enquire.

"I picked up a sports injury playing rugby last week. I'll have a go in the future. What's your excuse, Lucy?"

"My fear of heights had a lot to do with it."

"Is that all?" Jake pushed.

Matthew got between them and placed an arm around their shoulders. "Guys, it really doesn't matter. Right, on to the next one."

It hadn't taken Lucy long to realise this day wouldn't go down in her memory scrapbook as an enjoyable experience.

She made sure she smiled in all the right places and cheered Matthew on during his ventures, all whilst standing alongside Jake. Maybe *he* was the problem, the reason why she was struggling to relax and enjoy herself. Or was that an unreasonable suggestion?

After watching Matthew exert himself for a couple of hours, Lucy proposed he took a breather, and they all returned to the car. Jake took a car rug from the boot and laid it out on the grass nearby while she and Matthew retrieved the bags.

She unloaded them and both men appeared to be suitably impressed by the dishes on show.

Jake picked up a Scotch egg and asked, "Home-made?"

Lucy smiled. "I have to hold my hands up and confess. All of this is shop bought. I work full time, as you do, I imagine. Making this lot from scratch would've taken me days."

"He's teasing you, Lucy, ignore him. It all looks delicious. You have some of my favourite things here."

"Oh, such as?"

"Pork pie and those little fondant fancies. I couldn't get enough of those as a child."

Shit! What's he saying? That he thought the spread would be more suited for a children's party rather than a picnic for sophisticated adults?

"I loved them, too. That was my aim in selecting them, to relive my childhood, I suppose."

Matthew leaned in for a kiss. "Top marks. I think you achieved your aim. I love it."

Jake said nothing, his gaze drifting to a nearby family of two adults and three kids. He strained his neck to see what their lunch consisted of. "Oh look, they have virtually the same spread as us."

"Popular choices then, obviously," Matthew announced.

Lucy, however, died a little inside. At least her enthusiasm had for the hours of trouble assembling the food the evening before. She nibbled on a tinned salmon sandwich and cursed herself for not thinking to remove the crusts. And that was how she spent the next hour or so, tearing herself apart. Criticising every damn thing that was wrong with the picnic she'd worked so ruddy hard to put together. Why? Well, Jake was to blame for that.

Matthew laughed at the way his brother continued to tease her, however, it all left a sour taste in her mouth and spoilt the day for her. So much so that she even thought about feigning an illness to put a halt to the day. *Matthew has changed since his brother came on the scene, or am I guilty of reading far too much into his behaviour?*

"Come on, guys. I need to have another go at that wall," Matthew announced, jumping to his feet.

"You go ahead. I'll help Lucy clear up this mess, and we'll be with you in a mo."

Matthew rushed off without giving her a second glance. All of a sudden, being left alone with Jake, her anxiety levels rose once again. She fumbled with the containers, dropping the odd one here and there.

Jake rescued them before the contents spilled onto the blanket and said, "Clumsy."

Her head shot up, and he smiled briefly. Just being in his presence was having a detrimental effect on her welfare. Her emotions were almost strangling her. A pain clawed at her chest; she put that down to the tension mounting within.

Unable to cope, she excused herself and sprinted towards the toilet block on the other side of the car park. She ran a paper hand towel under the cold tap and placed it on the back of her neck. A lady in her fifties flushed the toilet and exited one of the cubicles. Lucy smiled awkwardly at her.

"Are you all right, dear? You look a tad peaky."

"Too much excitement for one day, I fear. It's all rather overwhelming for my system. I'll be fine in a second. Are you having fun today?"

"Me? No, I wouldn't be seen dead going on any of these torturous contraptions or rides. I value my life, not fond of risking it. I know, all the safety procedures in place would prevent anyone hurting themselves, but there's that tiny voice niggling away at me. I can guarantee, if anything was going to happen to anyone in this place, it would be to me."

She laughed. "I feel exactly the same way. Give me a day of sunbathing on the beach any time."

The woman pointed at her. "I said the same thing to my old man. He and the kids are loving this place, though, so it wouldn't seem right dragging them away when they're having so much fun. Anyway, I'd better get a wriggle on. Enjoy the rest of your day."

"You, too. Take care, and thank you for your kindness."

"Showing a little kindness never hurt anyone in this life, did it now?"

The woman left the toilet, and Lucy couldn't help the feeling of loneliness that enveloped her. She tried to shrug it off. There was no reason for her to feel that way, not now she had Matthew. Lucy studied her reflection, really studied it, and was shocked to see the worry lines that had recently disappeared had emerged again. Why? Was her sixth sense working its magic, picking up on something in Matthew, or Jake for that matter?

Maybe she was guilty of reading too much into it because she had barely spent any time with him and had been forced to spend time with Jake instead. But something was definitely in the air, and she had to admit it was unsettling her.

She shrugged, shook out her arms, trying to release the tension there, then she doused her face with cold water, dried it on a paper towel and left the toilet block to make her way back to the picnic area.

Jake was busy still clearing up. Most of the bags were half-filled, and there was only the rug left to fold. "Typical of you to turn up once all the work is done."

Although he smiled, she detected the bitterness in his tone.

"I'm sorry. As for that being typical of me, nothing could be further from the truth, but I'm willing to let you off this time, especially as you know so very little about me."

"And there lies the problem…"

She crossed her arms and stared at him. "Go on, don't stop there."

"As a family, and I'm including Matt in that, we know next to nothing about you."

"And you perceive that as a problem? Funny that, because I don't think Matthew does."

"There you go, that proves my point."

"What does?" she snapped, her annoyance now visible.

"He hates being called Matthew. Everyone in the family calls him Matt, except Mother when she's angry, of course."

She chewed on the inside of her cheek. *What am I supposed to say to that? I don't know why Matthew hasn't instructed me to call him Matt. It's as if Jake is blaming me for something. God, I wish I was anywhere else but here right now, stuck with him.* "Matthew has never told me to call him otherwise. When I say never, I mean in the few days I've known him. You make it sound as if I've known him a lifetime and you're punishing me for not being aware of the slightest details. I think that's harsh, don't you?"

He placed the rug and the last of the bags in the boot of the car. "Maybe, maybe not. Forgive me if I reserve judgement on you and my brother for the next month or so. He's been here before, several times over, in fact."

"What are you trying to say? That I'm like every other girl he's met?"

Jake shrugged. "If that's how you insist on interpreting it."

"But…we've had this conversation…"

"And what was the outcome?" Jake prompted when she paused.

She dipped her head and mumbled. "That's private and between me and Matthew," she replied, sticking to her guns and insisting on calling her new beau by his proper name until he told her to do otherwise.

"Whatever. I'm off."

"Where are you going?"

"I'm leaving. Tell Matt I got bored with the company and I'll see him at home later." With that, he threw her the car keys and marched away.

"But how will you get home?" she asked foolishly, searching for the right words to appease him in the hope he would stay.

"There's a wonderful invention called the taxi," he flung back at her sarcastically.

Lucy watched him walk away until he turned the corner. She blew out a breath, which puffed out her cheeks, and slammed her fists against her thighs. Was she right to blame herself for the outcome of their conversation? She was confused. As far as she was concerned, she hadn't said or done anything that Jake could have possibly found offensive. She shrugged, slotted the keys in her jacket pocket and went in search of Matthew, or Matt, or whatever she should call him. *How the hell had that man caused me to doubt myself?* She refused to go there again. Her life was on an upward curve, and she'd be buggered if the likes of Jake, or anyone else Matthew was acquainted with, was going to spoil what they had.

She located Matthew descending the tallest climbing wall. Once he was on the ground, he spotted her and excitedly trotted towards her. He swooped her up in his arms and planted a lingering kiss on her lips. "That was fantastic. I wish I could've shared the experience with you. Maybe one day we'll conquer your fear of heights together."

"Maybe. I can't make any promises, though. So glad you enjoyed it."

He scanned the area, and she sensed what was coming next.

"Where's Jake, in the loo?"

"No, he left. Said he had to be somewhere else." It was only a small lie, nothing major.

"He did? Did he say where?"

"No. Have you ever thought he might have felt a bit of a gooseberry, tagging along with us?"

"He was eager to meet you. When Jake wants something, it's hard to say no to him. You got on okay together, didn't you?"

"I think so. He packed the car up and then took off. He left me wondering if I'd upset him in some way, but I couldn't think of anything I might have said or done that could've offended him."

"You? Upset someone? I doubt that could happen." He flung an arm around her shoulders and steered her back towards the car. "I've had enough excitement for one day. You must be bored rigid, though. I appreciate what it's like when someone drags you somewhere which doesn't suit you."

"I'm fine, honestly. I don't mind hanging around here if you want to carry on." Another half-truth. She did mind, but she was prepared to put herself out for the sake of this man's enjoyment, unlike his brother, apparently.

"As much as I love you for saying that, no, let's call it a day and participate in doing something we can both enjoy."

Her heart swelled. "Are you going to give me a hint?"

"You'll see."

They chatted as if they'd known each other for years, and during the stroll back to the car, Lucy fell a little deeper in love with Matthew. "Can I ask you something?"

Matthew had started the engine and left the car park. He indicated and pulled over. He turned in his seat to face her. "Ask away, I have no secrets."

She resisted the temptation to wince. *You might not, but I have! What if, in time, those secrets come out? What will happen to our relationship then?*

He clicked his fingers in front of her face, bringing her out of her daydream. "Hello, Lucy, are you in there?"

"Sorry, I was miles away. Don't ask me where." She tried to laugh off her major slip-up.

"Okay, I won't. What did you want to ask me?"

"It was something Jake mentioned."

"Go on. I'm sorry, I'm not into reading minds, although I do have many other talents which you've yet to discover."

She tutted and groaned. "Stop, I'm trying to be serious here."

"I apologise, you have my full attention."

"When we were alone, he seemed to chastise me for calling you Matthew, even went as far to tell me that no one in the family calls you Matthew, and, well…oh, I don't know. He said you hated the name, is that true?"

"It's true. Saying that, and in my defence, whenever you say my name it does funny things to me."

She hadn't expected that response and giggled. "Oh right, I'm not sure what I'm supposed to say to that."

"Neither am I. Give me a kiss instead. I haven't had enough of those today."

They shared the most intimate of kisses which made them both moan with pleasure.

Matthew cleared his throat. "Oh God, right, back to plan B, and sharpish, I think, before we get ourselves in trouble."

"Which is?"

"You'll see. I'm going to lower the window, if that's all right with you? I need to cool the interior of the car down." He winked.

"Go for it, I'd welcome that myself."

Then he selected first gear and drove them to the ultra-secret location. The bowling alley in the centre of town. "Fancy a game? I take it you can play?"

"I can. I used to be in a league, many moons ago." As soon as the words broke free, she regretted airing them. *Shit! What if he decides to look me up and realises I'm lying? Except I'm not. I was in the league, only it was under a different name. What's wrong with me? I've kept my other life a secret all these years, but in the last few hours I've slipped up a few times.*

"You've drifted off again. Is there something on your mind, Lucy? Something you'd like to share with me?"

"No, I have no idea what's happening to me today. For some reason I keep thinking about the good times I spent with my parents, before their deaths."

"I'm sorry. I shouldn't have probed. You're entitled to your privacy, just like I am."

"Thank you. It's still early days, and sometimes it catches me out, so forgive me."

"Nothing to forgive. I'm fortunate enough to still have both of my parents with me. I haven't got a clue what it must be like to lose one of them, let alone both of them at the same time. I'm here if you ever need to unburden yourself, you know that, right?"

"I do."

She reached for his hand, and they strolled into the bowling alley. He was the perfect gent, and she left all the organising of the shoes to him. However, where the ball was concerned, she took an age to choose the one that felt right in her hands. That was the most important part to a professional, as she had once regarded herself.

Matthew insisted she should go first. She knocked down nine pins with her first ball. He was impressed, but she was disappointed at her rustiness. Annoyed even, that she wasn't allowed to do a couple of practice runs to get back into the swing of things.

His first throw ended with a strike, which meant she was playing catch-up from the moment they got on the lane. *Right, if that's the way you want it, buster, step aside and let me show you what I've got hiding in my locker—well, not all of it, just some of it.*

Her second ball resulted in a spare which blew him away. "Wow, that's some power you have in that slender wrist of yours."

If only you knew! "I told you, years of practice. I was lulling you into a false sense of security with my first ball. Game on now, honey."

"Game on, eh?" He selected his ball and took four large steps up to the line and released it. Yet another strike.

Her muscles tensed. She hadn't realised she had such a competitive streak. Not even when she'd played the game in the league had this streak come to light. Maybe Jake had wound her up the wrong way and she was eager to vent some of that anger by punishing Matthew.

The rest of the game went the same way, each of them stepping up and delivering the perfect strike. She kicked herself for not concentrating hard enough on the first ball but then chastised herself for being so harsh. It had been around ten years since she had last entered the lane.

They chilled out at the bar for about an hour, and then Matthew insisted he took her for dinner. One look at the outfit she had on made her decline his kind offer.

"I'll give that a miss in this getup."

"Not even a burger and chips?"

She placed a hand over her stomach. "I couldn't, I ate far too many carbs at lunchtime. Would you mind if we called it a day instead?"

"Are you all right? I thought we were having fun?"

"I'm fine." She wasn't really, there was something niggling her about the day, and she was struggling to shake the feeling off.

"Okay, far be it for me to push the issue. Can I see you tomorrow? I'll take you for a ride out in the country. There's a beautiful pub I know that serves a traditional Sunday lunch."

"Go on then, if you insist. Can you drop me back to Trisha's? I left my car there."

"Of course."

Twenty minutes later, he switched off the engine outside Trisha's house. "Are you sure you're okay?"

"Honestly, maybe it was too much excitement to cram into one day. I'll see you tomorrow. Where do you want to meet?"

"Shall I pick you up from home?"

"No, don't do that. Meet me here instead."

"Is there any reason you don't want me to know where you live?"

Her chin rested on her chest. "I'm ashamed of it. Trisha has asked me to move in. I'm hoping to do that in the next few weeks. I'm waiting on a call back from the landlord."

"This seems a nice area, I'm glad you're switching. Can I help you move your stuff?"

"You're so sweet. I'll be okay, I don't have many belongings, not really."

"The offer stands."

"Thanks. What time tomorrow?"

"Around twelve. I'll ring up and book a table for one o'clock, how's that?"

"Great. I'll see you then."

He leaned in for another kiss that appeared to starve her of breath, and she almost caved in, changing her mind about spending extra time with him.

She pulled away and smiled. "Until tomorrow."

"I'll look forward to it. Can I ring you later, if I get lonely?"

Lucy chuckled. "Of course. Not too late, a girl needs her beauty sleep."

"Some might, you definitely don't."

"Charmer. See you. Oh, and thank you for a wonderful day."

"I'll get your bags. What will you do with the extra food?"

"Trisha had her eye on a few things. I'm sure she'll take them off my hands."

He carried the bags to the door and kissed her on the cheek. She waved him off until he turned into the next road. Once inside, she dropped her bags and was suddenly overwhelmed with emotion. Trisha came into the hallway and found her crumpled and on her knees.

"Shit! Lucy, what's wrong? Has he hurt you?"

Tears stinging her eyes, she glanced up at her concerned friend. "No. He didn't do anything wrong. I've had a 'different day', shall we say."

"What's that supposed to mean?"

"I'll tell you over a coffee."

Trisha helped her to her feet, and between them they carried the bags into the kitchen.

"Sit! Tell me what's gone on. If he's hurt you..."

"He hasn't. It wasn't him. However, what occurred affected the rest of the day. I couldn't wait to escape. Oh God, even to my ears that doesn't make sense. My mind is so muddled. I've had to be on my guard today. A few things slipped out that weren't intended."

Trisha placed a mug of coffee on the table and sat opposite her.

"Dangerous things? You'll need to give me more than that, love."

She went over the day's events, starting at the adventure park. Trisha listened and nodded and gasped in all the right places, appreciating what she had gone through.

"So, this brother of his, tell me about him?"

"He's inquisitive I suppose would be the best way to describe him."

"Do you foresee him causing trouble between you?"

She shrugged. "I don't know would be the honest answer. When I was in his company…alone with him…I was back there, in my living hell, all over again. I can't go through that again, Trisha, I just can't."

"Did it alter things between you and Matthew, is that what you're telling me?"

"I don't think so and yet, I put an early end to our day. I'm so mixed up right now. My head's a mess. Do I continue seeing Matthew or not? What if his brother gets suspicious and starts digging into my past, what then?"

Trisha scratched the back of her neck. "Crap, you've had five years of putting your life back on track, only for Matthew to walk in and turn your once stable life upside down. I'm trying to put myself in your position, but I can't. Only you can truly say whether you're willing to continue seeing Matthew or not. You're going to have to balance things, see which wins, your heart or your head. If you have any doubts…"

"I should call it a day with him, is that what you're saying?"

"Love, honestly, I don't know what to suggest. If I tell you what to do and you go ahead and do it but end up spending the rest of your life miserable, then where would that leave us?"

Lucy sighed and shook her head. "I could never blame you. I trust you. You've always had my back through my troubled past."

"And I'm still here for you. Nevertheless, you've never been in this difficult situation before, either. I can't advise you what to do for the best, only you can do that. What I will say is, how do you think you'd feel if the truth came out?"

And there it was, the one question she failed to have a clear answer to.

4

---

*T*he next few weeks passed by like a dream. Matthew had treated her like the proverbial princess, wanting to see her either every day or every other day, never wanting more from her than a kiss. Sometimes they got a little heated, and had they been either in a hotel or at Trisha's house, in her bedroom, she had no doubt at all they would've ended up in bed together. As much as she wanted that to happen, she was also pleased that it hadn't. It meant what they had was built on mutual respect for each other and not just sex, like so many couples' new relationships.

During this time, Trisha had also made her feel at home in her new abode. Life as she knew it was definitely brighter, whichever way she chose to look at it.

That was until Matthew mentioned it was time to meet his parents. During the conversation, her inner panic mode went into full swing. She tried desperately to come across as excited, but even to her ears, her enthusiasm sounded false. She had a mountain to climb in the few days before the meeting took place, she knew that. Conquering her fears would be a daunting task. She'd already succeeded in conquering one fear, the week before when Matthew had surprised her by showing up at the house with a beautiful silver ballgown and sandals for her to wear to a gala ball with him.

Trisha had screamed and fawned over the stunning sparkly dress that just happened to be a perfect fit, when she laid eyes on it. The conversation had gone like this: "Girl, if you don't want to go, I'll willingly take your place. Bloody hell, he's got exquisite taste, for a bloke."

"I suppose he has. I didn't consider that. I can't go, Trisha. I'm not ready for this."

Trisha had stared at her open-mouthed for a few seconds and then shook her head. "I think you're wrong. I've seen you two grow as a couple over the past three weeks or so. You were made for each other. He hasn't pressured you to do anything you didn't want to do, has he?"

"No, not at all. It's in here…" Lucy held a clenched fist over her heart. "Something is telling me that it's all going to go wrong. I'm aware of that and trying to avoid getting involved in stressful situations. Going to a gala dinner is about as stressful as it can get, right?"

"I truly understand where you're coming from, but we're talking about Matthew here. There's no way he'll stand back and let anything happen to you, sweetheart. He's head over heels in love and treats you like a bloody goddess. Take my word for that, no man has ever looked at me that way before, let alone treated me the way he treats you. Stop putting obstructions in the way and live your life how it should be lived, filled with kindness and love."

"Jesus, that's a little over the top, even for you." She sighed heavily, more baffled than ever.

However, she had gone that night, taking hesitant steps into the unknown world of charity functions and, with Matthew alongside her, she had genuinely enjoyed herself. The circle in which Matthew was involved seemed very friendly and keen to make her feel at ease. With Matthew at her side she was, but the second he disappeared, either to visit the toilet or to collect another drink from the bar, she froze and became tongue-tied whilst speaking with someone. How she overcame that, God only knew, because she didn't have a bloody clue. Was it down to her self-confidence perhaps, or lack of it? Under the microscope, that was how she felt at times. Maybe that had more to do with the way Jake had treated her than anything else. She was worried about giving people a false impression. Let's face it, her whole life was nothing but a lie. That was what stuck out in her mind the most. But how the hell did she get past that and get on with her life?

Anyway, that evening was nothing compared to what lay ahead of her at the weekend. She'd researched the rest of Matthew's family, to prepare herself a little, however, there was only so much you could learn via the internet, and Matthew himself had warned her not to believe everything she read on Google. She had three days left to prepare her state of mind and to chill out about being in the same room as his parents, and Jake again, come to that. Maybe that was what was really behind her jitters, coming face to face with him again, after their last disastrous meeting.

It was Wednesday, Shirley's day off at the agency. Lucy started up the car. It kicked into life at the second attempt—she was aware it needed its yearly service, however, funds were tight at the moment but, on a brighter note, payday was just around the corner. Booking a garage slot would be at the top of her agenda once the figure in her bank was the right side of zero.

She was travelling along the dual carriageway on her way into the city centre; the road was fairly clear for this time of the day. Lucy switched on the radio and tapped her fingers along to an oldie but goodie from *Smooth Radio*, her mind wandering to the evening before which she had spent with Matthew at the cinema. He'd persuaded her to see the latest *Mission Impossible* film, which she had surprisingly enjoyed.

Bump!

The car bounced forward. She immediately looked in her rear-view mirror to see a car right up her arse. Turning her attention back to the road ahead, she shouted, "What the fuck do you think you're doing, mate? You've got the whole road to drive on and here you are up my jacksy."

The car surged forward from another shunt.

"Jesus, what is he doing?" She peered into the mirror, trying to make out the driver of the vehicle behind. It was impossible to see, the interior was too dark—no, the bloody person was wearing a ski mask.

Her throat instantly dried up, and her pulse pounded in her wrist as she clung tighter to the steering wheel. *Do I pull over? What if he attacks me? Or worse still, kidnaps me? How do I get out of this...alive?*

Was this karma paying her a visit? After all these years? *God, please help me.*

She looked behind her again; the car was gaining. She prepared herself for another shunt, and a sickening thought filled her mind: *what if the car breaks down? She's hardly in the best of health, is she?*

Her phone was in her handbag in the passenger footwell. She didn't have the courage to remove a hand from the steering wheel; it was taking all her energy to keep the car going in a straight line. She pressed her foot down on the accelerator, trying desperately to escape the bastard.

He followed her, kept to within a few inches of her rear bumper, intimidating her. *Bloody hell! What is wrong with him? Why is he doing this to me? What does he hope to achieve, and why isn't someone trying to help me?* The last part was simple, there was no one around to aid her. Which was probably why the fiend had taken the opportunity to attack her.

There was nothing for it, she had to try and get her phone. Gripping the wheel with her right hand, she dipped down and dragged her bag onto the passenger seat. Even in that time, her car had veered off course when the bastard had bumped her up the arse again. Her tyres squealed as she struggled to regain control. "Bugger, how am I supposed to call anyone? I need all my wits about me. Why? Why are you doing this to me?"

The car's engine whined; the vehicle behind was now pushing her. Bile rose into her throat as the fear mounted. Tears of frustration blurred her vision. "Please, stop it! I'm not sure how much longer I can hang on." Sweat poured from her forehead into her eyes. She blinked the droplets away.

She swallowed down the lump in her throat, but it re-emerged seconds later. *I must try and outsmart him, but how?*

This would be her last attempt to outwit the attacker. She zigzagged across the two lanes of the dual carriageway. At one point the aggressor got alongside her. She saw his head turn her way but couldn't make out his features, then he dropped back again. Lucy floored the car, but the driver remained on her tail. The roundabout sign appeared up ahead, and she breathed out a relieved sigh.

The shunt when it came was more aggressive this time. It snatched the steering wheel out of her hands. She screamed and frantically grappled with the steering wheel to maintain her position on the road but failed. She careened into the hillside and bashed her head on the steering wheel. Dazed, she found the energy to raise her head and watched as the driver flew past her. She broke down then and reached inside her bag for her phone. The first person she called was Matthew. His secretary said he was in an urgent board meeting and she'd get him to call back when he was free. *Great! Not what I wanted to hear.*

Then she called Trisha's mobile.

"Hi, hon. What's up?"

"I've been in a crash."

"No! Where are you?"

"At the roundabout, coming off the dual carriageway. Please, Trisha, hurry. Call the police, get help."

"Why? What are you saying? You're not making any sense, Luc."

"Someone did this."

"Oh my God. Stay there! Grr...that was dumb. I'll be with you in fifteen minutes. Lock the car. I'm going to ring nine-nine-nine now."

"Hurry, he could come back, I'm a sitting duck here, in no fit state to fight anyone off, Trisha."

"Don't worry. Have you locked the doors?"

"Yes."

"I'm going. Ring me if you're at all worried about anything. You've got this, hon."

"I hope so. Bye."

She scanned the road on either side of her, confused as to why there was no one else around, especially at this time of day. It was a struggle for her to think straight. She needed to speak to Matthew, to help put things back into perspective.

Around five minutes later, sirens filled the air, and a police car pulled up alongside her. A female officer left the vehicle and ran towards the car.

Lucy lowered the driver's window. "Please, you have to help me."

"Are you hurt?"

"A slight bump to the head. This was intentional. Someone did this to me."

"What? Drove you off the road?"

"Yes, you have to find them."

"How long ago did this happen?"

"I don't know, five, ten, fifteen minutes. My head hurts."

"I'll be right back." The officer stepped away from the car and spoke into her radio.

Another uniformed officer appeared beside her, a male in his thirties. He peered into the back seat. "Are you all right? Can you move? Do you want to get out of the vehicle or stay there?"

"I'll feel safer inside, thank you."

He took a step back to join his colleague, and they discussed the issue for a few seconds then returned.

The male asked, "Can you tell us exactly what happened?"

"I'll try." She held a hand up to hold her aching head. "I was driving along, normal speed, when this car started bumping into me from the rear. I tried to escape him…"

The male took out his notebook, and his pen flew across the page. "Him? Did you see the driver?"

"No, that was an assumption. He was wearing a mask of sorts. I think it was one of those ski masks."

"All right, do you know why he attacked you?"

She shook her head, and giddiness took over. "Oh God, I feel sick."

"It'll be the wound to your head. Try not to make any sudden movements. Has it settled down now?"

"Yes, a little. I can't answer that. There was only the two of us on this road. I thought that was strange. He bumped me and continued to do it until he drove me off the road."

"Have you fallen out with anyone lately?"

"No, nothing like that."

"Okay, it's rare for people just to pounce on someone out of the blue. Are you sure? Or is your head hurting that much, hampering your thinking?"

"I don't know. I'm sorry."

Just then Trisha drew up. She rushed out of the car and approached them.

"Stand back," the male officer said, raising his arm in front of her.

Trisha stomped her foot. "What? This is my best friend. I was the one who called you guys, give me a break."

"Okay, calm down, I'm not a mind reader, Miss. Give me two minutes, we're trying to ascertain what happened here."

Trisha raised her hands and stepped back a few paces. She kicked out at the earth beneath her. And then walked round in a circle. Lucy tried not to be distracted too much and concentrated on what the officer was asking her.

"What type of vehicle was it? Colour, make, model? Did you get the registration number by any chance?"

"No, no, I couldn't tell you. I was in the middle of fighting for my life, I'm sorry," Lucy replied, feeling a failure.

"Give her a break. Have you called for an ambulance? By the look of that cut on her head, I reckon she's suffering from concussion. Surely this can wait," Trisha shouted, her voice rising during her comment.

The female officer had a quiet word in her partner's ear and nodded. "Okay, we'll call it a day there. The offender will probably be miles away by now. We'll need to question you further when you're up to it, Miss."

"Okay, although I won't be able to tell you anything else," Lucy said, disheartened at the way things had gone with the police.

The male officer gestured for Trisha to come closer, and the two officers took a few steps back. In the distance, a siren wailed.

"Thank God, the ambulance is on its way, love. How do you feel?" Trisha reached inside the car and grasped Lucy's hand.

"Like my head belongs to someone else. Shit! I need to ring Shirley, it's her day off; I was supposed to be opening up today."

"Hand me your phone. I'll do that for you."

Slowly, Lucy sought out her phone and handed it through the window. "Thanks. Her number is in my contacts under 'Shirley'."

"You need to punch in your password for me."

Trisha angled the mobile back to Lucy, and at the third attempt she successfully opened up her phone. Trisha rang Shirley and explained the situation.

"I'm sorry, Shirley," Lucy shouted before Trisha hung up.

"She said to pass on her best wishes and not to beat yourself up about not opening up. She's going in herself."

"Bugger. I hate letting people down."

A paramedic hopped out of the ambulance and crouched at the window to speak to her. "Hello, I'm Sam, and you are?"

"Lucy Brent. Please, I don't want a fuss. Can you just check me over and send me on my way?"

"We'll see. I take it you hit your head on impact?"

"Yes. I didn't lose consciousness, if that's going to be your next question."

"It was. Okay, then that's a good sign. Can we get you out of the vehicle? I need to see if you can walk in a straight line."

He opened the door. Lucy unfastened her seatbelt and slipped her hand into the paramedic's. "Oops, I'm a little unsteady."

"Take your time, there's no rush. Follow that white line over there, if you will?"

Trisha took a step in Lucy's direction, but the paramedic shook his head. She remained in place and watched instead.

Lucy's legs wobbled slightly, not as much as she thought they would, and, in the end, she did well in her task.

"You get a gold star for that. Look, if you're feeling better already, then I'm not going to try and force you to go to hospital."

"Thanks, I'm sure I'll be fine in an hour or so. I'd hate to waste the medical staff's time. I'm aware of the stress the NHS is under."

The paramedic tutted. "Don't feel sorry for me, I'm here to make sure you're okay. I can take you in, no problem."

"I'd rather not. Trisha can take me home, if that's all right with the officers?"

The male officer nodded. "It's all right with us. We'll call a tow truck and get your car cleared. Sorry to have to tell you that I think they'll declare it a write-off."

"Crap, that's just what I need, not. Okay, time to start saving for a new one. Just when I was getting on my feet as well," Lucy complained.

Trisha rubbed her arm. "We can share mine, or I can give you a lift into town, no problem."

Lucy covered Trisha's hand with her own. "I owe you so much as it is."

"Nonsense. You'd do the same for me, I know you would. Did you ring Matthew? Maybe he'll put his hand in his pocket and buy you a car, you never know."

"Yes, he's in a meeting. I wouldn't want him doing that. It wouldn't feel right, not to me."

"Okay, ladies, I'm going to skedaddle now. Keep an eye on that head of yours. Any blurred vision or the sign of a thumping headache, promise me you'll go straight to A&E?" the paramedic said, his expression less stressed.

"I promise. Trisha will ensure that happens, too, I'm sure. She's my guardian angel."

"Take care." He waved and jumped back in the ambulance.

"I think you should have gone to hospital, love, you know, to get checked over," Trisha whispered.

"I couldn't. You know that. Think about it."

Trisha grimaced and shook her head. "Silly me. Okay, let's get you home."

"Leave the car with us. We'll take care of it and give you an update later on," the male officer said.

Trisha hooked her arm through Lucy's and helped her to the passenger seat of her car. Lucy buckled up. Trisha got in and kicked the engine into life. They had barely left the scene when the emotions came flooding out. Lucy bawled and covered her face with shaking hands.

Trisha indicated and pulled into a nearby lay-by. Without saying anything, she gathered Lucy in her arms. "Let it out, sweetheart."

"I was so scared, it brought dozens of bad memories flooding back. Why would someone deliberately target me?"

Trisha sighed and sat back. "I don't know. I'm not happy about leaving you alone. I'm going to take the rest of the day off and look after you."

"No, I'll be fine. I don't expect you to do that, not for me."

"I can assure you, I wouldn't do it for anyone else. You need me to be with you today. If I dropped you back to the house and shot off to work and came home to find a quivering wreck, well, how do you think that would make me feel? I'll ring my boss now, lay it on a bit thick."

Trisha made the call, told her boss they were on the way to hospital and that she would update him during the day. He also sent his best wishes to Lucy, making her feel guilty as hell.

Once they arrived home, Trisha fussed over her like a mother hen. She rushed upstairs and returned with the quilt and pillow from Lucy's bed and ordered her to lie on the sofa.

Lucy settled on to the sofa and, not long after, her mobile rang. It was Matthew.

"Hey, you! It's unusual for you to ring me at work, something wrong?"

"It's nothing to worry about…"

"Okay, whenever someone says that, it usually means the opposite. What's going on, Lucy?"

It was obvious how anxious he was. "I've had an accident. Please, I'm fine. Trisha picked me up, and she's taken the day off to look after me. I just wanted you to know," she rambled, not giving him the chance to interrupt her.

"What? Are you hurt? Have you been to hospital?"

"I'm shaken up, that's all. The paramedic was happy to send me home. Please, I don't want you all to fuss over me."

"Don't fuss? Are you kidding me? Of course we're going to make a fuss, we love you. Damn, I've got important meetings planned for the rest of the day. I won't be able to see you until later. I promise I'll drop round after work, if you don't think I'll be intruding, that is."

"I'd love to see you later. My head should be clear by then. Please, try not to worry, I'm fine, honestly. My nurse is taking good care of me."

"If you're sure. I can arrange for a private nurse to visit you, you only have to say the word."

"Don't do that. I'll be fine after a quick nap. I have to go now, my head is thumping, and I'm having trouble thinking straight."

"Okay, I get the message. Can you pass the phone over to Trisha?"

"Only if you promise to be nice."

"Have you ever known me to be otherwise?"

"Hmm...the truth is, I haven't known you long enough yet."

"You'll just have to take my word for it then."

"Passing you over now." She thrust the phone at Trisha who was sitting at the bottom of her makeshift bed. "He wants a word with you. Don't take any bullshit from him."

Trisha's face was a picture. "Me? Why does he want to speak to me?" she asked, her hand covering the phone.

"He'll be fine. Just reassure him that I'm okay, will you?"

She nodded and tentatively spoke into the phone. "Hello, Matthew...yes, she's fine...no, there's no need for you to send anyone else...that'll be fine...of course I'll ring if she takes a turn for the worse. Okay, speak soon." She exhaled the breath she'd been holding in. "Bloody hell. I've never known a man care so much. You've hooked a good 'un there, love."

"I got the gist of what he said." She smiled and snuggled under the quilt and dozed off.

The doorbell woke her a few hours later. Trisha walked into the room holding a large bouquet of flowers and a wicker basket.

"How beautiful. What does the card say?" Lucy asked, sitting upright. Her vision was slightly blurred, however, she was determined not to let on about that, fearing her life wouldn't be worth living if she did.

"Thinking of you. Enjoy lunch on me. Love you, Matthew XX."

"That's so sweet and thoughtful. What's in the basket?"

Trisha opened the lid and gasped. "Oh my, I don't think I've ever seen a grander picnic basket."

She emptied the contents onto the quilt beside Lucy.

"Oh my, neither have I. I fear it's going to be far too rich for my stomach today. Duck pâté, I don't think I've ever tried that before."

"Bloody hell. Look at this fabulous bread, it's still ruddy warm. How the hell has he managed that?"

"It must have come from that exclusive shop in Bath. What a waste."

"Are you crazy? Waste, why is it a waste?"

"Because it's going to be too rich for me. You carry on, though, don't let me stop you."

"I'm not going to eat your gift, don't be silly. All this stuff in the jars will keep, and the bread will last at least a few days. Let me sort out something light for you to eat. Fancy some cheese and bread?" Trisha held up a small baguette roll and some Camembert in a box.

Lucy nodded until she wished she hadn't. "Okay, you've twisted my arm, on one proviso."

"Which is?"

"You dig in and help yourself, don't hold back."

"Okay, I will, I promise. Want a coffee to wash it down or this?" She held up a bottle of red wine.

"A coffee might be better, the way my head feels." She winced, regretting voicing the words out loud.

"You heard what the paramedic said. We should get you to the hospital to get checked over."

"Please, don't make me go, it'll only cause extra problems. I don't have any medical records for a start. I've never thought about the ramifications of that side of things before."

"Bugger, neither have I. We'll put our heads together, excuse the pun, this afternoon and come up with something to combat the issue for the future. Pretty dumb of us not to have thought about that in the beginning." She placed her head in her hands. "Very dumb, in fact. What if you'd been lying in hospital in a coma now, what then?"

"I don't want to think about it, but I think we should come up with a plan. God, my head hurts even more now, imagining that."

"Then let's leave it for now and address the issue if it ever arises in the future. Deal?"

"Okay, I agree. I need to go to the loo. Did you mention something about a coffee?"

"I can take the hint. Can you make it up the stairs?"

"I'm sure I can manage. I'll give you a shout if I get stuck."

Trisha held out a hand and pulled Lucy to her feet.

After taking a steady trip upstairs, she came down again and entered the kitchen. Trisha had laid out all the goodies from the hamper on the table.

"Bloody hell, that lot must have cost him a packet."

"I was thinking the same. Here you go, cheese and bread, unless anything else has taken your fancy? How are you feeling?"

"My head is really muzzy. It might be because I'm hungry, though."

"True enough, hunger does that to me. Go back in the lounge, I'll bring it in."

Lucy passed by the window on her way back to the sofa. She peered out to see what the weather was like and gasped. Trisha came in the room behind her and rushed towards her.

"What's wrong?"

The car that was sitting outside the house sped away. Lucy's hand shook, and the words stuck to her tongue. Trisha placed the tray down on the coffee table and guided Lucy back to the sofa.

"Here, sit down. What did you see, love? Tell me?"

"I'm not sure I can. I thought…"

"What? Who was out there? Do you want me to call the police? Or Matthew?"

"No. Don't do that. Maybe it was my eyes playing tricks on me."

"Okay, but what did you think you saw then?"

"The car that ran me off the road today."

Trisha ran back to the window, cursing. "Are you sure?"

"No. That's just it. It was probably my mind working overtime, imagining things that weren't there."

"That's so unlike you. I'm going to go out there and take a look."

Lucy grabbed Trisha's hand and pleaded, "No, please, don't do that."

"Nonsense. I'll leave the door open. If he's out there, I'll come back in and call the police. I'm not having you live in fear like this. Look at you, you're breaking out in a sweat."

"Be careful. Why take the risk?"

"I'll be right back, don't stress out. I have to make sure there's no one out there for my own peace of mind."

Trisha left the room before Lucy could say anything else. She flipped back the quilt and peered out of the window again, not wanting to let Trisha out of her sight.

Trisha stretched her neck over the gate, turned around and shook her head. Lucy sighed with relief.

"Thank God for that." She tapped on the window and gestured for Trisha to come back in the house, then dived back under the covers.

"Nothing out there at all. I'll keep an eye open throughout the day. Stop worrying about it, love, okay?" Trisha stated, running a hand down Lucy's arm.

"I promise. I fear it's going to be easier said than done, though."

Trisha handed Lucy the plate of food she'd prepared and placed her mug of coffee on the floor beside her.

Lucy stared down at the food, her stomach churning still, and glanced up at Trisha. "I'm not sure I can eat this now."

"Nonsense, get it down your neck."

She nibbled on the bread, got the taste for it, and then slathered the bread with the cheese. "It's delicious. I'm over it, I'm sure it was all in my mind."

"That's my girl. You need to eat to put some colour back in your cheeks."

"What have you got?"

"I thought I'd try one of the pâtés." She took a bite and moaned appreciatively. "It's divine, never tasted anything like this before. I suppose the quality speaks for itself. Hey, you should get sick more often if this is how Matthew is going to treat you. I was joking, don't throw a wobbler."

"You're unbelievable at times. I'd be lost without you fighting my corner, though. Thank you for spending the day with me."

"You're welcome. I couldn't leave you here by yourself. You seem a little brighter, barring the mishap of what's just happened."

"I do feel more human after my nap."

"It gave me a chance to read a few chapters from my book, especially as I was forced to keep quiet, in case I woke you."

"You're so considerate. I'm sorry to be such a burden. You can do without friends like me hanging around you all the time."

"And you do have a habit of talking shit at times."

They both laughed. It eased her conscience a little.

"I love you."

"Ditto. We're a team, you and me, and it will always be that way, no matter who comes along in the future, right?"

"I'm going to make sure Matthew doesn't interfere with our friendship, that's for sure."

"Good. I get the sense he won't. I could be wrong, though."

5

$\mathcal{M}$atthew showed up at the house at around six that evening. He'd rung ahead to warn her, giving Lucy the chance to have a bath and make herself look half presentable. She had folded up the bedding she'd been snuggled under for catnaps most of the day. He sat on the sofa next to her, clinging on to her hand, almost as if he was too scared to let her go.

"Whoa! Why didn't you tell me about this earlier?"

"I didn't want to worry you."

"What did the police have to say? Could you give them a number plate?"

"No. He came out of nowhere…"

He pulled her close and gently kissed the bruise that had developed on her forehead. "My poor baby, I can't believe you had to go through that alone. Listening to you now, it's as if you've brushed it off as a minor incident. It wasn't, not if you think someone deliberately set out to hurt you."

"If he'd bumped me up the rear once, maybe I'd be willing to accept it was an accident, but I lost count of how many times his car made contact with mine. Look, I'm fine, all's well that ends well. The same thing can't be said about my car—that's a different issue entirely."

He waved his hand. "I'll get you a new one."

"What? I can't allow you to do that. I'll get a loan from the bank."

"Oh, no you won't. I'll pay. I know how proud you are; if you want to pay me back over time, that's up to you. We'll draw up a contract."

"That sounds doable. My funds are tight at present. Hopefully, now I've moved in with Trisha my balance will be looking a little healthier in no time at all."

"That's settled then. When do you want to go car shopping? Tomorrow?"

"Why not? Oh, wait, why don't we leave it until the weekend instead?"

Matthew chewed on his bottom lip.

"Is there a problem?"

He tutted. "No, I'm sure we can fit both in…it's a major deal picking the right car for your needs."

"Fit both in? What do you mean?"

"Don't forget we're meeting my parents this weekend. Mother rang today to remind me. We've been summoned for dinner."

"Summoned? Did she actually put it that way? I hadn't forgotten."

"No, that was me putting my spin on it. Are you up to meeting the rest of the family or would you rather I delayed it?"

Her heart pounded harder. "Will Jake be there?"

"I should think so. That'll help break the ice, won't it?"

Lucy gulped and then forced a smile. "I suppose so. What if I have a relapse in between now and then?"

"Then I'll postpone it. Do you think that's likely?"

"How do I know? My head is really fuzzy, despite me being asleep most of the day. Well, on and off anyway."

"It's bound to be. Is that a hint for me to get going?"

She slapped his arm. "Hardly, I like having you here. I've missed you."

He leaned over for a kiss. "Thanks, I've missed you, too. What are you having for dinner?"

"I haven't thought about it. Thank you for the picnic lunch, it was amazing, not that I managed to eat much of the contents. Mind you, Trisha did a lot of damage to it."

"Good, I'm glad you both enjoyed it. Where is Trisha?"

"She left to go to Neil's, giving us time alone. She's so thoughtful."

"She's a gem, to have taken the day off work to look after you. She put me to shame."

"Don't say that. You've both been amazing. Shall we have a takeaway?"

"I know an excellent Indian, if you're up for that?"

"I'd love one. Nothing too spicy for me, a nice korma, or I can share one with you. I don't think I'm up to eating a big meal."

"Okay, how about a chicken korma with a lot of side dishes and a keema naan and chips?"

She laughed. "Sounds fattening, go for it."

While Matthew placed the call, she wandered out into the kitchen to prepare the plates and cutlery.

Matthew joined her and slipped his arms around her waist. "You feel good. *This* feels good."

She spun around in his arms. "It does indeed."

He kissed her. "It's good to be alone with you. I can't remember what my life was like without you in it. If anything bad had happened to you today…worse than what did happen, I mean…well, I would've been devastated. Mum and Dad are going to love you."

"I hope so. It's always a risk meeting the family."

"I know. I wish I'd had the opportunity of meeting your parents. Hey, you've already met Jake and you got on all right with him, didn't you?"

"I did," she lied.

"Mum and Dad are just the same. You're going to get on well together, I can tell."

"If you say so."

She had three days to prepare her nerves for the visit. She hoped Jake hadn't put his spoke in and pre-warned his parents about what to expect from her. She'd hate them to get the wrong impression without even meeting her.

"Hey, where did you go?"

"Sorry, I was thinking what Mum and Dad's reaction would've been to knowing you, that's all."

"Sorry, love, it must've been awful to have lost them together like that. Oh God, I bet that's added to how all this has affected you today, too, am I right?"

"Perhaps. I don't suppose it helped, knowing they were killed in a car accident. You would've loved them and they you. Life is such a bitch at times. All we set out to achieve in this world is the right to be happy and successful. Why does it have to throw us a curveball now and again to steer us off track?"

"That's what life is all about, overcoming the challenges. We all come out stronger at the other end."

"Maybe not some of us. Losing my parents the way I did…well…it was hard. Took a massive toll on my well-being for a long time."

"I'm sorry to hear that, Lucy. I can't offer you any words of wisdom because I've never been in that situation. Know this, that going forward, I'll be here for you, always. I know we haven't been going out that long, but, well, we're meant to be together. Your problems are my problems from this day forward. No looking back on things you can't change that happened in your past. Okay?"

She raised her head, wanting him to kiss her. "What did I ever do to deserve you? We're definitely kindred spirits, not that I usually believe in that codswallop. I suppose you have to experience it to believe in it."

He smiled down at her. "I feel the same way about you."

The doorbell rang. Matthew volunteered to answer it and returned carrying a huge paper bag, filled to the brim with containers.

"Bloody hell, that was quick. Look at the size of it."

Matthew beamed. "I've heard that somewhere before."

"Cheeky. We'd better do this together otherwise it's going to get cold."

They got busy in the kitchen, and after all the dishes were empty and their plates were piled high, Matthew suggested heating them up in the microwave.

They enjoyed their meal. Matthew ended up eating most of hers as well as his own, and then they cuddled up in front of a film he spotted amongst Trisha's DVD collection. Lucy was asleep next to him when Trisha came home at around ten.

Lucy stretched. "Have you had a good evening?"

"The best. What about you guys?"

"Ditto. Sorry to have fallen asleep, though."

Matthew kissed the top of her head. "I didn't mind. I'm going to have to make a move now. Will you be okay, now that Trisha is home?"

"Of course. You could have gone sooner, you didn't have to stay with me all evening."

"Hush now, it's fine."

Trisha snuck out of the room and returned once she'd heard the front door close, signifying that Matthew had left. She sat next to Lucy. "How are you?"

"I'm feeling a lot better now, bloated, but good."

"Did you tell him about the incident outside?"

"No, I couldn't bring myself to say it. He kind of floored me..."

"Floored you? How?"

"He told me his parents have invited me for *dinner* at the weekend. I thought it was just going to be a quick visit, afternoon tea or something."

"Oh shit! Dinner, eh? How do you feel about it?"

"You took the words out of my mouth. Oh shit! How do I prepare for that? Especially after how tits-up the meeting with Jake went, not that Matthew knows about that."

"By being yourself. Who gives a shit what he thought about you? That's his problem, not yours."

"I hear what you're saying, but what if he's there? How should I react towards him? What if there's an atmosphere? He regarded me with contempt all the time we were alone together. He did the complete opposite with Matthew there, that's the perplexing part for me. How do I handle such awkward, or should I say, diverse behaviour?"

"By being you. Don't let him screw up what you have with Matthew. Do all you can to avoid being alone with him."

"You think? How difficult is that going to be? Grr…what a mess. I'm going to be dwelling on this right up until Saturday now."

"You won't. Put it out of your head. Hey, you have more important things to consider than what that wanker thinks of you."

"Such as?"

"What you're going to wear."

"Bugger! That thought never even crossed my mind."

"I have a couple of evening dresses that I think will be suitable."

"I can't keep borrowing your clothes, love. I could wear that dress Matthew bought me…"

"Behave, of course you can. Not a good idea. That one has been seen publicly already. Once you two get married, you can buy me a whole new wardrobe, how does that sound?"

"Talk about pre-empting things. Who said anything about getting married?"

"Umm… have you seen how Matthew looks at you? The guy is besotted, and I don't mean in a yucky way either. He's fallen hard, a bloody fool could see that."

"The thing is, I don't want to rush things."

Trisha inclined her head a little. "Don't want to, or you're too scared to get in too deep?"

Lucy covered her face with her hands. "Don't do this to me. I don't know how I feel."

Trisha gently pulled Lucy's hands away. "Why? Because of what happened before? You can't judge every man you meet by *his* standards, love."

"This is all so easy for you, isn't it?" she snapped. "I'm sorry, I didn't mean that. You've been so kind to me, more than that, the last thing I want to do is fall out with you over this. I need time, time to think, time to breathe. Maybe the incident today has blighted my relationship a little."

"Why? Do you blame Matthew?"

"No. Shit! I don't know. All this has stirred up the past I'd done my best to forget about. My head's a mess, and I don't just mean because of the bruising and possible concussion I have."

"Are you telling me you've had a terrible evening with Matthew? Because from where I was standing, you both seemed really happy in each other's company."

"See, I told you my head was a mess."

"You need to sort yourself out, Luc. If you start imagining problems that aren't in your relationship, well, you're only going to end up pushing him away. You hear me?"

Lucy rubbed at her tired, gritty eyes and nodded. "I hear you. I'm going to try and make sure that doesn't happen. What about the man?"

"The one who tried to run you off the road?"

"Yes, how do I figure out what he wants and why?"

"Now that I can't work out for you. Hang in there. The next time you see him, you need to shout, no matter who's around, just bring attention to yourself and him. I'm sure that'll do the trick."

"I'll try, if you think that's going to work."

"I do. Now, do you fancy a cup of Horlicks? I think I have some in the cupboard."

"Go on then, it might help me sleep, not that I haven't done enough of that already today."

Trisha smiled and went into the kitchen. Lucy waited until she left and then walked over to the window and discreetly looked out. She could see nothing through the darkness in the distance or in the nearby glow of the streetlight. She let go of the breath she was holding on to. Knowing that the house was well lit helped to reassure her and put her mind at ease a little. She returned to the couch before Trisha re-entered the room carrying two mugs and a plate of chocolate Hobnobs on a tray.

They drank and ate while they recapped their respective evenings and then called it a night. Trisha treated her like an invalid and supported her up the stairs first and then raced back down to collect her quilt and pillow, while Lucy nipped to the bathroom to have a wash and clean her teeth.

"Do you need anything else?" Trisha asked from the doorway.

"No, thanks for everything, Trisha. A girl couldn't wish for a better friend."

"You're welcome. Do you think you'll be well enough to go to work in the morning?"

"I think so, that's the plan anyway. Can I cadge a lift?"

"I was about to offer. Goodnight, love."

"Goodnight, sleep well, and thank you again."

Trisha switched off the main light, leaving only the bedside lamp on next to her friend. Lucy laid there for a while, her mind racing until she forced herself to calm down with a few useful breathing exercises Shirley had taught her at work, and then she turned off the light. Sleep came easily once she was snuggled up warmly under the quilt.

6

---

*F*ive years ago

I can't do this any more. What gives him the right to treat me this way? I'm such a wuss for putting up with this mental torture for years on end. It must stop soon. I have to get out of here before he makes good on his threat to kill me. Has it really come to this? We used to be so happy...in the beginning. I keep trying to think of when that happiness gave way to the hatred on show today. It glistens in his eyes, is evident in every tiny wrinkle in his face when he glares at me.

I'm petrified most of the day. He keeps me locked up in the house when he's at work. Drops me off at the supermarket while he sits in the car. Once I come out, laden down with bags, he interrogates me, demands to know what I spent his cash on. If he was that bothered, why didn't he do the damn shopping himself? Because it was women's work, just like every chore around the house. It was the man's job to go out and earn the money to keep the house going but a woman's role was to cook, clean, wash, and iron his clothes ready *for work every day. One unexpected crease in a shirt and she knew about it.*

He'd given her a few black eyes over the years and she'd been forced to go out to buy makeup so her friends and family never found out. Not that she had many friends nowadays. He'd driven them away with his vindictive tongue, not caring what he said to them if he found them in his house when he walked through the door at night.

She'd begged him to be reasonable on more than one occasion and ended up with a blacker eye than she had already.

Her parents knew there was something wrong—her father had taken her to one side during a visit one day, pleaded with her to confide in him. Dad was never one to interfere in a couple's relationship, but even she knew he was aware things weren't right between them. She had cried that night, once her parents had left. Patrick had insinuated that she'd been crying on Daddy's shoulder—she hadn't. That hadn't stopped him screwing her arm tightly at the wrist. What started off as a Chinese burn soon turned into him almost breaking it.

Of course, he was full of remorse after he saw the bruises, as usual. However, that was short-lived, the same as always. He'd be kind to her for a few hours to make up for it, drop some of the regimental ways with how he acted and treated her, but it never lasted. The hatred and evil tones would reappear, usually on the second day.

I loathe him. I'm trying to figure out a way to escape. I haven't come across one yet, otherwise I would be gone by now. My heart is heavy. I hate myself as much as he hates me for being such a wimp. How I overcome that is a conundrum for me. Here I sit, day after day— when I'm not busy keeping the house spotlessly clean, that is—trying to figure out what went wrong, when it went wrong.

Patrick wasn't always like that. Everyone who met him at the start of our relationship assured me I had a one-in-a-million on my hands. I've racked my brain numerous times trying to fathom out what the trigger had been for him to turn into this monster.

It's almost five now. The dinner is on the go. He'll be home at five-thirty, on the dot, and expect his meal on the table. It's his favourite tonight: lamb chops, mashed potatoes and greens. That's sure to put him in a good mood, depending on how his day at work has gone, of course. It's been a little traumatic lately, since the takeover. His job was secure, he was upper management at the factory, but he'd been forced to take on extra responsibility with no change to his salary. The beatings had increased lately due to this. I tried to talk to him about the situation, only voicing my concerns had increased his anger almost to the point of him nearly putting me in hospital.

She had found a bandage in the pharmacy while doing the shopping and wrapped it around her bruised ribs, fearing that he'd broken one or more of them, but he'd refused to take her to the hospital. He'd managed to talk her around, the way he usually did. However, she was getting to the end of her punchbag days now. Something had to give, she was conscious of that. Either she got out of there or he'd be forced to dump her body when things got out of hand. It was definitely heading that way from what she could tell.

If only I had the courage and determination to get out.

Shit! He's home early, and the dinner isn't cooked yet.

She upped the gas underneath the pots on the stove and boiled the kettle ready to make him his tea the way he liked it, not too strong and not too weak.

Recognising that he'd had a bad day, she smiled at him. It was the wrong thing to do. He stormed across the room, yanked her hair, twisting it around his hand, and sneered at her, his spittle flying and landing in her eyes and on her cheek.

"What are you grinning at?"

"I wasn't. I smiled at you to welcome you home, darling."

"Don't *darling* me. You think using endearments will soften the blow? It doesn't wash with me, bitch."

"I'm so…"

Words only inflamed the situation. The punches rained down on her as heavy as a monsoon. Before long she was lying on the floor, his feet ramming into her stomach. She pleaded with him to stop, but her pleas fell on deaf ears. He was in the zone and he wouldn't get out of it until it was too late.

His mobile rang, drawing her beating to a halt. He walked out of the room. Gingerly, wincing in pain, she rose to her feet. Her gaze rested on the knife block for the briefest of moments. She didn't have the courage to pluck one from its slot; instead, she tiptoed past the lounge, where he was talking to the caller, and up the stairs. Locking the bathroom door, she ended up spending the night in there, alone, shivering against the cold, which was preferable to facing another beating that could possibly end her life.

I have to get out of here…and soon.

7

"No! Please don't hurt me, not again!"

"Lucy, wake up, sweetheart. You're safe. Wake up!"

She shot up in bed and cowered from her best friend until the realisation of where she was hit her, and that she was indeed safe. The tears came then, and lots of them. Trisha didn't ask any questions. She simply hugged her, rocked her back and forth until the tears and shuddering ceased, then she released Lucy.

"Oh God, they've started again."

"What? The nightmares? Are you sure it wasn't about today's incident?"

"No. I was taken back to the dreadful days when he used to beat me. Bloody hell, will it never end? Just when I thought I had something to look forward to in my life, he crops up again, filling my head and my dreams."

"It was a silly dream, don't dwell on it, it'll probably be a one-off, love. Want me to make you a cuppa?"

"No thanks. I know you're right, at least, I hope you are, but it was so vivid. I was back there with him. I never want to go back there."

"You know that's not going to happen. Think positive about this. He can no longer hurt you, ever."

"Only in my nightmares, eh? What if I continue to have them? How do I explain them to Matthew when the time comes that we share a bed?"

"You'll think of something. Perhaps put it down to your parents' accident, tell him that it's a recurring nightmare that emerges when you least expect it to."

"Good idea. I wish I didn't have to go through them all the same, they're so draining. They also scare the crap out of me. It's like I'm back there, reliving the beatings and abuse."

Trisha touched her cheek. "I can imagine. It's time to move on. He can no longer hurt you. You have a new man in your life. I'm sure he won't turn out the same way."

"How do you know that? Patrick wasn't always a monster to begin with. That side of his nature developed after a few months." *His* face filled her mind once more, and she shuddered.

"Don't do this, love. The truth is, no one knows what someone is really like until you live with them and truly get to know them."

"So Matthew could turn out to be the same?"

Trisha shrugged. "Like I said, there are no guarantees in this life."

"Oh God. How will I cope if Matthew turns out to be like him? Look at his brother's reaction to me. Shit! You don't think that's why the nightmares have started again, do you?"

"If you want my opinion, it's more likely to be because of the accident today. I'll be right back."

Lucy watched Trisha leave and hugged the quilt around her. All she'd ever wanted was to feel safe and loved. She'd felt the opposite with Patrick. Was she wrong to think Matthew could be like *him*? Was that fair?

Trisha returned with a mug of tea. "This will do the trick— camomile tea, it'll soothe your nerves and calm you down."

"Thanks, love. I'm so sorry I disturbed your sleep."

"Don't be. I'll always be here for you, Lucy. Always, day or night, even if you end up moving in with Matthew, call me whatever time of day it is, got that?"

"I couldn't do that. Anyway, that's a long way off. I'm not about to jump in feet first with Matthew. I've sworn to myself that I will take the time to get to know him, inside and out, before I make the leap and move in with him. Not just him, I mean any man in the future."

"Good idea. That's one reason why I haven't committed fully to Neil, I suppose."

"Do you think it's a sign of the times?"

"Possibly. More and more women are keen on remaining single and doing things with their lives, including not sharing them with men. I'm not sure I'd go down that route, I'd miss the sex too much."

That eased the tension filling the room, and they both laughed and took a sip from their mugs.

"Why does life always have to be so complicated? Do you think anyone escapes the trials and tribulations it dishes out?"

"I doubt it. My mum used to always remind me how lucky I am that I have all my limbs when I used to complain how harshly I'd been treated in the past."

"That's true enough, there are always people worse off than we are."

"There are, however, that doesn't mean that we have to discount what's going on with you, that's not what I was saying in the slightest."

"I appreciate what you're saying, don't worry."

They finished their drinks, and Trisha kissed her goodnight. Afraid of what the darkness might bring, Lucy left the bedside light on for the rest of the night and fell asleep sometime around three.

She woke just after seven and jumped in the shower.

Trisha was waiting outside the bathroom for her. "You look a lot brighter today."

"I feel it. What time are you leaving?"

"Eight-fifteen too early for you? I'd like to escape the heavy traffic if at all possible."

"Sounds good to me."

. . .

*T*risha dropped her quite close to the edge of town, and Lucy walked the final ten minutes or so, eager to get some fresh air in her lungs after being cooped up at home the previous day. She'd tried to cover the bruise as much as she could with makeup and had even brought her cosmetics with her to top it up during the day, something that never usually crossed her mind.

Shirley gave her a huge bear hug the second she laid eyes on her.

Lucy pulled back and said, "I'm so sorry to have let you down yesterday."

"Hush now. It wasn't your fault. How are you feeling? Are you fit enough to be here?"

"I'm fine. Still got a slight fuzziness in my head, but it's miniscule to how it was yesterday. I'm fighting fit by comparison."

"Well, I'm not expecting you to tear around here, just take it easy, that's an order, okay?"

She mock-saluted her boss. "I will. I'm not an invalid, though, just to be clear."

"I get that. How about your car?"

"No good. It's a write-off. Trisha dropped me off on the edge of town this morning. Matthew is taking me car hunting at the weekend."

Shirley raised her eyebrows. "Wow, you've got a real gem there. Is he paying? No, don't answer that, it's no concern of mine, and I shouldn't have asked."

"Why not? I don't have any secrets. Matthew offered to buy the car for me, but I said I would pay him back once I get on my feet. Now I'm sharing with Trisha, I have more funds to play with."

"I could always give you an advance on your wages, you only have to ask."

"I definitely wouldn't want that, it would be a slippery slope for me. Thanks for offering, it means a lot."

"I value you as an employee, Lucy. Promise you'll ask if you need any extra time off or anything?"

"I will, although I feel bad about you giving up your day off yesterday. What are you going to do about that? Have tomorrow off instead?"

"Nope. What's one day in the grand scheme of things? I'm just glad to see you fit and well after your scare. Have the police been in touch?"

"Nope, not yet. I'm not sure they'll be able to do anything really. It's not as if I could give them any details about the car or the driver—he was wearing a mask."

"No! Why? Shit! That doesn't sound good. Do you think he deliberately targeted you then? Oh God, forget I said that. What a dreadful thought."

"One that I've definitely considered. The truth is, I don't know and I'm not likely to find out either."

"Another thing bugging me, why didn't you go to hospital? Didn't the coppers call for an ambulance to attend?"

"They did. That was down to me. I told the paramedic I didn't want to waste his time and that I felt okay. I didn't, but I knew the hospital would've sent me home and didn't want to waste their time, not when the NHS is under so much strain."

"You're a better woman than me, love, I'd have been milking it if I were in your shoes. Anyway, sit down. You answer the phone today. I'll jump up and down as and when the customers come in, you hear me?"

"If you're sure. Let me make us a drink, though, yes?"

"I never say no, you know that."

The morning flurry of customers started at around ten a.m., and the phones rang off the hook all morning. It wasn't until eleven that they had a chance to catch their breaths. It was around this time a delivery driver entered the agency and asked for a Miss Brent.

Shirley smiled and nodded in Lucy's direction. "That's the lucky lady over there."

The driver presented Lucy with a brightly coloured box with a purple ribbon around it and asked her to sign his machine accepting the package. She waited until the man left the shop and then opened the box.

"Oh my God, that's perfectly exquisite," Shirley said, coming behind her and looking over her shoulder.

"Isn't it? It's...well, it's breathtaking." Lucy lifted the gorgeous silver gate bracelet from the velvet interior, and Shirley fastened it on her slim wrist.

"Wow...I thought it was silver, but the label in the box is telling me it's white gold. Get you."

"Really?" Lucy asked, flabbergasted. "Bloody hell, what did I do to deserve a man like Matthew?" she whispered, casting aside all the dubious thoughts she'd had during the night. He was definitely one in a million, not that she was keen on him spending his money on her—that meant nothing really. It was the thoughtfulness behind the gifts that truly set her heart on fire.

"I'll make us another drink. I suggest you ring that young man and tell him his beautiful gift has arrived safely. I'll give you some privacy."

Lucy's cheeks heated up. "Thanks." She searched in her handbag for her mobile and rang Matthew. He answered after the second ring. "Hello, you."

"Gosh, I'm so glad you called, I didn't know whether to ring you or not, in case you were having another day off and in bed sleeping."

"Why did you send your gift to the shop then?"

"Just in case. Oh bugger, don't ask. I added that address to the order before I bloody realised. Do you like it?"

"I'd be pretty dumb not to. It's exquisite, or *perfectly exquisite* is how my boss described it. Why? You're spoiling me, and there really is no need. In spite of what you think, your money means nothing to me. I'm with you because you make me feel good about myself and..."

"And?" he asked, sounding like an eager child in a vast toyshop.

"And because I love you."

"Phew! Me, too, I mean, I love you, too. I wanted to show you how much. Don't prevent me from doing that, please."

"There's no need, Matthew. Look after your money. This is far too good for me, it must have cost you a fortune."

"I wanted you to have something nice to wear on Saturday when you meet my folks. Shit! Not that you don't already look nice in the stuff you do have. Bugger! I'm bloody screwing this up, aren't I?"

"No, well, maybe a little. I realise it's unintentional, though. You're too kind. Would there be any point in me asking you not to keep spoiling me?"

"Ha! None whatsoever. Are we still on for going car hunting on Saturday?"

"Yes, if you insist. We close at one. Do you want to pick me up from here or shall I meet you somewhere else?"

The door opened, and a bearded man with a deerstalker hat walked in. Lucy noticed he had a limp and lowered her voice a touch while she finished her conversation and the man browsed the brochures for the Middle East.

"I'll pick you up from there, it's no bother. I've gotta go, I'll ring you later. Oh, by the way, how are you feeling?"

"I'm good, thanks. I have Shirley fussing over me here today, and Trisha dropped me off this morning. I don't know what I'd do if I didn't have you guys to fall back on, so to speak."

"We care about you. Speak later. Enjoy the rest of your day and always remember that I love you."

"I love you, too."

The man glanced in her direction as she hung up.

"Hello, sir, are you after anything in particular?" She left her chair and crossed the room to join him.

The man ignored her, grunted and flicked through a brochure. She was used to his type; mostly they were timewasters who ventured in out of the cold to have a nosey.

Shirley came out of the back carrying two mugs and set one down on her desk. "Is he all right?" she whispered.

"Yep, I've asked. Just a browser."

"Oh well, his type aren't going to make us rich, are they?"

Whether the man overheard them or not, he left the shop. He continued to eye the special offers in the window for a moment or two and then went on his way.

Shirley shuddered. "Well, he was a weird one. I'm sooooo glad he didn't hang around for too long."

"I agree."

"How was Matthew?"

"Fine. He told me he loved me. I chastised him for spending so much on me. I told him I wasn't with him for what I could get out of him. He said he realised that and just wanted me to have something nice for the weekend."

"How sweet. Wait, what's happening at the weekend, another gala dinner?"

"I wish, it might be easier for me."

"What are you talking about?"

Lucy chewed her lip and tapped her pen on the desk. "I'm going over there to meet his parents."

"Whoa! That's about as serious as it gets. Are you up for that at this stage?"

"I'm not sure is the truthful answer."

"You'll be fine. When are you going?"

"On Saturday."

"Quite an eventful day ahead of you then, what with buying the new car et cetera."

"Yeah, I can see me having a right tussle with him about that as well."

"Don't knock it, kiddo, accept the gifts, if that's what he wants to do. It's his money after all. If he wants to spend it on you, then don't stand in his way. That would be my advice."

"Noted. I can't help feeling bad about that, though. I've never been one to stay with a bloke for what I can get out of him, unlike some women I've known in the past."

"I hear what you're saying. You only have to read the bloody newspapers to realise the extremes some women are prepared to go to get their man to place a ring on their finger."

Lucy chuckled. "Yep, does that make us both cynics of the worst kind, do you think?"

Shirley opened her mouth to answer but was interrupted by the door opening and a man and woman entering. She slipped into efficient business owner mode, and within half an hour the couple had spent over ten grand on an exotic beach holiday at a select resort in the Caribbean. They left, and Shirley rubbed her hands together in glee. "Good to see I haven't lost my touch. Boy, did we need that sale? It's been a dire April so far."

"Oh? The phones haven't stopped this morning. I thought things had picked up a little."

"Yes, we might have sold more holidays than March, however, their quality has been inferior compared to what we sold in January and February."

"Ah, I see. I take it you were concerned about that. You should've told me, I would've worked harder on the limping bloke earlier."

"It's fine. I should never burden you with the finer details of running the business, you have enough on your plate to worry about. I'm not an ogre of a boss who has high expectations of the staff."

"I realise that. Shirley, I would never fall out with you if you ever felt the need to kick me up the arse now and again. Want me to stand on the corner with some flyers or something? Because I will, if that's what's required of me to keep my job."

Shirley took a sip of her coffee and appeared to be mulling over the idea. "Now you're being plain ridiculous, although, if things don't pick up soon, it's definitely an idea to fall back on. Who knows where Brexit will leave us? I thought after being bailed out by that consortium last January that Flybe would be safe, but now they've gone to the wall. Lord knows what disruption and heartache that's likely to cause for the staff and those people who work at the airports who were reliant on their services."

"It all happened too quickly, didn't it? It must have been floundering anyway, surely. Mind you, these companies sometimes look for a likely excuse and pounce on it, don't they? Look at the uproar which has come about since we opted for a Brexit exit. As far as I know, the country is still going strong, isn't it?"

"We won't see the effects of Brexit for a little while, I fear. Anyway, enough of this doom and gloom, back to things we can do to bring in extra business, apart from selling our bodies on the bridge in town."

"Go on, it sounds like you've come up with something. You know I'll give it my all to help this business survive."

Shirley patted Lucy's hand. "That's because you're a caring and compassionate individual and why I think the world of you."

"Aww…right backatcha, Shirley."

"It's all about the teamwork with us. Right from the word go, I don't think I've ever regarded you as just a member of staff."

Tears blurred Lucy's vision. Shirley had always treated her fairly, never made any outrageous demands on her time, unlike her previous bosses. She was lucky to have found a job she loved and a boss she'd go out of her way to do anything for—within reason, that was. "You're so sweet. I've loved working alongside you these past few months. I want to reassure you that my relationship with Matthew won't have any negative effects on my job here. Hey, I could even use this weekend to try and sell his family an exotic holiday or two, how's that?"

"You're a card, you are. Don't force the issue, not this time round. At least get to know them first." Shirley sniggered. "In all seriousness, I was thinking about putting on an enticing buffet. I have collected a few freebies from some of the travel companies we've dealt with over the past year. We could put those in a raffle. Maybe throw in an adventure weekend or something along those lines. What do you think?"

"Sounds like an incredible plan to me. All we need to do is get the people through the door and pounce on them. I could tie a few up and threaten not to let them go until they've purchased a holiday worth five grand."

Shirley opened and shut her mouth rapidly, imitating a fish out of water. "I think we'll stick to my idea for now, there's no need to go to those extremes."

Lucy roared. "You didn't think I was serious, did you?"

Relief flooded Shirley's face, and her shoulders slouched. "I did bloody wonder there for a moment or two. You sounded rather convincing."

"Okay, in all seriousness, I think it's an excellent concept and one that I'd be willing to get behind. When are you thinking about doing it?"

"It's going to take a little while to organise, maybe in a week or two, does that suit you? That young man of yours isn't likely to sweep you away anywhere before then, is he?"

She laughed. "If he does, I'll make sure he books the trip through us."

"I have you well-trained, that's excellent to know."

The rest of the day was spent bouncing ideas off each other and serving the odd customer in between. Nothing major, a couple of weekends away for two elderly couples, one in The Lakes and the other to Cornwall. Enough to keep the rent going on the agency for the next few months, Shirley said. They locked up together, and she walked a few roads with Shirley to where she'd arranged to meet Trisha. It wasn't until she was seated in the car that she saw the man with a limp.

"That's strange. He was loitering in the agency today." Lucy pointed to the man.

Trisha observed him and shrugged. "He's probably a local then. Did he buy a holiday?"

"Nope, only eyed a few brochures. Appeared to skedaddle once Shirley pounced on him, not literally."

"Crikey, I think I'd do a runner, too, if your boss ever did that to me. I can't stand being pressured into buying something, especially something as expensive as a holiday."

They drove past the man who was fiddling around with his mobile. Lucy glanced back in the wing mirror and saw the man turn their way once they'd passed by. He appeared to be studying them, enough to make the hairs on the back of her neck stand to attention.

"Did you hear me?" Trisha asked, placing a hand on her thigh.

"Sorry, what was that?"

"What's got into you?"

"There's something about him which is freaking me out."

"Like what?"

Lucy ran a hand over her long hair, tugging it into a ponytail at her neck. "I don't know. Ignore me, I'm probably being foolish. What were you saying?"

"It was a lifetime ago, I've forgotten now. Oh no, I remember, I asked if you were seeing Matthew tonight."

"For now, no, although he did mention he'd ring me later. Damn, I forgot to show you this." She switched on the interior light and jangled the bracelet on her wrist in front of Trisha. "Another gift from the man himself."

"Bloody hell, that's beautiful. He's definitely got the hots for you, girlie."

"He told me he loved me over the phone today."

"Wow, that's huge! And what did you say in return?"

"I told him I loved him, too. I can't say I'm looking forward to Saturday, though, meeting his folks."

"Why? What harm can they do if you've both professed your love for each other?"

"Perhaps the accident has knocked my confidence a little. Oh, I don't know."

"Possibly. Hey, if you're not seeing Matthew tonight, why don't we stop off at the local and grab a meal there? On me, of course."

"Sounds like a great idea. We could make a night of it and leave the car there and walk home."

"Stagger home, you mean. I'm just in the mood to go on a bender."

"I'll let you do it, I need to take it easy. My head still isn't as it should be. A nice meal and a few drinks are just what the doctor ordered. Providing you let me pay."

"We'll see. Right, that's sorted. I fancy one of their huge plates of fish and chips. My tyrant of a boss forced me to work through my lunch hour today."

"Why? As punishment for you taking the day off to look after me yesterday?"

"He said it wasn't and that he wouldn't be as petty as that. I know differently. Bugger him, I couldn't give a toss what he thinks, my mate needed me, I couldn't let you down."

"I appreciate that, love, but if I thought it was going to cause a rift between you both..."

"Nothing of the sort. Forget I mentioned it. It's a bloke thing. Most men hate the thought of any woman getting the upper hand on them, you know that."

"Only too well," Lucy mumbled, her thoughts going back to her previous debilitating relationship.

Only too well. He hated me having an opinion, and doing anything off my own bat was totally out of the question. I'm well rid of him. It's been over five years now, I shouldn't be thinking about what he did or said to get me through the day. So why am I? Why, after all these years, is this man haunting my dreams again? Is it the thought of being in love again? Is that why my experience with Patrick has resurfaced? Or is the accident to blame? Either way, I need to rid myself of the images of Patrick, once and for all, but how?

Trisha tapped her on the leg once they'd parked up. "Are you sure you're okay? You keep drifting off. If you'd rather go home and chillax, that's fine with me."

"No. I'd like to spend the evening with you, chatting and forcing food and drink down my throat."

"Whoa! I'm glad you're not in the restaurant trade, they'd come down on you hard if you ever tried to sell an evening package in that way."

They laughed and left the car. The public bar was heaving at The Red Rooster.

Trisha pulled a face and pointed to a door off to the left. "Let's go in the Lounge Bar instead."

The room was a lot quieter, and they found a table in the bay window overlooking the kids' play area at the rear of the property which was lit up and had a haunting feel about it.

"What are you having? I'll place the food order at the same time."

"I fancy a lasagne and chips. But I'm paying." Lucy took a twenty out of her purse and slid it across the table.

Trisha tutted and accepted the money. "It'll go towards it."

"No, I insist." She took another tenner from her purse and forced Trisha to take it.

Trisha put in the order at the bar. She waited patiently for the barmaid, who was servicing both bars, to make an appearance.

During Trisha's absence, Lucy eyed the play area outside. She drifted off, her imagination working overtime as certain shapes from the trees above formed creepy shadows over the equipment. She would have loved it out there at this time of night as a child, or would she? An unseasonable wind suddenly got up, and a branch slashed at the window, scaring the shit out of her. She yelped and placed a hand over her heart. Trisha rushed over to see if she was okay.

"I'm fine. Silly me. Sorry to cause you concern."

"Don't be. What's freaking you out so much, hon?"

"I wish I knew. I've never been this petrified by the wind getting up before. My heart is racing."

"Do you want to go home? I haven't placed the order yet."

"No. Just ignore me. I'll be fine in a second. Quick, the barmaid has appeared."

Trisha rushed back to the bar. Lucy glanced sideways, cautiously eyeing the play area again just in time to see the shadow of a man disappear into the darkness. She blinked and rubbed at her eyes then peered in that direction again. There was nothing there, not this time. The question was, was there someone there before or was it a case of her imagination getting the better of her?

She shifted uncomfortably and rotated her head from side to side in an attempt to rid herself of the tension which had crept up on her during their brief stay at the pub.

Her eyes continued to be drawn to the spot where she thought she'd seen the man during the course of the evening, even though she was annoyed at herself for letting a few shadows spook her half to death.

8

*T*he rest of the week passed by without further incident, thankfully, which only made Lucy doubt herself even more. Saturday morning arrived, and work was heaving. Shirley spent most of the morning sporting a huge smile and even made the decision to remain open for the rest of the day. Lucy was disappointed about letting her down. If she hadn't already made plans to go car hunting with Matthew, she would have remained there to give Shirley a helping hand.

Shirley had chastised her for thinking that way and virtually pushed her out of the door at one o'clock on the dot. Matthew was there to meet her. They set off and did the rounds of a few dealerships. She left it up to Matthew to choose a suitable car for her. To Lucy, a car was just an object to get one from A to B. She didn't go in for all this alloy wheels and how many revs the engine was capable of, although she did ask Matthew to make sure a make and model was efficient to run on her meagre wages.

He told her to leave it with him. They took several cars for test drives and finally settled on a Vauxhall Corsa in a stunning royal blue. The car was around three years old. The ticket on the screen was an eye-watering six grand, but Matthew assured her he wouldn't pay anything near as much as that. He negotiated hard. She started off the meeting embarrassed the way he went in with his lowest offer. The salesman smiled and came back with a counter offer a few times. He didn't appear to be offended at all, in fact, there was a lot of laughter filling the tiny office by the time they finally shook hands on a deal.

Matthew reached over for a kiss before he signed the sales document. He'd managed to get the salesman down to five grand, due to the high mileage on the clock. She gulped. How the hell she was supposed to find that sort of money was totally beyond her. Matthew assured her on the journey back to Trisha's that there was no need for her to pay him back, not for a while. The salesman even promised to throw in a full tank of petrol for when she picked it up during the week.

They were celebrating the deal over a cup of coffee in the kitchen.

"I can't thank you enough, Matthew. I insist we put a payment scheme in place soon, okay?"

"Whatever, it's a drop in the ocean. Why are you so worried? You're not about to do a runner on me, are you?"

She slipped onto his lap and ran a hand through his short hair. "Not likely, you're stuck with me for good."

Their kiss was interrupted by Lucy's mobile vibrating across the table. She ignored it for a few seconds until Matthew drew back and insisted she answer it, if only to give them some peace.

Shirley's number filled the tiny screen. "Shirley, hi, what's up?"

Heavy breathing filtered down the line, and then a woman's scream.

Matthew snatched the phone out of her hand. "Who is this?"

The line went dead.

Matthew swiftly pushed Lucy off his lap. "We must get to her. Do you think she's at work?"

Lucy glanced at the time on the phone. It was five-fifteen. "She usually locks up around five, but who knows, maybe she'd already left if it went quiet this afternoon. Should we ring the police?"

"No, let's get over there and see for ourselves first."

They slipped on their shoes and jackets, and Matthew sped into town, weaving his way expertly through the heaving Saturday afternoon traffic. He screeched to a halt on the double yellow lines outside the agency.

"Shit, the door's open." Lucy reached for the handle.

Matthew stopped her. "No. You stay here. I'll take a look. If I don't reappear within five minutes, call nine-nine-nine, got that?"

"Yes. Oh God, please be careful."

"Don't worry about me," were Matthew's final words as he left the vehicle.

She watched him enter the building, unaware she'd stopped breathing until her lungs seared with heat. She inhaled a restorative breath which left her gasping. *Please let her be okay, let them both come out of there in one piece.*

Matthew reappeared. He shook his head. She didn't know what that shake of the head implied and was eager to find out.

Remaining in the car, she wound down the window to ask him. "Is she okay?"

He withdrew his phone from his jacket pocket and punched in a number. "Police, please...yes, at Shirley's Travel on the high street. Yes, there's a dead body."

"No!" Lucy screamed.

She opened the door to get out of the car, but Matthew held out an arm to prevent her from going into the building.

"Don't, love. It's not pretty."

He ended the call and hugged her. She rested her head against his chest, her breath coming in short sharp gasps as the thought of Shirley lying there rampaged through her mind.

"There, there, let it out. There was nothing either of us could have done."

Sirens wailed in the distance. Tyres squealed, and everything happened with the speed of a Charlie Chaplin movie, the type she used to watch with her grandfather as a child. Oh, to have his comforting arms around her now.

"I'm DI Terry Warren. Did you report the incident?"

Matthew nodded. "Yes, we were at home and received a call from

Shirley—sorry, she's the victim. Well, Lucy did. Sorry, I'm not making much sense, all this has hit us pretty damn hard."

"I can imagine. If you could stick to the facts, sir," the policeman said, his tone as stern as a headmaster's.

Matthew apologised again and then informed the inspector about the events that had led to them being at the scene.

"I see. Okay, we're going to need to take a statement from you both. Was it only you who entered the building, sir?"

"Yes, I instructed Lucy to remain here, outside."

"Why don't you both get back in the vehicle? I'll need to wait for SOCO to arrive before I can get in there."

"No, you can't do that. What if she's not dead, just unconscious and needs assistance?" Lucy blurted out.

"That's not the case, love. There's blood everywhere," Matthew assured her.

"But it doesn't mean to say she's dead."

Matthew sighed. "Shirley's throat has been cut, Lucy. Take my word for it, she couldn't survive that."

Lucy buried her head in her hands and sobbed. "No...no...no. Not Shirley...she can't be dead. She can't be."

"As I said, it would be better if you both got back in the vehicle. I'll take a peek inside, if it'll put your mind at ease," DI Warren suggested reluctantly.

"Thank you, it would."

Matthew hugged her tighter and kissed the top of her head. "She's gone, love."

The inspector emerged seconds later and shook his head, just like Matthew had moments earlier. "I'm sorry, she's gone."

Lucy let out a whimpering howl, and her knees buckled. Matthew held her firm and steered her back to the car. He opened the door and eased her into the passenger seat. He got in beside her and gathered her in his arms. His hand smoothed her hair flat against her head.

"I'm so sorry, Lucy."

"Why? Who would do such a violent thing to one of the nicest people to ever walk this planet?"

"I don't know. I'm sure the police will do their best to find out."

"Why? Sorry to repeat myself, but none of this makes sense." She gasped, pulled back and stared at him. "You don't think this has to do with the accident I had the other day, do you?"

"Why would you say that?"

"Shit, I'm talking bollocks. My head is all over the place. I can't think straight." But the words were out there now, and she couldn't stop herself from dwelling on them. *What if there is a connection? My God, how can this be happening? Shirley didn't deserve to die.* "Do you think it was a robbery? I knew I shouldn't have left her; it was too busy for one person to cope with alone."

"I'm glad you were with me and not here. I don't know, perhaps. The police will figure it out, all in good time."

"Should I tell the inspector about the accident? It might help the investigation. Shit! I've been watching too many cop shows on TV. None of this is going to bring Shirley back. Why her?"

"I don't see the point in mentioning it. Saying that, it can't hurt. There would be a record of it down at the station anyway, wouldn't there? I'm so sorry, love. No one deserves to go out like that."

The tears fell again, and she shook her head. "I have to tell her husband, Keith."

"I wouldn't. I'd leave it to the inspector to do that. Poor bloke. Have they been married long?"

"Over twenty years, they're devoted to each other."

He hugged her again and kissed her forehead. "When you find the love of your life, it's hard to deal with something of this magnitude."

More vehicles arrived, and white-suited men and women entered the property. Lucy and Matthew watched the inspector and another man get suited up and join the SOCO team inside. He emerged moments later and tapped on the passenger window.

"I don't suppose you have a phone number for her husband, do you, Miss?"

He must have seen the wedding ring on Shirley's finger. "Not his mobile number, but I have their home number."

"That'll do. I'll need to inform him before the journalists get a chance to air the news; the pack is already gathering." He motioned across the road with his head.

Lucy flicked through her contacts and located Shirley's home number. The inspector punched it into his phone as she read it out to him. Then he stepped away from the car to talk to Keith.

"Damn, he won't tell him over the phone, will he?"

"I doubt it, he'll probably make arrangements to go and see him. He's coming back."

"Okay, I'm going over there to break the news in person now. Can we make arrangements to get a statement from you both?"

"Can't we do it here and now?" Lucy asked.

"We could, if that's what you want?"

Lucy glanced at Matthew. He nodded. "Yes, we'd both prefer to get it out of the way. I need to ask if this was a robbery or not."

The inspector held her gaze and shrugged. "My honest opinion would be no. Burglars rarely kill their victims."

Lucy remained in a daze on the drive back to Trisha's. She was at home when Lucy let them into the house.

Trisha could tell instantly there was something wrong, and a frown crinkled her brow. "Jesus, what's wrong? You both look terrible."

"I need a stiff drink." Lucy slid into a chair at the kitchen table.

"Coming up. Matthew?"

"Please, it was terrible." He dropped into the seat next to Lucy. He covered her hand with his.

Trisha reached to the back of the lower shelf of the larder unit and withdrew a bottle of brandy she always kept there for medicinal purposes during the winter months. She poured three glasses and handed them around, then sank into the chair opposite Lucy. "Don't keep me in the dark, I'm going out of my mind with worry. Are either of you hurt?"

"No. It's Shirley…" Lucy took a huge gulp of the soothing drink.

"What about Shirley? Has she had an accident of sorts?" Trisha urged, her brow pinched into a tight crease.

Lucy and Matthew stared long and hard at each other. He seemed as shell-shocked as she did, even though he'd never met Shirley before.

Lucy turned her attention back to Trisha. "She's dead!"

Trisha fell back in her chair as if she'd been hit in the chest by a speeding bullet. "What? How? Oh my God, that poor woman. Where did it happen?"

"At the agency. I received a weird call from her. Heavy breathing and a woman's scream. Matthew and I rushed back to the agency to see if we could help. Matthew found her inside. That was around an hour ago. We had to wait for the police to arrive, and SOCO."

Trisha sat upright, her eyes widening. "Dear Lord! Dead..."

Lucy nodded as fresh tears bulged and stung her eyes. "Yes. I didn't see her. Matthew said her throat had been cut."

"Oh fuck! This can't be happening. Was it a robbery? Do you even keep cash lying around there?"

Lucy stared down at her drink. "No, the police doubted that was the case. We keep a small amount, nothing special, though." She covered her face with her hands and sobbed. "Why her? She was such a sweet lady. Why would anyone want to hurt her, let alone kill her?"

Trisha left her chair to comfort her. "It's all right, love, I'm sure the police will find the person responsible."

Lucy dropped her hands and stared at Trisha. "You don't think...?"

"Think what?" Trisha asked, perplexed.

"This has anything to do with the incident the other day?"

Trisha shook her head, slowly at first until it gained momentum. "No, don't think like that. It's not possible, is it?"

"Why? How do you know that?" Lucy countered, her head filled with a tornado of reasons both for and against.

"Ladies, please, don't overthink things, not yet. Let the police try and piece what happened together, first."

"Matthew's right. The last thing we should do is make any outlandish assumptions. We need factual evidence, right?" Trisha agreed.

"Okay. I'll try not jump ahead of things. But she's dead. She was such a lovely lady, and now...I can't believe I'll never see her again. She's been like a second mother to me since I joined the agency. We grew close really quickly. She was thrilled I'd met you, Matthew. No teasing when you sent me gifts, pure pleasure lit up her face. Dare I say it, a proudness that only a mother usually radiates. I'm going to miss her so much. I dread to think where this is going to leave me now. I know I shouldn't really consider that at this moment..."

"You have every right to be concerned about your job." Trisha returned to her seat. She took a large swig of her brandy and shuddered.

"Trisha is right, you have a right to know where you stand."

"I don't want to think about it now. I'll contact Keith over the weekend, or should I ring him tonight? Oh God, I don't know what to do for the best. What will he think of me if I don't call him?"

"I'm sure you're overthinking things. He'll welcome a call at the right time," Matthew assured her.

"When is that likely to be?"

"And now my question is going to seem just as selfish," he replied.

"Go on, ask it anyway," Lucy prompted.

"Are you still on for tonight?"

She ran a shaking hand over her flushed face. "Oh, shit! I forgot all about the dinner with your family. What would they think of me if I cancelled? I couldn't do that, I wouldn't be able to live with myself. On the other hand, I'm not going to be in the mood to sit there with a permanent smile on my face either. What would you do, Trisha?"

She held her hands up. "Whoa! Leave me out of it. You have to do what's right for you. I'm sure Matthew and his family will understand if you decided to pull out at such short notice."

"Of course we would. Lucy, there's never any pressure from me." He left his chair and placed an arm around her shoulders then pecked her on the cheek. "Why don't I leave you two girls to debate the pros and cons? You can give me a ring with your decision in half an hour or so. I'll make arrangements for my driver to pick you up at seven, if you decide to come."

She glanced at her watch. It was already six o'clock. "Shit, that doesn't leave me much time to get ready."

"I'll leave it up to you. Ring me when you decide."

Lucy saw him to the front door. They shared a comforting kiss, and she waved him off then stepped back into the kitchen to discuss the issue with Trisha. "What do you think?"

"You're going to have to meet them sometime. I know the timing is bad, however, sitting around here moping about Shirley all night isn't going to help you either."

"Yeah, I get that. Would you go, if you were me?"

"With the caring Matthew by my side, yes, I would. He'll be there if things get tough, sweetie. Come on, I'll help you get ready, if that's what you want."

Against her better judgement, she allowed Trisha to sweep her up in the excitement. Before she knew what was happening, she was standing naked under the shower with Trisha sitting on the toilet, discussing what dress she should wear.

Thirty minutes later, she bit the bullet and rang Matthew to arrange for the driver to pick her up. He was thrilled that she'd decided to attend this evening's soirée, as he'd put it.

She sat on a chair at the kitchen table while Trisha applied her makeup, the results of which took Lucy's breath away. "My God, is that really me?"

"You'd better believe it, girl. Matthew is a hell of a lucky bloke. If I wasn't straight, I'd be in there, no kidding."

Lucy couldn't help but chuckle at that. "You crack me up. What would I do without you by my side? I love you dearly for what you do for me, tonight and all this, opening up your home to me."

"Don't you dare start blubbing, not now I've completed your makeup. I love you, too, and it's my pleasure to always help out when I can. You're like a sister to me. I think we're closer than sisters most of the time, if that's possible. You're going to knock Matthew's family sideways tonight. They're going to love you as much as Matthew and I do."

"Maybe even Jake will see me in a different light this evening, or is that going to be too much to hope for?"

"Who cares what he thinks? Come on, princess, upstairs. Let's get you tarted up and ready. Crikey, look at the time."

9

The driver arrived on the dot, just as Trisha was slipping the gold sandals onto Lucy's feet near the front door. He knocked and inclined his head.

"Miss Brent, are you ready?"

"I am. I'll be right out."

He nodded, took a step backwards, spun around and headed back to the car.

"Well, this is it. You look amazing. Matthew, or any man, come to that, would be the proudest man in the room with you accompanying him. Have a wonderful time. Try and put aside what's happened today, you hear me?"

"That's going to be so difficult. I'm glad I didn't go in there and see her, I would've definitely backed out of this evening. Thanks for everything, love. Don't wait up."

"What? I have to…at midnight your dress will turn into rags and…"

Lucy laughed. "Shit, don't say that. I'm going to have enough on my mind already without that added stress."

"Knock 'em dead…shit, me and my big mouth, you know what I mean." She squeezed Lucy tightly.

"Life goes on, eh? I wish I didn't have to do this, of all evenings. Wish me luck." She exited the front door, feeling posh in the sparkly black evening dress Trisha had insisted she wore.

"You're not going to need it. They'll love you. Just be you."

"I will...well, maybe not the true me," she whispered back, her ugly past rearing its head. *Shit! Why did I have to go and spoil things by mentioning that?*

Trisha tutted and shook her head. "I expect to hear all about it when you get home."

"Don't wait up, it'll probably be a late one."

The chauffeur smiled and opened the back door for her. She slipped inside. There was a bottle of champagne on ice and a long-stemmed glass.

The driver started the engine and peered in his rear-view mirror. "Help yourself to champagne, ma'am."

"Oh, I couldn't. I think I need to keep a clear head for what lies ahead of me, but thank you for the offer."

He nodded again and closed the little window between them. There was no getting away from it. Lucy surveyed her surroundings and found it impossible not to be impressed by the limo's luxurious interior. The smell of new leather had always seemed an extravagance to her. She remembered when Patrick and she had bought their first car together and he'd taken her for a celebratory ride out to a country pub. That was when they had first got married, when he worshipped her, before things had gone drastically wrong between them. She closed her eyes, blocking out the image.

Why did he insist on cropping up? Was it because she'd found true happiness at last with Matthew? Or was there something else going on here? Was it her subconscious warning her to be careful? Reminding her of how things used to be between Patrick and herself until things had gone drastically wrong? It was all so confusing, and she was having trouble deciphering what her feelings and thoughts truly meant.

Putting an end to her dodgy thoughts, she sat back and tried to relax on the short trip out to Matthew's place, or should she say, Matthew's parents' place? The driver entered a large sweeping drive.

At the entrance was a relatively small hexagonal gatehouse. It was cute. She wondered if Matthew would allow her access for a nose around and then laughed off the idea, thinking it was probably home to some of the staff who cared for the magnificent-looking mansion that had come into view ahead of them. She'd never laid eyes on something so grand before, except on the TV screen, of course. Her nerves rattled her bones, and her mouth immediately dried up to the point she now regretted not having a glass of the champagne on offer.

Matthew was waiting for her at the top of the grand steps. He raced down them and opened the back door as soon as the driver brought the car to a halt. He leaned in, kissed her gently on the lips and offered her his hand. "You look...well, words fail me, and I assure you, that's never happened before."

Her cheeks warmed up. "You're just saying that. You look pretty dapper yourself in your tuxedo." Once she got out of the car, she whispered an admission, "I'm scared. How do I overcome my fears of meeting your parents? Any tips?"

"There's no need for you to feel that way. They're human, we have the same colour blood running through our veins, I promise. You're not scared of me, are you?"

"Of course not. I love *you*. That's different, though."

He pecked her on the cheek. "I love you, too. Don't be scared, don't let your wayward thoughts spoil the evening ahead. I'll be by your side every step of the way, you have my word on that."

"Phew! That's a relief. Have they said anything about me?" she whispered as he led her up the steps.

"Only that they're thrilled to be finally meeting you."

"Finally meeting me? It's only been a few weeks since we started out on this incredible journey together."

"I know. Maybe they're keen to meet the girl who has stolen my heart where so many have failed in the past."

"You're adorable. I can't imagine my life without you now."

"Ditto. Deep breath. Are you ready for this?"

"No. But with you by my side, anything is achievable."

He placed his arm through hers and laid his other hand over hers to reassure her everything was going to be okay. A butler was standing on ceremony in the hallway ready to greet them. He dipped his head at Matthew.

Lucy smiled awkwardly at him, unsure of what the protocol should be with the staff as a guest. Matthew pointed out a few of the portraits on show going up the staircase, not dissimilar to the one in *Gone with the Wind*. They were of his ancestors who had previously owned the mansion. She was in awe of the grandness and was totally overwhelmed by the time he showed her into the drawing room where his parents were waiting for them.

Her steps faltered. Matthew sensed her apprehension and squeezed her hand to keep her calm, and together they continued to walk towards the two people she imagined could make or break their relationship.

Matthew introduced them. "Lucy, this is my father, Arnold, and this is my mother, Cynthia."

His father took a step forward, gathered her hand in both of his and shook it exuberantly. "It's so wonderful to finally meet you, my dear. Matt has been a different person since you came into his life."

"That's wonderful to hear. It's so lovely to be here and to meet you both. Thank you so much for having me. You have a magnificent home."

"Thank you. We can't take any credit for its structure. Our input, since taking over the upkeep, can be seen in the grounds. Although I have to credit my darling wife for her contribution in that area. She has an expert eye for things of that nature."

Matthew's mother held out her slim hand for Lucy to shake. "I'm delighted to meet the girl who has stolen my son's heart. You're a beautiful young lady. I admire his taste, this time."

"Thank you. I'd love a guided tour one day, if you'll allow me?"

Cynthia tilted her head. "How charming. Of course. Not this evening, some other time perhaps."

"Oh yes, that would be super. Have you lived here long?" she asked, already searching for something interesting to say.

"Since my father passed away, around fifteen years ago," Arnold replied. "Come now, take a seat."

A maid stepped forward with a tray of drinks. "Champagne, ma'am?"

Matthew took two glasses from the tray and motioned for Lucy to take a seat on the Chesterfield sofa opposite. Once seated, he handed her a glass. She sipped her drink and resisted the threatening shudder. She'd never liked the taste of champagne, had always put that down to the quality she'd tasted in the past and, after sampling what was on offer, her opinion hadn't changed in the slightest.

"Tell us about yourself, Lucy. Where are you from?"

Shit! With all that's gone on during the day, I forgot to prepare for the onslaught of questions.

"I'm from a little town on the east coast, near Norwich."

Cynthia fluttered her eyelashes and grinned. "How charming. Does this town have a name?"

"Wadestown," she replied, saying the first thing that came into her mind.

"Ooo...I loved geography at university. That one is a new one on me, I'll be sure to look it up later."

Nervous laughter escaped Lucy's lips, and she took another sip of the vile drink, imagining it was the brandy she'd been fortunate to have earlier.

"And your parents? They still live there, do they?"

She kept her smile in place but couldn't prevent the sadness descending. She glanced at Matthew for help. He patted her thigh.

"Mother, can we leave the interrogation for now? I should have said something sooner. Lucy has had a rough week, and it was topped off today...well, by her boss being murdered."

"What? Murdered you say, how?" his father asked, scratching the side of his face.

Cynthia's expression was a picture of fear and dread. "How dreadful. Do tell us more, if you're up to it. Oh my, listen to me, how insensitive of me. Of course you wouldn't want to talk about it."

"I'm fine. It was a shock, that's all. Matthew gave me the option to back out of tonight's dinner. I dug deep; I couldn't let you all down at such a late stage."

"Nonsense," his father said adamantly. "We wouldn't have thought any less of you, dear girl. Rough week? What exactly has that entailed?"

Matthew spoke on her behalf again. She loved him for that alone. His support meant the world to her.

"She was in an accident; her car was a write-off. We went out this afternoon and replaced it."

"Oh my, what a devastating thing to happen, all in one week." Cynthia shook her head, her gaze fixed on Lucy.

Lucy placed a hand on Matthew's thigh. "If it hadn't been for Matthew's support, well, I'm not sure what I would've done. Today has been an emotional roller-coaster ride, what with searching for a new car and all the euphoria that brought, to dropping by the agency to find Shirley…"

"Agency? What type of agency? Are you a model?" Cynthia asked, a weak smile drawing her ruby lips apart.

"A travel agent's. That's what I do for a living, I sell holidays." For some reason, Lucy felt the need to pull her shoulders back and announce her role proudly.

"Ah, I see. Posh holidays, are they, dear?" Cynthia grinned.

"Mother! Just holidays. Let's leave it at that, shall we?" Matthew pounced.

"I was merely asking, dear. There was no need to bite my head off."

"Cynthia, please, leave the poor girl alone. Don't you think she's been through enough as it is today?" her husband stated.

"Pardon me for showing an interest. Consider me told. It's nice to meet you, Lucy. Maybe you could join me for lunch at the club one day and we'll continue this conversation without these two jumping down my throat. I really am eager to get to know you more."

Lucy smiled and nodded. "I'd like that. I won't know what arrangements I can make for the week until Keith informs me if I still have a job or not."

"Oh my. What will you do if it turns out he no longer wants you?"

She shrugged. "I have no idea. It's not as if I have any formal training to do anything else."

Matthew leaned over and placed his head against Lucy's. "Don't worry about it for this evening, we'll sort something out, even if it means me setting you up with your own business."

Lucy pulled away and stared at him. Her cheeks warmed under everyone's gaze. "No! I can't accept that, Matthew. Thank you for the offer, but I'd rather stand on my own two feet, it's what I'm used to."

"Quite right," his mother interjected.

Matthew shot a warning glance at his mother, and Lucy shuddered a little. The change in him was unsettling to say the least. She'd never seen this side of him before. She'd only ever seen the charming, devoted, happy Matthew. *What the hell is going on here?*

"Don't do this, you two, not in front of a guest," Arnold's voice cut through the icy atmosphere.

Neither Matthew nor his mother apologised. Thankfully, the maid reappeared and announced that dinner was served.

"Thank you. Shall we go through to the dining room?" Cynthia smoothed the creases out of her velvet skirt as she rose.

Arnold accompanied his wife, and Matthew remained seated.

Lucy was unsure what to say or do next. "Are you going to tell me what that was all about?"

He kissed her on the lips. "Mother's inimitable way of digging deep, trying to get to know someone quickly. Well, she can pack it in. I've had enough of her grilling you for one day. I'm sorry, sweetheart."

"It's fine. I expected a certain amount of questions, Matthew. It's only right she should be curious about me."

"You know what they say, curiosity killed the cat."

She raised her eyebrows. "Seriously? Why are you so upset about this?"

He shuddered out a long sigh. "The truth?"

"Yes, the truth."

"Mother is notorious for grilling the girls I bring home, never for them to return."

"What? She scares them off, is that what you're saying?"

"Yes." His head dipped.

She placed a finger under his chin and raised it so their eyes met. "I promise you, I'm made of strong stuff. She won't scare me off, got that?" She hugged him and kissed his cheek. "Idiot. This is about you and me, not those around us. More fool your other girlfriends for allowing her to get under their skin."

"You're amazing. The way you manage to see through people so quickly."

"Years of experience. I'm aware of the masks some people choose to hide behind."

"You are? May I ask what you're referring to?"

"I'll tell you later. We should go. I wouldn't want to give your mother further ammunition to have a pop at me."

He rose and held out a hand for her to take.

She smiled up at him. "Why, thank you, kind sir. Please, don't ever let that smile slip again, I hate it when it does."

"I promise. I shouldn't have let you witness that side of me. Let's just say that sometimes Mother brings out the worst in me."

"Then you need to develop a shield against that. I didn't like what I saw."

He gasped. "It wasn't intentional. Years of frustration welling up, that's all. I love my mother dearly, but sometimes I don't like her and what she stands for. If that makes sense? Actually, later, we need to discuss what I mentioned earlier about starting you up in your own travel agent's."

She shook her head. "I'm not about to change my mind on that, Matthew. I love you for who you are, not for what I can get out of you. Am I making myself clear?"

"Perfectly. However, if it's something I want to do, then surely…"

She wagged a finger and turned to leave the drawing room. "End of discussion. Your parents are waiting for us."

He trotted up behind her. "Umm…I'd better lead the way, otherwise you're likely to find yourself stumbling around in a maze. I'll give you a guided tour after dinner if you like?"

"I'd love that. I've always been eager to see how the other half live."

He sniggered. "We do okay. I prefer living in my humble abode, though."

"Which is where?" She slotted her arm through his.

"You passed it on the way in, the little gatehouse."

"Wow! Really? That place is so intriguing. I wouldn't mind a guided tour around that later."

He winked. "The master bedroom is the *piece de resistance*."

She slapped his upper arm. "Cheeky."

As they entered the dining room, they were still giggling. His mother shot them a wary glance while his father seemed at peace with the way Lucy and Matthew were with each other. They took their seats on opposite sides of the table. Was that another intentional ploy by his mother to put distance between them?

Three members of staff entered and served the meal. They were about to start eating when Jake walked in. Lucy's heart sank, although she was wise enough not to let it show and kept her smile firmly in place.

"Well, well, if it isn't Miss Lucy. How are you?"

Jake sat next to her. She sighed inwardly, and her stomach clenched into a painful knot of discomfort. "Hello, Jake, I'm well, and you?"

"I can't grumble. It's been a good week at work. We secured a massive deal."

"Jake, I've warned you about discussing business in front of guests at the dinner table," his mother cautioned.

"That's all I was going to say, Mother, I promise."

"Good, let's keep it that way. *Bon appetite,* everyone. I hope you like salmon, Lucy?"

"I do, it's my favourite fish, thank you. It looks delicious. Do you have a personal chef?"

Cynthia laughed. "Yes, I'm afraid my cooking skills aren't up to par, not where entertaining is concerned. Do you cook?"

She smiled and nodded. "Yes, I've always enjoyed cooking."

"I can vouch for that. The picnic she supplied the other day was amazing," Jake said.

Lucy turned to look at him. His expression unreadable, she couldn't tell if he was mocking her or not. He knew the food she'd supplied had come out of packets. She'd been open with Jake and Matthew about that. *What's going on?*

"Sadly, time didn't permit me to create that sumptuous spread, Jake. I thought I mentioned that on the day, didn't I?"

"Yes, she did. It was still divine, and you put it together with love, which meant more than anything to me," Matthew piped up.

"Ah yes, you did say. Sorry, I totally forgot that for a moment there. You'll have to invite us round to your house for a family meal soon then, won't you? You know, to show off the cooking skills you're so proud of."

She put down her knife and raised a finger. "As much as I'd like to, I don't think it would be appropriate as I'm house-sharing with a friend at present. Maybe when I get my own place, yes?"

"And when is that likely to be?" Cynthia was quick to ask.

"Mother, give her a break, you're aware of what's happened this week."

"Yes, of course, forgive me, Lucy."

"I'm not aware," Jake exclaimed. "Care to fill me in?"

"I will later, not now," Matthew jumped in.

The rest of the meal consisted of minor small talk centred around the family's recent activities which didn't involve work. From what she could gather, they all led very active social lives. Lucy felt exhausted just listening to them. After an exquisite chocolate fondant dessert which was to die for, they retired to the lounge, or drawing room as Cynthia preferred to call it, for after dinner drinks.

It was all rather grown up. She didn't feel out of her comfort zone until half an hour later when Matthew did something that left her speechless.

They were standing next to the piano, his father expertly tinkling the ivories, entertaining them all. Matthew suddenly slumped to his knee beside her. At first she'd thought he'd dropped something on the floor and got down to search for it. Realising what was going on, she gasped.

"Lucy Brent, the love of my life, will you do me the honour of marrying me?"

Her eyes misted up, and her heart skipped several beats. Everyone else in the room drifted into the background, her attention fully on Matthew and his handsome face, etched with expectation. She hadn't even noticed the rock of a ring he was holding in his hand, until now.

"Really? Oh, Matthew, I truly don't know what to say."

"Yes, would be good." He chuckled.

She placed a hand on either side of his face and kissed him. "Yes, a thousand times over, yes."

Matthew slipped the ring on her finger. It was the perfect fit, and then he rose to his feet again.

"Congratulations!" His father came forward and kissed her.

Her gaze drifted over his shoulder to Matthew's mother. Her stare was intense, to the point it narrowed her eyes.

Her father stepped back, allowing his wife to approach them.

She turned to Matthew and kissed his cheek, then she placed her hands on Lucy's shoulders and kissed her, too. "Well, this is a surprise. Are you sure it's not too soon?" she asked her son.

"My head and my heart are both saying otherwise, Mother. I'm glad you're happy for us both."

"I am. Have you decided on a date yet?" Her smile seemed genuine enough towards Matthew, and yet it appeared to alter when she turned to face Lucy.

"Give us a break, I've only just asked Lucy. You could see how surprised she was."

"Weren't you expecting it, Lucy?" his mother asked in a sickly sweet tone.

"No, this has come as an utter shock to me."

"And yet you accepted without faltering," his mother added.

What was that supposed to mean? "I love Matthew. Yes, it's only been a while since we met, but, well, we've been inseparable since that first meeting. I think that counts for something, don't you?"

"Yes, I've heard Matt has been distracted at work recently," his mother bit back sharply.

"What? Who said that?" Matthew demanded to know.

His mother waved his question away. "I have my sources." She held out an arm for Lucy to slip hers into. "We won't be long, boys. Time for a girlie chat. Come along, dear."

Panic filled every nerve ending, and Lucy glanced over her shoulder at Matthew as his mother tugged on her arm and led her out of the room and into a grand study. She deposited Lucy in one of the studded dark-brown leather chairs and then sat daintily in the other chair.

"Now then, we're going to need to put our heads together over the coming months."

"Regarding the wedding arrangements?"

"Yes, that's right. I'll sort everything. There are certain standards we'll need to maintain, after all."

"I'm not adverse to you lending a hand, although I think the majority of the decisions should be made initially by Matthew and myself."

Cynthia's eyes bulged. "I disagree. As I've already stated, we have certain standards we need to adhere to. A history to uphold."

"I don't doubt that, that's where I'm going to need your guidance. Please, I don't mean to be rude, all this has come as a shock to me. Matthew has never even mentioned the M word, not until five minutes ago. I love him, and we'll do what's right for everyone, I'm sure."

"I understand. My greatest fear is that you'll exclude us."

"Exclude you? Why would we want to do that?"

"I don't know. Youngsters of today have a tendency to want to elope to Gretna Green for some reason."

Lucy laughed. "Not me, I can assure you. Please, bear with us. We need to sit down and have a serious chat ourselves first, and then we'll include you in our plans, if that's what you want?"

"I do. It's my forte, you see. Putting on extravagant functions for our friends and relatives to attend. Will you have many to invite on your side? I'll need the numbers fairly soon."

"Fairly soon? And no, there will just be a few friends I'd like to invite. I have no family to speak of, now that my parents are no longer with us."

She gasped. "Then who will give you away?"

Lucy inhaled a large breath and shook her head slowly. "I don't know is the truthful answer."

"Oh dear. Well, I'm sure we'll overcome that nearer the time."

"Can we rejoin the others now?"

"May I ask why? I thought we were discussing the arrangements."

Lucy resisted the temptation to roll her eyes. Cynthia was coming on stronger than she could imagine now, and she was at a loss how to combat her overenthusiastic nature. She didn't know whether to be pleased at her taking an interest in the wedding or offended that she wanted to do things all her own way. "I'd prefer to leave all this until I've got used to the idea."

Cynthia launched herself out of the chair and stormed towards the door. "Very well, come on then."

Lucy marched after her. They both entered the drawing room under the watchful gaze of the men. That was when Cynthia switched back to doting mother mode. Lucy took a leaf out of Cynthia's book and smiled broadly as she sashayed her way across the room to her new fiancé.

Matthew kissed her gently on the cheek and whispered, "You survived then?"

"Only just," she whispered back. "Why did you ask me tonight?"

"I couldn't wait any longer. I love you, Lucy, and wanted to let everyone present know how much."

"It was a grand gesture. Shocked everyone, including me."

He rested his head against hers. "You could have turned me down."

"No way. Wow, what a week this has been, truly memorable in so many ways."

"I wanted to take all the angst and pain away. I hope I've succeeded?"

"You definitely have. I love you so much, Matthew. Your mother asked when the wedding is likely to be. I couldn't answer that."

"The sooner, the better for me. Mother is likely to object to that, but if you're up for it, we can sort out some of the arrangements ourselves."

"I'm more than up for that. I don't think your mother will be too happy about it, though."

"We'll discuss it later. All I wanted was to put a smile on that gorgeous face of yours and I think I've succeeded in doing that this evening. You're the reason I get up in the morning and why I go to bed every night with a smile on my face."

"You're so charming. Thank you for coming into my life the way you did. You've turned it upside down in a few short weeks and made me extremely happy. A happiness has draped itself around me which I never knew existed until now. I'll always be grateful to you for showing me that."

"You can show me how grateful later."

She frowned.

"When I show you around the gatehouse. I'd like you to stay over, if it's what you want?"

Her heart thundered. "More than anything."

Jake appeared beside them. Lucy wondered if he'd been eavesdropping in on their conversation.

"What are you two talking about?"

"Wouldn't you like to know? Always been a nosey parker, haven't you, bro?"

"Actually, I was going to offer my services as best man." Jake grinned at his brother.

"Hold that thought," Cynthia interrupted. "Lucy might need you to give her away yet, Jake. Males are sorely unrepresented on her side of the family."

Lucy's mouth gaped open.

Matthew shook his head. "Now, Mother, it's not up to you to decide who gives my future wife away. She should be the one to make that decision."

"A huge decision like that shouldn't be taken lightly. I'll get back to you, if that's okay, Jake?" Lucy said, not bearing to look at him.

He shrugged. "Suits me. I have other duties to perform anyway, right, bro?"

"You seem pretty confident I'm going to ask you to be best man. I haven't even thought that far down the road yet. I'll be in touch."

"Whatever," Jake replied and stormed out of the room.

"Was that necessary, Matthew?" Cynthia chastised, using his full name.

"Yes, he occasionally needs bringing back down to earth. He's fine. He knows it's a no-brainer and that I'll have him as my best man. Chill, Mother."

"Hmm…I can see this wedding being trouble with a capital T," his mother stated quietly.

The atmosphere had become chilled again.

"I need the loo," Lucy whispered, conscious she'd leave a puddle if she didn't go soon.

Matthew excused them and escorted her from the room. He gestured to a downstairs toilet. "Can you make your own way back? I need to have a word with Mother."

"Sure. Don't be too hard on her, Matthew."

"I won't. See you soon."

He walked away, and she opened the door to a powder room the size of Trisha's kitchen. After spending a penny, she washed her hands with the soap and then used the moisturiser. She studied herself in the ornate mirror in the shape of a sun with its extended rays. *What a day it has been. One I'll never forget.* Her biggest regret was not being able to share the news of her engagement with the ones nearest to her. They were all gone now. She only had Trisha left. Lucy reached for her mobile and dialled home. There was no answer, and she realised halfway through the call that Trisha had mentioned something about going over to Neil's tonight. Therefore, there was no excuse for her not to spend the night at Matthew's with him. A flash of what lay ahead of her coloured her cheeks. If only she didn't have makeup on. She would have doused her face with water.

After running a comb through her hair, which didn't really need it, she opened the door and left the toilet. During the walk back up the marbled hallway, she had a feeling someone was following her. She peered over her shoulder and found Jake barely three feet from her.

"Sorry, I didn't see you there."

"You weren't supposed to," he muttered, his eyes narrowed into tiny slits.

"What's that supposed to mean? Have I done something wrong, Jake?"

"The day you started seeing Matt, is the day you're going to regret, lady."

"What? Explain yourself."

"I don't need to say more, the warning should be enough. Just ask the other girls. They took heed of the warnings I dished out. You will, too, if you know what's good for you."

"Are you telling me you drove all Matthew's previous girlfriends away? Why?"

"That's right. You'll find out the damage I can cause if you persist on seeing him. You have forty-eight hours to call the wedding off, you hear me?"

"And if I don't?"

He hitched up a shoulder and marched past her. "Wait and see."

Lucy's feet froze to the spot. Her heart rate rose and fell like a wave in a turbulent storm. *My God, did he just threaten me? What did he do to the other girls? I need to know, but what if Matthew is unaware of how his brother reacted to them? Bloody hell, what do I do for the best? Dump Matthew for fear of what Jake will do to me if I don't?*

Matthew appeared in the doorway of the drawing room. "Hey, you, did you get lost?"

She forced a smile in place to disguise how upset she was. "I think I took the wrong turn back there. Jake was kind enough to point me in the right direction."

"Good old Jake, never one to leave a damsel in distress."

He held out his elbow for her to slip her arm through the gap, and they rejoined the group. The evening progressed slowly, too slowly for Lucy's liking. Thankfully, Jake excused himself not long after the incident in the hallway. Matthew said goodnight to his parents around eleven and got the driver to drop them back to his gatehouse. Lucy's gaze darted everywhere. She had a fascination for tiny places like this that had a history of their own to speak about. Except this was unlike any other gatehouse she'd had the pleasure of visiting in the past. The interior was ultra-modern, to the point of her wondering if the building's integrity hadn't been compromised by the alterations.

"Wow, well, this is different."

"I'm sensing it's not what you expected, Lucy."

"Hardly. Who did this? Not you, surely?"

He visibly cringed. "Umm…are you going to hate me if I say yes?"

"No, but I might demand to know what you were thinking when you spoilt the look of such a beautiful building. Damn, did I say that out loud? I didn't mean to. You have every right to change the interior, it's just that…"

"You detest it." He laughed and gathered her in his arms.

"Damn, are you offended?"

"I would be if this was going to be our home in the future. It's not, by the way."

"Phew. The last thing I want to do is upset anyone else this evening."

He pushed her gently away from him. "Who have you upset? Not mother, that's just her way. You'll get used to her."

"I thought I had, sorry, maybe I was wrong. When did you alter the interior?"

"Around five years ago, under the guidance of an interior designer an ex put me in touch with. I hated it too at first, now I'm used to it. It grows on you. Don't feel bad for speaking your mind, it's one of the things I admire most about you."

"Good, because that's me. I wouldn't want to change in the future either."

"And I wouldn't want you to change at all. You seemed shocked by my proposal tonight."

"Very shocked. I know we've both told each other how much we're in love, but to do that to me in front of your parents, who I'd only just met…"

"I know. I'm always one to jump in and do things first and think of the consequences later."

She tilted her head. "Does that mean you're likely to regret your actions?"

"No. Bloody hell, I'm cocking this up."

His mouth covered hers in a demanding kiss that led them into the bedroom. Another room that took her breath away, but that was nothing compared to what happened between the sheets that evening.

10

Five years ago

"No, please, don't do it. I didn't mean to do that."

His fist struck her jaw, and she staggered against the wall in the lounge. She levered herself away from the new wallpaper and saw the blood outlining the embossed pattern. That pissed her off more than him striking her for some reason.

She ran from the room, didn't have a clue what to do next. All she knew was that she had to make plans to get away from him, or risk being six feet under within a few months. The beatings had become more frequent in recent weeks. If someone riled him at work, he suppressed his anger until he laid eyes on her and then let rip. She always witnessed the satisfied grin covering his face once he'd unleashed what was eating away at his soul. Invariably, she did nothing wrong. She cared for him as a wife should, cooked, washed, ironed, cleaned, all this on top of working extremely long hours herself. While he, well, his chores consisted of working full time, putting out the bin once a week and maintaining both the cars, his better than hers. Generally, he put a fiver's worth of petrol in the tank to see her through the week. Some weeks, if she had to make an extra trip to the supermarket to top up the cupboards, she barely had enough in the tank to see her through.

He didn't allow her money of her own. All her wages went into a joint bank account only he had access to. He put sixty pounds on the kitchen table every week. She had needed to learn how to be frugal from the outset really. No luxury items ever found their way into her basket. She should've left him as soon as she noticed the decline in the marriage. The controlling influence he had over her. Her mother had always instilled in her that men knew best and she encouraged her to take on board their advice where finances were concerned. It got her wondering if her own parents' marriage had been similar. She doubted it. Her father adored her mother, worshipped the ground she walked on and treated her like a lady. Or was that for her benefit? What truly happened behind closed doors? No one really knew, did they?

She heard him thumping up the stairs. Her eyes tightly shut, she pulled her knees up to her chin and leaned against the headboard. She was aware the beating wouldn't end until he saw fit. Without saying a word, he laid into her again. Blood spattered the pretty pink wallpaper behind the bed. She grunted and groaned with every punch. Maybe she should stop making the noises, perhaps they were turning the warped bastard on. She had to pretend he'd knocked her unconscious for him to back off. She froze in position, listened to him come around the other side of the bed. He roughly laid his hands on her, checking several pulse points to make sure she was still alive, and then walked out of the room.

As soon as the coast was clear, she sat upright and stared at her reflection in the mirror. A weak, miserable excuse of a woman stared back at her. Bloodied and bruised, beaten inside and out by a man who supposedly loved her. *How in God's name did I allow this to happen? How did it escalate to this?*

Her nights ended up being filled with terror, either in her sleep or while she stared up at the ceiling for hours, listening to him snoring, teetering on the edge of the bed. She'd often considered grabbing her pillow and suffocating him, however, in reality, she knew she didn't have the bloody strength left in her frail body to combat him if he cottoned on to what she was trying to do.

Her life as she knew it was over. In truth, it had been for years...

11

---

*L*ucy woke up in a sweat, cradled in Matthew's arms. He was propped up on an elbow, gazing down at her, his eyes overflowing with love.

She stretched, yawned and smiled. "Good morning. Have you been awake long?"

He lowered his lips to hers and kissed her until she used up all the breath in her lungs. He pulled away and ran his tongue over his lips, tasting her. "Did you sleep well?"

"Sort of, strange bed and all that. Did you?"

He traced his finger over her cheek. "Off and on. You had several nightmares which scared the life out of me."

She sat up and pulled the quilt around her naked body. "I did. In what way did I scare you?" *Shit! Did I try to attack him, or worse still, try to kill him?*

"You scared me by what you said. Has something gone on in your past, darling? Have you been traumatised in some way?"

Her gaze drifted off to stare at the black chest of drawers against the wall close to the door. "No. Why, what did I say?"

"A mixture of things. Some of them hard to decipher, but you were clearly distressed."

"It's been a harrowing week, what with the accident and Shirley's murder. I suppose it's only natural I should react and for it to affect my sleep."

He gathered her in his arms and placed her head on his chest. "Of course. You'd tell me if there was anything else, wouldn't you?"

"I promise. I'm so happy with you, truly elated for the first time in my life. Why would I do anything to harm that?"

"You couldn't. However, I want you to know that if you ever need anything, I'm here for you. I'll always be by your side, from this day forward until the day we die."

She wiped away the unexpected stray tear that slipped down her cheek. "I know, ditto, Matthew. We have a powerful love that others might try to destroy. We won't allow that to happen, will we?"

He raised her head to make her look at him. "Did you have someone in mind?"

"No, not really. It was a figure of speech, that's all." She'd meant his brother, Jake, and was adamant she would raise the subject one day. But not yet, not until she was sure of Matthew. After all, they barely knew each other really, and yet here they were, engaged to be married.

"Come on, I'll cook you my speciality for breakfast." He eased her aside and shot out of bed.

Her gaze didn't wander. It remained on his face while he pulled on a pair of jogging pants.

"What's on the menu?"

"You'll see. The en suite is in there, and you'll find my dressing gown behind the door." He left the room.

She stared at the ceiling, smiling, and wondered how, and if, she deserved the luck in love she was having at the moment. He truly was the most special man, who clearly loved her deeply. Everything was going too well, that was what was niggling her. Nothing was ever this perfect in life, she'd more than recognised that over the years.

Pots clattered in the kitchen, forcing her to get out of bed and get a wriggle on. She scrutinised her face in the bathroom mirror and groaned. "Bloody hell, how could he love someone who looks like Frankenstein's bride first thing in the morning?"

She lathered up the soap in her hands and scrubbed at her face, regretting the fact she hadn't brought an overnight bag with her. Normally, she avoided using soap on her face, except in emergencies, which this was.

"It's ready," Matthew shouted, five minutes or so later.

Lucy tied the silky dressing gown, seeped in his aftershave, around her waist and stepped into the kitchen to find a pile of American-style pancakes, bacon and lashings of maple syrup poured over the top.

"What the…you made all this?"

He raised his hands, expelled a breath on his fingertips and rubbed them against his smooth chest. "I did. I'm a dab hand in the kitchen, I'll have you know. When the mood takes me, that is."

"Wow! To say I'm impressed would be an understatement. I hope it tastes as good as it looks." She winked.

He gestured for her to take a seat at the marble-topped island. "There's only one way to find out. Sit and enjoy, lovely lady. Coffee?"

"Now you're spoiling me. It's been ages since I had a fresh pot of coffee in the morning. Mum and Dad always had a pot on the go when they were alive," she added quickly, shielding off any questions he might have had.

"You must miss them?"

Her gaze drifted to the pancakes he was piling on a plate. "I do, every day. It's going to be sad walking down the aisle without them being there, or without Father on my arm to give me away."

"I wish we'd met sooner." He passed her the plate. "Dig in."

"I do, too. It would've solved so many problems." She cringed, her mouth running away with her. She'd need to be conscious of that in the future, if she was going to successfully conceal her past from him.

He tilted his head. "Meaning?"

"Oh nothing, just talking crap as usual. I'm deliriously happy and I think it's addled my brain. I've never had a man cook breakfast for me."

"About that…I was wondering why you never talk about your past."

She shrugged. "I could ask you the same thing. I've never had regrets in this life. I prefer to live in the present. I suspect you're the same, right?"

"You're correct, and that's why I think we're the perfect match. I can't wait to have you with me permanently, as my wife. The truth is, I don't know how I've survived this long without having you in my life. I hope you feel the same way I do?"

She reached across the island and covered his hand with hers. "Of course I do. I can't describe how deep my love is for you. Sometimes I have to rein my emotions in, otherwise they'd overwhelm me. I love you so much, you make me feel complete, as if all these years I've felt a part of me was missing. Does that even make sense?"

"It's incredible. I feel exactly the same way; you put it perfectly." He leaned across and kissed her.

"I need to eat this before it gets cold. Tell me, how did you know pancakes were my favourite breakfast ever?"

"Call it a lucky guess. I'm so pleased you stayed last night. Waking up with you beside me, well, it tops everything I've ever experienced in this life."

"You're such a romantic. I'm lucky to have you."

"I'm the fortunate one. That first night you blew me away with your beauty and you continue to do that, every single day I'm with you."

Her heart pounded rhythmically as if it were fit to burst. They chatted generally over breakfast. Lucy leaned back in her stool, the metal support digging into her back, and patted her stomach. "I don't think I'll be eating another thing all day."

"Get away with you. I bet you do. Do you have any plans for the day?"

"No, not really, although I should visit Keith later, to offer my condolences."

"I could come with you, if that's what you want?"

"I'd like that. Now, what did you have in mind for the rest of the day?" She grinned, mucky thoughts running through her head.

He pointed a finger at her. "Get your mind out of the gutter. I was thinking I'd give you a guided tour of the property."

"Umm…you're forgetting one thing."

His brow furrowed. "I am?"

"I don't have a change of clothes with me."

He dropped a clenched fist on the counter. "You're right, silly me. Want me to drop by your place and pick up some clothes for you? Either that or I can sort out a pair of shorts and a T-shirt that'll probably fit you."

"Sounds adorable. I still can't go around the estate wearing high-heeled sandals, though."

"I've probably got some flip-flops or deck shoes that will do."

"You've thought of everything. I'd love a guided tour."

"Great stuff, I'm looking forward to showing it off to you. One day, all this will be ours."

"What? Are you kidding me?"

He chuckled. "That's right. I'm the heir to Fledgling Hall as I'm older than Jake."

"Wow, I had no idea. Where will we live until then?"

"Not here, that's for sure, not after your reaction last night."

She covered her eyes, ashamed. "I'm sorry, me and my big mouth. I wouldn't mind. We could make a few adjustments. It has a cosy feel to it, sort of."

"I sense a 'must try harder' comment coming my way." He laughed, which set Lucy off.

"I'm sorry. I shouldn't have voiced my opinions openly last night. I didn't mean to sound disparaging of your efforts."

"You weren't, at least, I didn't read it that way. You're entitled to your point of view. I never want to suppress that in the future, you hear me?"

"Does that go for the wedding plans, too?"

"Of course. What makes you say that…? No, wait, yes, Mother can be dominating at times. You'll need to speak up if there's an element you find you're uncomfortable with. Promise me?"

"All right. The last thing I want to do is step on your mother's toes, love."

"You won't. I'll have a word with her, tell her to back off, if that's what you want."

"No, don't do that. We'll see how things progress first and seek changes if we need to, how's that?"

"Sounds as perfect as you are."

"Get away with you. Right, can I jump in the shower?"

"We could always have one together."

She rolled her eyes, slipped off the stool and kissed his cheek. "Easy, tiger, we have plenty of time ahead of us for those sorts of shenanigans."

"Spoilsport! There's a spare towel in the bathroom cupboard, take your pick."

*H*alf an hour later she was in the bedroom, admiring her ensemble in the full-length mirror. Matthew had managed to source a royal blue T-shirt and a pair of white shorts which ended just past her knees. He also managed to locate a pair of yellow flip-flops at the bottom of his wardrobe. Yes, they were five sizes too big for her, but they'd do.

Matthew exited the en suite wearing a crisp white shirt and black jeans. "Are you ready for this, Mini-Me?"

He earned a slap for his cheek. "Not bad for what was to hand. What's first?"

"That's up to you, or should I say the weather? If it's nice, we'll take a chance on the grounds. What say you?"

"Agreed."

He held his arm out. She slipped hers through the loop, and they set off. He regaled her with the details of his mother's exploits in developing the grounds into something that was both picturesque and breathtaking at the same time.

"This is incredible. Does your mother have any formal training as a landscape gardener?"

"No. She has, however, studied numerous books about Capability Brown, who was her inspiration."

At the bottom of a long grass pathway was a stunning lake. In its centre was a magnificent fountain which changed shape every ten minutes or so.

"Bloody hell, I could stand here mesmerised by this display for hours on end."

He smiled. "Most of the visitors say the same."

"I'm not surprised. How do your parents feel about people traipsing all over their grounds?"

"They accepted it's a necessary evil. It takes a fair amount to maintain the mansion."

"I can imagine. Show me more." There was a thrill shooting through her veins. She could never have imagined being fortunate enough to date someone with this amount of history to their name, let alone be marrying them. She considered herself a very lucky girl indeed.

They rounded a slight mound and slipped into a wooded area. Something caught her attention through the trees. Her heart sank when she realised it was Jake and he was heading their way, carrying a gun. She gripped Matthew's arm tighter. He sensed her tensing beside him and patted her hand.

"It's okay, it's only Jake. He often comes out here to shoot the game."

"Ugh...how awful. I hate the thought of innocent creatures being murdered for pleasure."

"Hardly, but I'm not going to get into an argument about that and spoil our wonderful day together."

She stopped and stared at him. "Are you telling me you're pro hunting?"

"Most people are in our situation."

"What's that supposed to mean?" she asked, her voice rising through the octaves.

Jake was closer now. He deliberately took a shot. Lucy squealed and shook her head.

"Was that for my benefit?" she seethed.

"Nope. Enjoy your walk," he replied, going past them back to the house.

"What's wrong with you?" Matthew placed a hand either side of her face.

She turned her head away. "Nothing. I hate guns and what they stand for. Nothing ever good happens when someone fires one. I'm sorry if I'm not conforming to what you guys think…"

"It's okay. Please, if you have a differing opinion to us on hunting then so be it. The last thing I'd want to do is fall out with you about it, Lucy."

She held his hand tightly. "Promise me you won't go hunting in the future?"

He shook his head. "I can't promise that. We have certain traditions we need to uphold."

She stormed away, in the direction of the gatehouse, she hoped.

He caught up with her within seconds. "Lucy, what's wrong with you? Why are you so against guns? Speak to me, please."

A vivid image ran through her mind. Patrick holding a handgun to her head, threatening to pull the trigger. The day he started torturing her like that was the day she realised she had to get away from him and the day she started planning his demise. But how could she tell her fiancé that? The truth was, she couldn't, not if she wanted to still be in his life.

"I can't explain it, sorry, it's something that has stuck with me from my childhood. I respect animals and their place on this earth. I wish other people did the same. I don't want to fall out with you about this, Matthew, just don't ever try to include me in any hunts in the future. Okay?"

He raised his hands and took a step back. "You have my word. I'm not one for forcing people to believe in things against their will."

"Good. Would you mind taking me home now?"

"What about the tour of the house?" He seemed shocked by her announcement.

That's tough. I need to get away from here. I know I'm overreacting, but it's been a hell of a week, and now this. I can't be around people who take pleasure in robbing defenceless creatures of their lives. It isn't fair, and I want no part of it.

"Please, Lucy, won't you calm down?" he asked from his seat on the bed. He watched her strip off and replace his clothes with the dress Trisha had lent her.

"I'm perfectly calm. I need to go home."

"And I'll drive you. Tell me we're okay, Lucy? I couldn't bear it if we fell out over something so..."

She rounded on him, her anger mounting, and finished off his sentence for him. "What? Trivial? Just leave it, Matthew. If you value our relationship, you'll leave this topic well alone in the future, unless you're telling me that I'm not allowed to have an opinion of my own now that we're engaged."

"Whoa! Talk about going over the top. Where the hell is all this coming from? One minute we were enjoying a wonderful walk together, and the next all this has blown up. I don't understand and I'm not likely to unless you confide in me."

"I've stated my reasons already. If you choose to ignore or discount what I've said, then there's no hope for us."

He marched out of the room. Tears pricked, and she had to fight hard to prevent them from falling. She realised she was probably taking things to the extreme but she was battling what she'd been subjected to in the past. She left it a few minutes and then followed him out of the room. Matthew was leaning against the back of the sofa, shaking his head. She walked up behind him and placed her hands around his waist.

"I'm so sorry."

He swivelled and hooked his arms over her neck. "No, I should be the one to apologise. It's obvious we have a lot to learn about each other. Do you want to call the wedding off?"

Her eyes widened. "Do you?"

"No, not at all."

"Then let's ignore what happened today and move on with our lives."

"If only it were that simple. Don't take this the wrong way, but I won't allow you to dictate what I can and can't be involved in. Countering that, I will never do the same to you. Is that clear?"

"Okay, if that's the way it has to be. I'd like to go home now."

"If that's what you want. I'm sorry the day was spoilt."

"Why? You didn't spoil it, Jake did."

"Jake was doing what comes naturally to him, to us."

She swallowed noisily. "If I love you then I'll have to accept there are grave differences between us."

"Differences that you're going to have to adapt to, or…"

"Or our marriage will fail, is that what you were going to say?"

"Possibly. I'd hate it to be that way."

"Maybe it would be a good idea if we took a break from each other for a week or two, if that's how you feel."

His arms dropped, and he pushed away from her and headed for the door. "Are you ready?"

She wanted to break down and cry, tell him that she regretted her actions and her snarky comments, but she couldn't. She had made a vow to herself that she would never be subservient to a man ever again. She had a mind of her own and she was determined that no man would alter her way of thinking about anything in the future.

Lucy followed Matthew out to the car. The tension on the journey home was palpable. He dropped her off outside Trisha's house and left without giving her a farewell kiss. She unlocked the door and let herself in. Trisha was waiting for her, her arms open wide for her to walk into. Trisha knew, *how,* she didn't have a clue, but she knew things had gone desperately wrong between them.

"Come on, don't cry. Tell Auntie Trisha all about it."

Her friend led her into the kitchen. She poured a couple of glasses of brandy and handed one to Lucy who downed her shot in one go.

"I've screwed up," Lucy moaned.

"Jesus, I'm not sure how you make that out. Look at the size of the rock you're wearing."

"I might as well take it off. I've ruined things between us."

"I thought something was up when he dropped you off without kissing you goodbye. Want to talk about it?"

They sat in the kitchen, and she spilled everything over two cups of coffee.

"Go you for standing up for yourself. I hate any form of hunting, too," Trisha said, emptying her cup at the sink.

"But is it good to have principles when there is so much on offer? And I don't mean the money side of things. His love and adoration I was talking about."

"You don't have to point that out to me, I know you're no gold digger. The truth is, I don't know how you're going to get around it unless you sit down and thrash it out with him. I'm sure you'd be able to meet a compromise between you, if that's what the pair of you want."

"It's what I want, not sure about him. Things were really tense between us."

"Doh! I could see that for myself. My advice would be to leave it a day or so, see if he calls you first. If not, then you're going to have to be the one to reach out to him—if you want to continue seeing him, that is."

"I do. I've never felt like this before, I know we're right for each other. But I refuse to give up on my principles."

"Then you're going to be at an impasse, Lucy."

She covered her face with her hands and growled, then she dropped her hands again. "Me and my big mouth. I think it was the shock of seeing Jake coming at us with a loaded gun in his hands…"

"And it brought back the dreadful memories, yes?"

"Yes."

Trisha stared into the distance as if contemplating what to say next. Eventually, she said, "Well, now, don't go biting my head off when I say this, but maybe you should confide in him."

"Oh God! I couldn't! Not yet. Maybe a few months or years down the line, but not now. The last thing I'd want to do is scare him off."

"I promise you, I don't suppose you could ever do that. He's head over heels in love with you."

"So much so that he neglected to kiss me goodbye after a silly little tiff? That's what I'm struggling to come to terms with. I need to get out of these clothes. Thanks for lending me the dress, sweetie, everyone loved it."

"Okay, but once you've got your Sunday slouchies on, I want an in-depth account of what happened with the parents and how Matthew proposed to you."

"I'd rather forget about it and talk about something else, if that's all right with you?"

Trisha smiled and shrugged. "Whatever you want to do is fine by me, love."

Lucy bashed a clenched fist against her temple. "Actually, what I really need to do is go and pay Keith a visit."

"I'll take you if you want. Any news on when you can pick up your car?"

"I've arranged to collect it in my lunch hour on Monday, if I get one."

"You've gotta eat. You'll have to shut up shop for an hour."

"We'll see. I can always postpone picking it up. I'll play it by ear and see what Keith has to say first."

12

_A_n hour later, Trisha drew up outside Shirley and Keith's house. Trisha remained in the car while Lucy entered the couple's beautiful home. Tears filled her eyes the moment she laid eyes on all the photos of the extremely happy couple sitting on every surface. Keith may have smiled to greet her, but the smile soon disappeared. He seemed like a lost soul as he moved around the downstairs, going from room to room as they spoke.

"Keith, why don't I make you a drink?" Lucy asked, fearing for his state of mind.

"I don't want a drink. All I want is to know why? Why my Shirley of all people? The police said nothing was taken, so why? And where were you? You should've been there with her." He pointed an accusatory finger in her direction.

"Please, please don't blame me. You can't make me feel any worse than I do already. Shirley wasn't only my boss, she was one of my dearest friends."

"Phooey! You barely knew her. I've loved that woman half my life. They've been the happiest years I've spent on this earth, and now... she's gone." His shoulders dipped, and he bowed his head.

Lucy was unsure what to do next, whether to cross the room and comfort him or remain where she was. "I can't tell you how sorry I am. Shirley insisted that I should go at lunchtime. I had an appointment and, as it was busy in town, she decided to work on."

"I know. She rang me. Oh God, if I miss her this much already, what the fuck am I going to feel like a week from now, and beyond?"

"They say time is a great healer…"

He waved the suggestion away. "Bullshit. Don't go spouting that rubbish, not within spitting distance of me, Lucy."

"I'm sorry." She sighed, her own emotions getting the better of her.

They sat there in a tension-filled, poignant silence for a few minutes.

Finally, Keith blew his nose on a man-sized tissue and straightened his back. "There's the business to consider in all of this. I don't want anything to do with it. I have a career of my own to contend with. Any suggestions?"

"I haven't had a chance to think about that side of things yet. Umm…if you're asking if I'd be willing to carry on working there, then yes, without a doubt, the answer would be yes."

The words were barely out of her mouth.

"That's settled then. You can run it for me. I'll promote you to manager. We'll have to discuss the ins and outs about the salary and so forth another time when my head is somewhat clearer."

"Oh my! Well, if you're sure?"

"I am. Shirley had nothing but good things to say about you and your work ethic. Don't let me down, Lucy."

"I won't. I swear I won't. Umm…you want me to run the place single-handedly?"

"Of course not, you'll be responsible for advertising and inter-viewing for a girl Friday as it were. Are you up to that?"

"I think so. Keith, I promise you, I won't let you down. I'll do this for Shirley."

"Thank you, I was hoping you'd say that. Now, if you'll excuse me, I need to continue calling the family to break the news. Then I'll have the funeral arrangements to consider."

"Will you be able to do that yet? What with the ongoing police investigation, I mean?"

"I don't know. No one has told me a damn thing."

"I could ring them for you, if you'd like me to?"

"Would you? I'd be grateful. I'm not sure I could handle speaking to that detective again. He was rather off when he broke the news, not what I'd call compassionate at all."

"I'm sorry he treated you that way. Leave it to me. I'll ring in the morning. Is there anything else I can do for you while I'm here?"

He rose from his seat and shook his head. "No. I'll cope. Thanks for coming, Lucy, and for accepting the promotion."

She walked towards him and hugged him. Keith hugged her back, tightly, enough to suffocate her a little.

"I'll be off then. I'll give you a call tomorrow, once I've spoken to the detective in charge."

"Thank you. Shirley thought the world of you, I can see why now."

"I loved her like a member of my family. The place won't be the same without her smiling face around."

He nodded. "I hear you on that. Thanks, Lucy, I apologise for laying the blame at your door earlier."

"Don't be. You know where to find me if you need to vent at all, okay?"

"Thanks. I just need to get through the next few weeks."

"We both do," she said, only her mind was on her own overwhelming circumstances.

She left the house and got back in the car.

Trisha tossed her Kindle aside and asked, "How did it go?"

"As expected. He's asked me to run the place for him."

"Wow, that's so cool. Sorry, was I a little overenthusiastic about that?"

"Let's go, and yes, a touch. I have to employ someone else. I'm supposed to take over my role straight away, and tomorrow I've volunteered to ring the detective in charge to see what's going on with Shirley's body." She shuddered. "Keith wants to start making the arrangements for her funeral ASAP."

"He's not hanging around, is he?" Trisha drove away from the house.

"I think I'd be doing the same in his shoes. The poor man is beside himself. They meant the world to each other."

"Any kids?"

"No, I'm not sure if that makes a difference or not. Less responsibility for him, but it also means there's no one there to help see him through this."

"You're there."

"I know. As if I don't have enough on my plate already, eh?"

"You're resilient, made of strong stuff, as you've proved time and time again over the years."

"I hope you're right. There's only so much trauma a girl can take in her life, and up until now, I'd say I've had my fair share of it, right?"

"You're not wrong. Fancy lunch out today? It's on me."

"You don't have to do that. Umm...I need to go home and get changed first."

"We both do. I insist, my treat."

*T*hey dashed in, got changed, and then set off again. Lucy knew exactly what Trisha was up to. She was an expert in distraction techniques. Anything she could think of to keep Lucy from dwelling on her turbulent relationship and having to contend with Shirley's death at the same time. They ended up at a small gastro pub on the outskirts of Bath. They were lucky to get in. The waitress squeezed them in at a table in the corner where they ate a hearty roast beef dinner, foregoing the dessert menu as they were too full.

After the meal, and with the sun finally making an appearance to brighten their day, Lucy suggested they take a stroll along by the river. They chatted and put the world to rights, talking about every subject that had reared its head in the last week or so. By the end of it, Lucy was adamant about what she should do about Matthew and sent him a text to apologise for her behaviour.

He must have been waiting for her to contact him because he replied instantaneously. Then he rang her as they got back in the car.

"I'm so glad you got in touch. I've been a lost soul without you."

She sniggered. "I think that's a slight exaggeration on your part, Matthew."

"I swear it's not. Look, I want to see you, but I've been called away on business. I have to go to Scotland for the week."

"That's a shame. It doesn't matter. I have news of my own to share."

"What's that?"

"Keith has made me manager of the travel agent's, so I'll be flat out all week anyway."

"That's brilliant news. I'm so proud of you. It looks like everything is slotting into place perfectly."

"It is. If we can get past our little falling out."

"It's forgotten about, I promise. Can I see you at the weekend?"

"Saturday night? I might have to work all day on Saturday. It depends on how busy I am during the week. I need to employ a member of staff to fill my shoes as well."

"You're going to be under the cosh. Don't forget to pick up the car on Monday."

"I won't, already pencilled that into my schedule. Will you ring me during the week?"

"Every evening, if that's all right?"

"It is. Matthew, I love you and regret my actions today. They were silly and inconsiderate."

"I know you do. You're entitled to your point of view, just like we are. All we need to do now is find a happy medium, to keep us both happy. I have every confidence we'll be able to do that."

"Good. Speak soon. Have a good trip."

"Thanks. I love you, Lucy Brent, don't ever forget that."

"I won't." She ended the call wearing a huge smile.

"See, that wasn't so bad, was it?" Trisha said.

"No, you were right. I shouldn't have flown off the handle like that."

"He's forgiven you by the sounds of it."

"Yep, thankfully. I'm going to miss him this week, while he's away."

Trisha laughed. "I'd say it was great timing, what with what lies ahead of you this week."

———————

13

*T*risha turned out to be right. The next six days were frantic but enjoyable, nevertheless. First thing Monday morning, she had called the detective in charge of Shirley's case. He'd informed her that it was far too soon to release Shirley's body and that it would be another week or so before that was likely to happen. She relayed that information to Keith. He was far from happy, however, he accepted the position for what it was.

The next job she crossed off her extensive to-do list was to contact the job centre to place the job vacancy. She also decided to run an advert in the local newspaper at the same time. Lucy had needed to close up the shop to pick up her smart new car. The rest of the week consisted of her selling numerous high-value holidays and being kept on the go from nine until five daily. She let out a breath once home time came and promptly fell asleep on the sofa after she'd prepared and eaten her dinner every night.

On Friday of that week, she arranged to interview three candidates for the job. The first was an elderly woman in her sixties, who she considered ideal—the woman later turned down the job as the hours didn't suit her. That left a young girl in her teens, who Lucy didn't quite gel with, and a woman close to her age, called Kathy, who had a bubbly personality and seemed eager to please. She rang Keith and informed him that the position had been filled and that Kathy was due to start on Monday the following week. He appeared delighted by the choice but also a little subdued at the same time.

During the week, Matthew showered her with gifts of flowers, beautiful trinkets and jewellery. Although, she found it perplexing that he'd sent her a skeleton keyring one day, a single red rose, and a single white lily on another occasion.

On the Saturday, Lucy decided to stick to the usual routine and close at lunchtime. Business had been booming all week, therefore, she didn't see the need to push herself more than necessary. She went home and got ready for her date with Matthew. This time, she wore a dress that she'd splashed out on from the boutique next door to the agency. It was a classic midnight-blue dress which clung to her slim figure in all the right places. She also made sure she packed an overnight bag this time as well, although she had second thoughts while packing her bag, wondering if Matthew would deem it presumptuous of her.

She needn't have worried. He sent the driver to pick her up at six. He stepped out of the gatehouse as the car pulled into the drive and twirled her around as soon as she exited the vehicle. "I've missed you so much." He placed her on the ground and delivered a kiss that left her legs shaking. He took a pace back and glanced down at her evening dress. "That's beautiful. Is it new?"

"I treated myself."

"It suits you."

The driver went to the boot, removed her bag and set it on the ground beside them.

"Sorry, thought I'd come prepared this time."

"I'm glad, I was unsure whether to mention bringing a change of clothes or not, after the faux pas last time."

She smiled and wrinkled her nose. "It's forgotten about, remember?"

"It is. Thanks, Jim. I'll ring you if I need anything else."

The driver tipped his cap and drove the car up to the main house.

"What's on the agenda for this evening? You never mentioned it when you made the arrangements."

"Sorry, I should have forewarned you. Mother's having a little soirée in our honour this evening."

"Ugh…you could have warned me."

"What are you stressing about, you look perfect to me, as usual."

"You're biased."

He picked up her bag, took hold of her hand and led her inside. They'd scarcely got through the door when he pounced on her, his lips brushing across her face and neck.

She slapped his arm. "Hey, calm down. A girl has her makeup to consider."

"Sorry, overenthusiastic in your company, as always. I wish it could be you and me this evening."

"So do I. It's been a long week without you. Not sure I'm up to interacting with people I don't know. Can't we get out of it?"

"Not really. Once Mother has sent out invitations, there's no going back, not unless you want to piss her off."

"Thanks for the warning. Hey, you, I've got a bone to pick with you."

He stood back and frowned. "Have I done something wrong? Wait, I shower you with gifts all week and you have a bone to pick with me? Well, that's gratitude for you." Although his words were chastising, his tone wasn't, and there was a sparkle in his eyes.

"Actually, it's about the presents. Quite a mixed bag this week, I might add. By the way, I've told you before that I don't need you buying me gifts. It's not that I don't appreciate them, well, some of them, but I don't expect them. I know how much you love me, there's no need for you to continue trying to get me into your bed. You've won my heart."

"Bloody hell! The gifts aren't about forcing you into my bed. Anyway, what are you talking about? Mixed bag. Which ones didn't suit your tastes? I thought they were all as nice as each other and I'm a little put out by what you're telling me."

"Umm…maybe I should have kept quiet then."

"Nope, it's too late now, spill." He crossed his arms and tapped his foot, the twinkle never leaving his eye.

"Well, I'm not sure what the hell the single white lily was about. Or the skeleton keyring for that matter."

He tilted his head and stared at her in confusion. "I didn't send you those. Why would I?"

She slapped at his hand. "Stop messing about. Of course you did."

He shook his head, and his mouth turned down at the sides. "I swear I didn't. Where did they come from? All my presents can be easily traced back to the store where they were bought."

"You know what, I didn't think to check. I just presumed they were from you."

He glanced at his watch. "As much as I'd love to continue this conversation, Mother is expecting us to make an appearance before the guests arrive at seven."

"Okay, can we revisit this later, when we're alone again?"

"You bet. I want to get to the bottom of this mystery as much as you do."

Her mind was swirling during the drive up to the main house. *If Matthew didn't send the gifts, then who did?*

They entered the main hall to find Matthew's mother and brother, Jake, welcoming some early guests. Jake looked up and glared at her for a split second. Suddenly, all her doubts seemed to make sense. She hadn't heard from him since he'd threatened her, warning her to dump Matthew. Was this his way of letting his presence be felt? *Was Jake behind the weird, possibly nasty gifts? Aren't white lilies supposed to be the flowers which represent death? No, it can't be, he wouldn't do something like that, would he?*

Before she knew what was happening, Matthew had transported her a few feet and she was standing in front of his mother and brother.

"Hello, darling, you're late," his mother reprimanded Matthew under her breath, her smile fixed in place.

"Sorry, Mother, only a few minutes, and those guests were early," Matthew defended himself.

"Hello again, Lucy. What an adorable dress, is it new?"

"Thank you. Yes, it's lovely to see you again, Mrs Wallender."

"Now, now, none of that, you must call me Cynthia. I've been meaning to ring you all week. We'll speak later if we get the chance. I have a lot to discuss regarding the wedding."

Uncertain how to react, Lucy turned to face Matthew who was deep in conversation with Jake. They were laughing about something and nudging each other in the ribs.

She turned her attention to Cynthia again and said, "That would be wonderful. If we don't have time this evening, maybe we can discuss matters tomorrow."

"You're staying over?" she asked, her voice high-pitched.

Lucy wished a hole would open in the marble beneath her feet. "Yes, that's right," she replied, trying her best to sound confident and forthright.

Cynthia muttered something Lucy didn't quite catch before she moved away to welcome yet another guest. With the two men still deep in conversation beside her, she felt a little uncertain what to do next. In the end, she sidled up to Matthew and slid an arm around his waist.

"Hi, sorry, got involved there for a moment. Are you all right?" Matthew asked.

"Can I have a brief chat with you?"

He glanced over his shoulder at a crowd emerging through the front doors. "It's going to have to wait, love. Duty calls. You stand next to me, and I'll introduce you to everyone, okay?"

Her heart sank. "Okay, I suppose."

The next thirty minutes were some of the longest in her life. Dull and mind-numbing, and her cheeks hurt at the end of it as she was forced to smile throughout the daunting experience. Once they'd completed their duty, Matthew led her into the vast dining hall and placed a glass of champagne in her hand.

"You did really well, considering we threw you in at the deep end."

"Thanks. I wanted to have a chat with you about your mother."

Matthew lowered his voice. "What about?"

"She said she wants to discuss the wedding details. I don't know how to handle that, Matthew. We haven't even had the chance to speak about what we want ourselves."

He shrugged. "Can't you leave her to it?"

She gasped. "Is that what you want?"

"No, ideally we'd do it all ourselves, but you've just been promoted, and I've been away all week. Let's face it, neither of us have had the time to sit down and go through any plans."

"I can't do that. I don't want someone else planning my wedding, do you?"

"It's not just anyone else we're talking about, it's my *mother*, Lucy. I can't see the problem, not really."

"You can't? Seriously?"

He sighed. "Look, we'll discuss it later. If you decide you want my mother to take a lesser role in all of this, then we'll ask her to back off."

"That's not what I said at all. I'm just saying that I want to have some input into our big day."

"As you should. Don't get upset, we'll have it out with Mother later."

"I'm not getting *upset*, I'm perturbed by the intrusion and want to get it sorted sooner rather than later, that's all, Matthew."

He kissed her on the cheek and whispered, "Keep your voice down, you're making a show of yourself."

That was when a warning alarm went off in her head. Should she ignore it or act upon it? That was the dilemma running through her mind at present. She decided to give Matthew the benefit of the doubt and fixed a smile in place for the time being. After ten minutes of tiresome introductions, to people whose names she'd instantly forgotten, her duties were apparently over, and Matthew took her to one side to have a chat.

First out of his mouth was an apology. He kissed her gently on the lips. "I'm sorry, love, I shouldn't have snapped. I hate these kinds of events, they always set me on edge."

"I wasn't happy about the way you spoke to me, although I'm willing to let it slide this time."

"This time?" he queried, his head tilting.

"You heard me. I'm an independent woman, Matthew. I've fought hard to find my status in this world, and I don't expect you, or anyone else for that matter, to assume I'm going to conform to their way of thinking or doing things."

He raised an eyebrow. "Umm...yes, I think we've already established that last weekend. Can we call a truce?"

"I suppose so. But I still want a say in our wedding plans, if that's all right with you?" she added, her tone laced with sarcasm.

"And you will. Look, you'll get used to Mother in time. She's only trying to help. Use her experience in dealing with large functions, that's all I'm suggesting."

"I've never objected to her having an input, I welcome it. What I'm displeased with, if you will, is her *telling* me that she's arranged things."

"Has she said that?"

"Not as such. I can't help sensing that's the way it's going to be, though. This is our day, yours and mine."

"Ooo...are we having a lovers' tiff?" Jake interrupted, sneaking up behind Lucy and almost giving her a heart attack.

She turned to glare at him, huffed out a breath and went in search of a drink with Jake's and Matthew's laughter filling her ears.

When Matthew eventually caught up with her, she was gazing out of the large full-length window at the garden, which was lit by pastel shades dotted between the shrubs.

"Friends?" Matthew whispered in her ear.

She sighed. "Yes, I never said we weren't."

"That's not the impression I got. I know folks have mentioned it in the past, you know, about a wedding being one of the most stressful times in a couple's relationship. I just never expected it to be this stressful straight out of the starting blocks."

"Believe me, neither did I. Maybe it's the wrong time to be organising a marriage, after all that's happened in the past few weeks. Heck, it's only been about a month since we first met."

He shrugged and stared at her with lost puppy dog eyes. "My love, if you want to call it off, all you have to do is say the words."

She returned her gaze to the floor again, insecure about what to say or do next.

"Your silence is worrying me," he prompted.

"I hate being out of control of my own future. There, I've said it, that's all I'm prepared to say on the subject. So, either you have a word with your mother and ask her to work with me on this or..."

She raised her head and saw that he was frowning.

"Or? I can't believe you're willing to give me an ultimatum."

"I'm sorry. I feel overwhelmed, I suppose, and out of control. I hate that."

"I understand. I'll have a word with Mother, see if we can't put everything right before things go too far, how's that?"

"I appreciate it. I hope it doesn't stir up a hornet's nest. Your mother seems the type who would take offence to someone telling her to back off."

"You're probably right, but it's a risk I'm willing to take if it'll make you happy."

"I don't mean to cause any bother, Matthew. I swear."

He slung an arm around her shoulders and pulled her in for a hug. "I know. All I ask is that you're open with me. I don't want you to dwell on things to the extent that they start to eat away at you."

"I promise. I'm so lucky to have you."

"You are," he agreed.

She jabbed him in the ribs. "Oi, you!"

"Come on, we should mingle. That's another thing you're going to have to get used to doing. It goes with the territory, darling."

"I'll get used to it. My head is in the wrong place right now. I'll do my best."

"That's all I can ask. I'll be right back. I want a quick word with Mother while she's alone."

Lucy watched Matthew hurry across the room and was startled when someone whispered in her ear from her blind side.

"Are you causing bother again?"

She spun around to find Jake barely six inches away. "Excuse me? I'm doing nothing of the sort."

"I don't believe you. A word of warning, you won't win."

"Win *what*?" she asked, her eyes narrowing to match his.

"If there's a contest going on between you and Mother, she'll always turn out to be the victor...just saying."

"Thanks, not that there is anything of the sort going on. It's all in your imagination, Jake."

He smirked. "You keep telling yourself that. I know the signs."

"What signs?"

"Of a relationship when it's about to implode due to Mother's interference."

"Seriously? Are you all there?"

"Flinging insults my way isn't going to improve things either."

She crossed her arms and demanded, "Pray, tell me, what will?"

"Get used to there being three people in your relationship, that's all I'm prepared to say."

"By that I take it you're referring to Cynthia?"

"Of course. I'd say you're quick to cotton on but so far I've had to point every nuance out to you."

"You really are a piece of work, Jake. How come you're never willing to show your true colours when Matthew is around?"

He smirked again, leaned in and said in a menacing tone, "Where would be the fun in that?" Then he strode away from her, leaving her seething.

She gulped down the rest of her drink and walked into the hallway and out the front door. The cool evening breeze whipped her hair around her face and chilled her a touch. Warm hands grasped the tops of her arms, and she leaned her head back.

"It's cold out here, come inside."

She swivelled to find Matthew smiling down at her. "I'd rather be at your place, tucked up in a nice warm bed."

"Me, too. Only a few hours to go until we can achieve that tempting ambition."

"That's a pity. How did it go with your mother?"

"She was fine. She's asked if you'll join her in the morning to go over things."

"If I must," she replied, cringing.

"Will you do it for me if I show you a good time tonight, in bed?"

"Oh God, you sure know how to wear a girl down. All right, I'll do it for you, providing she doesn't start being heavy-handed with me about the arrangements."

"She's promised me she will be on her best behaviour."

*L*ucy spent the rest of the evening in a lighter mood and she found herself actually looking forward to the scheduled meeting with his mother the following day. They retired to the gatehouse at around eleven. His mother pecked her on the cheek and reminded her to be punctual the following morning.

Lucy assured Cynthia she would show up at ten-thirty. Everything seemed fine between her and Matthew again. She hated falling out with him, especially as he meant the absolute world to her.

He brought her breakfast of scrambled eggs on toast and bacon at nine, giving her enough time to get ready to meet his mother at the house. She thought her stomach would be tied up in knots as she walked through the grounds at ten-fifteen, but it wasn't.

The house was in sight now, and her mind was elsewhere, thinking up different ways of saying, 'No, I think we should do things this way', when a gunshot splintered the area close to her. The noise startled her so much she let out a scream and placed a hand over her frantically beating heart.

Before she had a chance to recover, another shot sounded. This time, it was louder and appeared to be closer. It was quickly followed by a third shot. She upped her pace to a trot, rushed through the main entrance and slammed her back against the door, panting. She stayed in the same position for a few minutes to capture her breath.

"Lucy? Whatever is the matter?" Cynthia asked, coming into the hallway from the drawing room.

"Someone was shooting out there, it scared me. I'll be fine in a moment or two."

"I'll send for some coffee. Why don't you come through and have a seat?"

Her legs just about had the strength to carry her into the drawing room. She almost backed out again at what she saw on display. The dominating feature was a flipchart at the head of a long table. Sitting on the table were an array of folders and albums the size of wallpaper sample books you get in a DIY store. *Oh heck! What have I let myself in for here?*

"Isn't it amazing? I've collected so many samples over the years in readiness for one of our sons' wedding. You're the lucky recipient of all this."

"It truly is, and overwhelming at the same time."

Cynthia hooked her arm through Lucy's and guided her closer to the display. "Take a proper look. There's a pad and pen at the end. I want you to pick out what takes your fancy. It'll be fun to see if we agree or not once you've finished."

"You expect me to do all this today? I thought we were just going to have a brief chat about things. I'm not sure I'm ready for all this, Cynthia."

"Whyever not? All you have to do is swiftly sift through the books. You can do that, can't you? It's not beyond you to spend thirty minutes of your precious time devoted to such a task, is it?" Cynthia stated.

Lucy faced her and frowned. Cynthia's tone was one that warned her not to retaliate, at least, that was how she read it. "Excuse me? You're expecting me to decide every aspect of my wedding within thirty minutes—that is what you implied, isn't it?"

Cynthia tutted and wagged her finger. "No, I think you misunderstood me a little. We'll get the basics down today and then work out the nitty-gritty later on."

"Okay, by basics, what exactly does that involve?"

"You know, the flowers, dresses, then we'll go on to what type of food we want to put on for the main meal and the evening reception."

"I see. To me, that's everything then."

Cynthia waved her hand in front of her. "Nonsense, there's far more to a wedding than that, my dear. That's why I suggested leaving everything to me."

"I didn't want that. I'd like some say in it."

"And so you shall. Start at the top there. Grab the paper and pen and jot down anything that takes your fancy."

Another shot sounded outside, and Lucy cringed.

"Ignore that, it's just Jake getting in some practice with his father. We have a new hunt gathering next weekend."

"Hunting what?"

"There's always woodpigeon around at this time of year."

Lucy shuddered. "The less said about that, the better."

"Ah yes, Matt mentioned you were a little touchy about hunting."

"*Touchy*? I'd say more than that, I despise it."

"Oh dear. My advice would be to get used to it as all the boys in the family take part, including Matt."

"We've spoken about it. I'd prefer not to get involved in any way, and Matthew is okay with my decision."

"As you wish. That remains to be seen once Matt inherits this place. You'll be expected to play hostess to the hunt."

"Or I could employ someone to do it for me." Lucy smiled tautly.

She watched Cynthia's breasts rise and fall in annoyance a few times.

"Tell me more about your background," Cynthia asked.

"Er…what in particular do you want to know about?" she tried to avoid the inevitable for a few seconds longer.

"Your upbringing. What school you went to, any awards you achieved, things like that, dear."

"I attended a general higher-education school where I obtained eight GCSEs, all grade B or above."

"What about university?"

"I didn't go. My parents didn't have the money to waste on sending me to further education facilities. I was okay with that. I started my first job at the age of sixteen and proved my worth right away. It was a thrill handing over two-thirds of my wages to my mother for keep."

"Two-thirds? And no further education, and yet you're a manager now. It doesn't seem possible."

"My father used to have a pop at people who chose to go on to university."

"Oh, do tell. What did he say about them?"

"High intelligence most of them, but very little common sense. In my experience, that's true, too."

"Oh, is it now? Well, I dispute that. My sons are both highly intelligent, and they also possess a lot of common sense, so that's poured water on your father's theory."

Lucy grinned. "There are always exceptions to the rules, I guess."

"There are. What work did you do before starting at the travel agency?"

"This and that," she replied evasively.

"Let's get on then, shall we? We can chat more later."

"If you insist."

"Oh wait, I have a very important question to ask."

"I'm all ears," Lucy said.

"Your family members—how many will there be at the wedding?"

"That's simple, sadly none. There's no one left. I'm the last of the…Brents."

"No one? Come now, I can't believe there isn't a distant relative somewhere out there."

"Take my word for it, there isn't."

"Oh well, that'll ease the costs a little," Cynthia murmured.

"Talking of costs, I know traditionally it should be down to the bride's family to foot the bill…"

"There's no need for you to concern yourself about that, it's all in hand. I know money is tight for you at the moment."

"It is, extremely tight. If this was up to me, Matthew and I would elope and get it over and done with."

Cynthia staggered back a few paces. "Goodness me, you nearly gave me a heart attack."

"Why? It would make sense and save a lot of money in the process."

"Hush, I won't have that said in this house again, do you hear me? Hopefully, Matt will only get married the once. We'll push the boat out for him, and you, of course."

"All I'm saying is that you needn't go to the added expense. None of this really matters to me."

"May I ask why?" Cynthia tilted her head and frowned.

"Money, I think it's a waste. One day in the life of a couple, and what? Some people, not you, of course, but some families end up burdened with debt. Why?"

"We're never going to agree on the whys and the wherefores, Lucy. Take it for what it is and enjoy it. There are plenty of girls out there who would willingly change places with you."

"I don't doubt that. What about your wedding? Did you have a grand affair?"

"I did. In this very house. Arnold and I were married within the gardens. I wouldn't have dreamt to having it held anywhere else."

"Any regrets over the years?"

"Regrets? Of marrying Arnold?"

Lucy nodded.

"No, never, he's the love of my life. He's given me two wonderful sons to be proud of. I see it as my job to carry on the tradition and help to find suitable wives for them."

"Do you think I'm *suitable*?"

"Honestly? I have my doubts at this point, but that's only because I hardly know you. The trust will come once I find out more about you, I'm sure."

"Why do you distrust me?"

"Who said anything about distrusting you?"

"I can see it in your eyes," Lucy said, not pulling her punches.

"Is there a reason I shouldn't trust you, Lucy?"

"No, I can't think of one." *Which is a lie. I could think of plenty. The main one being what happened five years ago!*

"I know you have a secret." Cynthia's words came as a sucker punch to Lucy's stomach.

"Excuse me?"

"You heard. You might play the innocent, doe-eyed woman to Matt, but I can read the signs a mile off. Women have a sixth sense, in case you haven't realised."

"Is this why Matthew has never been married? Because of your interference and accusations that are totally off the mark?"

"No, the right girl has never drifted into his life before."

"And has she now? Or aren't you willing to go that far?"

Cynthia sighed. "I haven't quite made up my mind on that one yet."

Lucy swept her hand across the books on the table. "And yet you've gone out of your way to put all this together for us."

"Any mother would do the same for her child."

"Most mothers' heart would be in it. Yours clearly isn't, is it, Cynthia?"

"You think you know me. You don't, young lady. You have no idea how dangerous I can be."

"Is that some kind of threat?" Lucy challenged.

"Not in the slightest. We've gone totally off subject here."

"I don't think we have, not really. It's clear how much you're willing to do to remain in your son's good books."

"Nonsense. I'm doing this because of the love I have for my son." She lowered her voice and issued yet another warning. "If you hurt my son, like any of the others before you did…"

"Please, don't stop there." Lucy pointed at her. "You're not brave enough to say the words, but I have enough common sense to know what this is all about, Cynthia."

"Go on, do tell."

"You think I'm a bloody *gold digger*."

"And now you're going to tell me I've got it all wrong, aren't you?"

"Yes, totally. However, I don't expect you to believe me. I love Matthew, none of this matters to me. If he had a tenner in his pocket, that would suit me down to the ground. It's him I want, not any of this. If you want to go into battle for his love, then who am I to stop you? I pity you if that's the case. What is it you're truly scared of? Another woman stealing his heart or just a poor woman, like me?"

"You haven't got a clue what you're talking about, and for what it's worth, I object to you speaking to me like this."

"Enough for you to want to tell Matthew about this little contretemps?"

Cynthia bowed her head in shame. "No."

"Well, I can assure you, I will. Because at the end of the day, Cynthia, I think too much of Matthew to hide the truth from him." She bit down on her tongue, and the taste of iron seeped into her mouth.

Cynthia's head rose, and their gazes met.

"I know you're hiding something. All this is your way of disguising the truth. I'm going to dig deep into your past and uncover what you're keen on hiding and, when I do, I'm going to expose you as the fraud I know you are."

"And I'm going to repeat myself in telling you that nothing could be further from the truth. I love Matthew, and he loves me. I'd be wary of interfering if I were you, in case it backfires on you and he decides he prefers my company to that of his mother's for the rest of his life. Be warned, Cynthia."

"Your threats mean nothing. Jake is of the same opinion. And yes, we've discussed you and your motives at length, don't worry."

"Why am I not surprised to learn that? I'll tell you what, I'll go back to the gatehouse now and return with Matthew. We'll all sit down, and you can explain all these accusations to him. See what he makes of it all, because I don't have to put up with this bullshit, Cynthia. You may have driven a bunch of his previous girlfriends away, but your attitude doesn't scare me."

"So you've already said. You've set me a challenge there, Lucy. Go, bring Matt back, if that's what you want. We'll see who's standing by his side at the end of the confrontation."

"I can do that, or we can try and sort this out between us. Either way is fine by me."

"I can't do this now, you've spoilt the mood. I was thrilled when Matt popped the question and at the thought of preparing the wedding for you, but I have to say you've done your very best to destroy any enthusiasm I might have had."

Lucy hitched up a shoulder. "You can try and play the wounded soldier with me, but it truly makes no odds. I can go back now and explain things to Matthew, or we can sit down in a civilised manner and discuss the arrangements calmly. I have never said I didn't appreciate what you were doing for us. All I was getting at is that I have a mind of my own and would dearly love to use it. If you object, then I can't see a way around this, can you?"

Cynthia's eyes welled up. Lucy sensed that was more out of frustration than anything else.

"Okay, let's try again."

After their pact was set in stone and each of them recognised the strength of the other, they took a seat and went through the wedding plans like the adults they were. As it was, the choices Cynthia had made turned out to be very much to Lucy's liking. After an hour, they wrapped things up. Both ladies rose from their seats, and Cynthia leaned forward to peck Lucy on the cheek.

"I'm glad we came to a suitable understanding."

Lucy nodded. She should have had the sense to have left it there but she refused to. "It's amazing what we can achieve together. We could be a force of nature instead of warring enemies, if only you made an effort to accept me, Cynthia."

"We'll see. We might have accomplished something this morning, however, we have a long way to go yet before I accept you as part of this family."

"Eh? After what we've selected together, how do you work that one out?"

"I've done all that for my son's sake, *not* yours."

Lucy heaved out a sigh. "I had a feeling you were going to be stuck in your ways and dig your heels in, I just didn't realise how much. In one respect, I admire your tenacity but, on the other hand, I feel sorry for you and your boys, because let's face it, no woman is ever going to live up to your exacting standards in this life, is she?"

"I think someone will, eventually. I still have grave doubts about you and the secrets you're keeping from us all, *including* Matt. If you break his heart, I will come after you."

"Yadda, yadda, Muma bear. There's no fear of me hurting Matthew, ever, not unless an outside influence plays a dirty hand or two. I've dealt with fiercer people than you in my past, so forgive me if I don't put much weight behind the threats you've issued today."

"And what's that supposed to mean?"

"You tell me. Dig deep enough and I have no doubt you'll learn the truth, or maybe you won't," she added cryptically. She smiled, left the room and made her way back to the gatehouse. She should have felt triumphant, but Cynthia's warning churned in her head during her speedy walk back.

14
---

*O*ver the next few weeks, her life as she knew it was conducted in a blur. Matthew was scarcely around, buried in work up in Scotland and only coming home at the weekends. She accepted it for what it was. It gave her the chance to get her own business, because that's how she regarded the agency now, up and running. Kathy, her new girl Friday, turned out to be the dream choice. They got on so well that the business seemed to turn around instantly, despite Brexit. People were voting with their pockets, booking holidays months in advance, hoping against hope that the economy would remain buoyant.

With every holiday booked, Lucy insisted that clients should take out travel insurance as a precaution.

Keith called in to see them halfway through the second week. He was suitably impressed by how busy they were and told Lucy that he was delighted she'd chosen Kathy as an assistant and that his wife's legacy was thriving. He also brought with him the sombre news that the coroner was releasing the body, and Shirley's funeral was due to take place on the thirtieth of May. And as a mark of respect, he asked Lucy to close the agency and to attend.

Obviously, she had agreed, and together they issued an invitation to Kathy, who showed no sign of hesitation in accepting the invitation.

The rest of the week had gone according to plan. Matthew's daily gifts brought a smile to her face and an ache to her heart. She missed him, more so in the evenings, when she was at home. Although he rang her every night, it wasn't the same as holding him in her arms.

The wedding plans appeared to be in full swing. Every now and again she received a text message from Cynthia, bringing her up to date and assuring her that everything was in hand. It was a relief not having the arrangements on her shoulders as well as the business. She had finally conceded that Cynthia knew her stuff in that department. But her biggest thrill was how the agency was performing in such troubled times. Kathy had proven to be an ideal colleague to work with. She even put Lucy to shame, coming up with dozens of exceptional promotional ideas that they had put in place the very first week.

Everything was going swimmingly until something very strange happened towards the end of the first week, when a wreath arrived at the shop. As soon as she saw it, she thought it was in memory of Shirley. Someone local perhaps had heard when the funeral was going to take place. She didn't even bother to read the card on the damned thing, not until midway through Friday afternoon during a lull in business.

*I*N LOVING MEMORY OF PATRICK.

*W*ell, her heart appeared to stall for several seconds. She sucked in a breath and studied the card, reading it over and over. *This can't be happening! This must be a mistake. The wreath must have come to the wrong place; there must have been a mix up along the way. But that name...Patrick, is so personal to me, it has to be meant for me, doesn't it?*

Her thoughts were caught up in a tornado, swirling angrily inside her mind. *Is this to do with Cynthia? Has she made good on her threat? Has she uncovered the truth? That my husband is dead? And that I killed him?*

But then the logical side of her brain told her that there was no way on earth Cynthia could have found out, even if she'd hired the best private investigator money could buy. So, if this wasn't down to her, then who was trying to rattle her cage and shake things up a bit? And why now, after five years of not hearing or seeing his name? Furthermore, how the hell was she going to find out who was responsible?

Kathy was astute. She could tell how upset Lucy was and asked her what was wrong. She'd grown close to her new colleague quickly and was tempted to share her secret with her but decided against it at the last moment.

"It must be a mistake by the florist. Silly me, I didn't think to check the day it came, I just presumed it was meant for Shirley."

"Can I do anything to help?"

"No, that's sweet of you, I'll sort it. I'll ring the florist, see what they have to say. You make the coffee, I'll do it now."

Lucy placed the call from her desk. The florist was no help at all. The woman informed her that the request had come in over the phone. She'd taken the call herself.

"Did a woman place the order?"

"No, it was definitely a man. Sorry I can't be more help. I have to go now, we're very busy."

"No problem. Thank you for your time." She hung up and stared out of the window.

Kathy nudged her out of her daze moments later. "Your coffee is beside you. Any luck with the florist?"

"No, nothing at all. It's all rather puzzling. Never mind, the weekend is just around the corner. Do you have any plans?"

"Not really. I have a first date with Chris to look forward to."

"Oh, do tell. Where did you meet him?"

They spent the next ten minutes sipping their drinks and telling each other about their past boyfriends, except Lucy cautiously neglected to fill Kathy in on the nastier parts of her relationship with Patrick. She was doing her best to keep those locked away. If only the nightmares hadn't started up. She'd suffered the past week in particular, had found Trisha in her room on a few occasions, truly worried about her after she called out Patrick's name in her sleep.

Good old Trisha, she'd know what to do about the wreath. Lucy had tried to call her a few times, but it was obvious she was busy as her phone had gone directly to voicemail each time. Never mind, they could discuss it over their usual Friday night takeaway instead.

She had arranged to meet Matthew for dinner on the Saturday with a stipulation they stay away from the main house. She wanted some *me* time with him. He'd agreed and said he had something special he was bringing home for her from his latest business trip.

Lucy had locked up for the night, said farewell to Kathy, and was en route to her car when Trisha finally returned her call.

"Hey, you. Are you on your way home?"

"Yes, sorry, haven't had time to even take a piss today at work. He's such a bloody slave driver, worse when there's a show around the corner. How are things with you? What was so urgent that you've left me five messages throughout the day?"

"Nothing much, I'll tell you once you're home. Actually, I'll show you," she said, holding up the wreath she was carrying.

"Okay, I'm just coming down Johnson Way now. Shit…"

"Trisha? Are you okay?"

"No, I'm bloody not. The brakes have gone. I can't stop the car."

"What? Try again."

"I am trying. There's no response. Oh God. I'm speeding down this bloody road. Tell me what to do."

"The handbrake, can you use that?"

"I've tried, it's no good. Shit! Shit! Shit!"

"Stay calm, don't panic. I'm on my way."

"Great! What do I do in the meantime? There's nothing in front of me, but there are cars on the other side of the road. What if the steering fails next and I drift over?"

"Don't think like that." Lucy ran the short distance to her car, got in it and sped towards Johnson Way to see if she could intervene in some way. All the time she was driving, she kept chatting to Trisha. "I'll be there soon. Hang in there!"

"Like I have other options open to me. Jesus, I've got no control now. The car is shaking. I'm getting closer to the bottom of the hill."

"Good, the speed should die down then. I'm with you in spirit. Stay strong."

"I can't, my arms are killing me. I'm holding on to the steering wheel for dear life, and please, don't tell me to relax my grip. I can't do that, the car is trying to pull to the right, into the oncoming traffic. Fuck! No! Fuck!"

Those were the final words she heard Trisha say. They were followed by an almighty scream and a crunching sound, then silence.

15

"Trisha? Are you there? Can you hear me? Speak to me. Dear God, please let her be all right." She pushed her foot down hard on the accelerator, not caring one jot if she got pulled over for speeding. This was an extenuating circumstance, surely. Her friend was in dire need of help. The line was still open. She kept trying to call out to Trisha, to see if she'd respond. Her attempts were met with silence, each and every time. She brushed away the tears forming at regular intervals. "Remain focused, the last thing I need is to have an accident as well." She was in two minds whether to hang up and dial nine-nine-nine, then she thought better of it, hoping that someone at the scene would have the sense to do that for her, for Trisha. Her Trisha, the one constant companion in her life since their schooldays.

The one person who knew the truth, every tiny detail about her life, past and present.

"Oh shit, please, Trisha, don't you dare leave me."

She arrived at Johnson Way and hurtled down the hill towards the melee of cars at the bottom. The first thing she did was check her brakes. They were fine. What had gone wrong with Trisha's? Why had they stopped working?

It seemed a lifetime had passed before she made it to the bottom, and during the drive she tried to imagine the terror Trisha must have felt as she plummeted down the hill. Her neck strained as she peered over her steering wheel at what lay ahead of her. The closer she got, the more her fear levels spiked. The damage to Trisha's car devastated her. *Jesus! How could she survive the impact? Please let her still be with us.*

She ran towards the vehicle. "Please, let me through. She's my best friend. I need to get to her."

A heavily built man blocked her path. "Love, I wouldn't advise it. The car's a mess. I doubt she's survived."

Lucy braced herself and hurtled around the man, shrugging off the arms seeking to restrain her.

"Stop her, someone, for her own good. Don't let her get near," the man shouted from behind.

Several people ahead of her tried to prevent her from getting closer, but she managed to push them aside. Her struggle to get to Trisha was real and proved to be extremely forceful come the end.

So, here she was, standing next to the car, staring down at her beautiful friend. Trisha's face was crushed in on one side. Her eyes were closed, though, which gave Lucy hope. If they'd been open, she would have feared the worse.

"Okay, stand aside, please. Stop gawping there. Come on, move out of the way," a police officer said close to her.

He tugged on her arm, and she shrugged it off, like she had the others who had tried to keep her away.

"Trisha Wallace, her name is Trisha, and she's my best friend."

"Okay, Miss, thank you for the information. We've called for the fire brigade to assist us, they should be here soon. I'm sorry, I'm still going to have to ask you to stand back."

"I can't. Please, don't make me do that. She needs me."

"I'm sure you're right, but the emergency services will need access to the car—unhindered access. Come on, let's go, now."

Lucy turned to face him, tears streaming down her cheeks. "Is she still alive?"

"Let's get you back and away from here." He craned his neck and pointed. "The ambulance and the fire brigade have arrived. Come on, let's not get in their way." His touch was firm but gentle, and he guided her to the side of the road, to stand amongst the other onlookers.

She didn't want to be with them, she wanted to be with Trisha. Her dearest and most loyal companion.

Everything appeared to happen in slow motion after that. Witnessing her friend's rescue for thirty minutes seemed to her like watching a scene from *Casualty*, or worse still, *Silent Witness*. Only Trisha was thankfully, and remarkably, still alive.

"Please, I want to go with her to the hospital."

The paramedic and the officer who had restrained her exchanged glances.

"Okay, I'm fine with that, if you are," the officer replied.

"Thank you. I promise to behave myself. I just want to be there to support her. My car is that one over there. I can drive it to a safe spot and return later to pick it up."

"All right. Go ahead and move it. I think the brigade have almost got her free."

Lucy turned her back on the fireman using the Jaws of Life to cut Trisha free. She tore over to the car and raced back just in time to see four firemen gently lifting Trisha's broken and twisted body from the wreckage. They had placed one of those spinal boards under her back. Lucy closed her eyes and offered up a silent prayer, ashamed she didn't really believe in God—only at times such as this.

Trisha was transferred to the rear of the ambulance, an oxygen mask in place, and the paramedic set to work inserting a drip into her right arm. Once that had been connected, they set off for the hospital. Trisha was wheeled into the triage room in the Accident and Emergency Department. Lucy was instructed to wait in the family room. She collected a cup of coffee on the way and sat in a chair at the back of the windowless room. She picked up a magazine and leafed through it, not taking in any of the words. Her anxiety forced her to put the magazine back on the table and take up pacing the room.

Her mobile rang fifteen minutes later. "Oh God, I've been dying to speak to you. I thought you'd be on the road by now…"

"Wait, slow down. You sound strange, is something wrong?" Matthew replied, concerned.

"I'm at the hospital."

"What? Why? Are you hurt?"

"No, it's Trisha. She's had an accident." The tears fell, and a lump clogged her throat.

"And? Is she all right, Lucy?"

"No, Matthew. She's on the brink of..." Unable to finish her sentence, she dropped into her chair and sobbed. "I need you here with me."

"Fuck, I'm driving back now. It's going to be at least five hours before I can get there, love. I'm sorry you're going through this. Have you spoken to a doctor yet?"

"No, they're still working on her. Shit! I can't lose her, I just can't. She's all I have left."

"That's not true, you have me," he was quick to add.

"It's not what I meant. I'm sorry, I'm confused. I don't know what I'm saying. Please, hurry. No, don't, drive safely. Shit, see, I'm contradicting myself. Take care."

"I will. Don't worry about me. Ring me as soon as you hear anything, okay?"

"I'll do that. What if she dies?"

"Don't think that way. You need to think positively about this, love. She's a strong lady, she'll get through this."

"I'm not so sure. You didn't see the state of the car. Her body was all, well, twisted. I fear for her. Not knowing what's going on is driving me nuts."

"Be patient. If she's as bad as you say she is, they'll be working on her, doing their best to save her. I'll be there as soon as I can, Lucy."

"I'll ring you if I hear anything. Thanks for calling. I love you."

He professed his love for her and ended the call. She felt drained, as if all her energy had been extracted from all her limbs in the last hour or so. Had it only been that long since Trisha had rung her?

The door opened, and a sombre-looking man in his fifties entered. "Are you Lucy Brent, Trisha's friend?"

"That's right. How's she doing?"

He inhaled a large breath then let it out slowly. "She's surviving, so far. We've managed to stabilise her the best we can. We suspect she has internal bleeding going on as her blood pressure is dropping. We're going to send her for an MRI now, and then on to surgery if she needs it. The team are prepped and ready to go. Are you her next of kin?"

"I'm the nearest thing she's got. Why?"

"Precautionary question. Nothing is set in stone from here on in. She seems to be a fighter. Most people would've died from their injuries by now."

"Oh shit! Don't say that. What about her face? Can you fix that?"

"In time. Our priority remains to see what's going on inside. We've assessed the damage to her face, and reconstructive surgery will be necessary, eventually."

"Thank you for letting me know. Can I see her?"

"Not just now. We're going to transfer her in the next few minutes. I suggest you make yourself comfortable, or maybe go and get something to eat, to while away the time. You'll be in for a long night if you insist on sticking around."

"I'm fine. I couldn't eat, my stomach is tied in knots with worry."

"Very well. I'll come and see you as soon as I have more news."

"Thank you. Please do your best for her, Doctor."

"It goes without saying."

He marched out of the room. She watched him go down the nearby corridor and disappear through the swing doors at the bottom. Unsure what she should do next, she returned to her seat and picked up another magazine to zip through. This time, not even the pictures registered. Her mind was full of the doctor's words, which set her fear rising to yet another level.

Lucy stayed in the suffocating room for the next forty-five minutes and then decided to head over to the hospital canteen to grab something to eat to keep her strength up for the long wait ahead of her. She nibbled on the tuna and sweetcorn sandwich and glanced out of the window, at the beautiful sunset looming over the houses in the distance. Such a remarkable event that would usually be the cause of celebration, and instead, here she was, petrified, uncertain whether her friend was about to pull through or not.

She wandered back to the family room, and her weariness overwhelmed her. She huddled in the corner, rested her head against the wall and drifted off. The hospital's general hubbub woke her several times, but it didn't deter her from drifting off again. A hand touched her cheek hours later.

"Matthew, you made it."

He held out his arms and hugged her. She openly sobbed, unable to keep her true emotions in check.

"Hey, now, come on. Have the doctors not told you what's going on yet? I can go and demand to know, if you want me to?"

"No, damn, I forgot to ring you. They took her for an MRI earlier. The doctor warned me I was in for a long wait. He thinks she's got internal bleeding. They had an emergency team on hand and were going to operate once they had the results from the MRI." She inhaled a large breath.

"Okay, that doesn't sound too good. It's been hours. You should've heard by now. I'm going to see what I can find out."

"I'll come with you. I was exhausted and fell asleep. I shouldn't have done that, my head is bloody muzzy now."

"You stay here. I'll be back as soon as I can." He kissed her temple and left the room.

Despair lay heavily on her shoulders. However, the feeling was short-lived. Matthew returned within a few minutes.

"She's been taken to the Intensive Care Unit. They were about to come and tell you, only an emergency case came up and, well, time got away from them."

"That's all right, shit happens. Did they say how she is?"

"Alive, only just, apparently. Come on, let's go and judge for ourselves." He took her hand and led her out of the room and into the lift which took them up four floors.

They emerged and searched the signs for the direction in which they needed to proceed next. The nurse on duty appeared at the door and ran through the procedures with them. They used the hand sanitiser and entered the unit. All the beds were full, and Trisha was lying in the one closest to the window on the right.

"Shit! I'm not sure about this," Lucy said, taking a hesitant step onto the ward.

"I'm here. She's alive, keep telling yourself that." Matthew gripped her hand tighter and smiled. "Come on."

They approached the bed and stopped at the bottom. Silence rippled between them while they stared at Trisha. The blood had been cleaned up, but there was no mistaking the pain she was in, judging by the impact on her face.

"I didn't think she'd be this bad," Matthew muttered.

"I hope she pulls through. You can see why I was so distraught over the phone, can't you?"

"I can, love. We need to remain positive about her condition. She's in the best place possible."

"I know. I wonder how the operation went."

"Want me to ask the nurse to come over and fill you in?"

"If you wouldn't mind."

He left her side.

She inched forward and moved around the side of the bed. She rested her hand on top of Trisha's and squeezed it gently. "Come back to me, sweetheart. You can't leave me, I'd never forgive you."

Matthew and the nurse returned.

"The operation went as well as could be expected. The internal bleeding was detected and stopped. I'm afraid now we're in for a waiting game. At present, your friend is fighting tooth and nail to stay with us."

"She's a fighter, there's no doubt about that. How long will it be before she regains consciousness?"

"We don't know. We'll continue to monitor her closely. Look, why don't you go home and get some rest? We can contact you if there's any change."

"If you're sure. I've been here for hours. I'd feel bad deserting her now, though."

"That's only natural. Honestly, family members and friends need to realise that it's better for them to take advantage and to get the maximum rest at this early stage. That would be my advice. You can always ring us if you want to check on her progress. You won't be letting her down, I assure you."

"Okay, if that's what you think would be for the best. I'll leave you my number. Please, ring me day or night, and I can be here within half an hour. She means everything to me."

"Don't worry, I understand."

Lucy gave the nurse her mobile number, and she and Matthew said goodbye to the unconscious Trisha and left the hospital. Once outside, Lucy suffered a mini panic attack. She doubled over and struggled to grasp her breath.

Matthew pulled her upright and encouraged her to suck in a few deep breaths which she let out slowly.

"Thank you. Bloody hell, it suddenly dawned on me that she might pass away during the night and I won't be here."

"She won't. I promise you she's going to get through this, love. There's no point in you getting yourself worked up over this."

She glanced across the lawned area to the left and nodded. Something caught her eye. A man staring at her. She frowned, recognising him from somewhere. It wasn't until he started walking away that she noticed he had a limp. *What the hell is he doing here? Is it a coincidence?*

"Better now?" Matthew asked.

"I'll be better once I'm in the car." She shook her head to clear it from the dangerous thoughts running through it and allowed him to lead her to the car. She peered over her shoulder a few times, only to see the man had disappeared from view.

Her mind was a whirlwind of dangerous scenarios, most of them centred around the strange bearded man with the limp. *He shows up at the agency, and within days Shirley is murdered. Trisha is in an accident in her usually reliable car, and now I see him lingering outside the hospital. What's that all about? Should I report this to the police? They'd probably think I'm an idiot. What proof do I have that he's done anything wrong? Who is he? And what does he want?*

Matthew dropped her back to Trisha's house. He boiled the kettle and made Lucy a strong, sweet cup of tea. "Are you hungry?"

"Peckish, I couldn't eat a lot. I think I'd bring it back up again. Sorry, was that too much information?" She smiled weakly.

He hugged her and kissed the top of her head. "No, love. I bet your insides are tied up in knots, aren't they?"

"They are. My mind is thinking up all sorts as well. Oh God, what if she doesn't pull through this? What will I do without her? She's my rock."

He squeezed her tightly. "Don't think that way. You have to think positively, otherwise you might as well ring the funeral parlour now. She's in the best place possible. The doctors and nurses will see her back on the right road. I'm sure."

"You think? Her face…it was all mashed up. What if her brain has been affected? What then?"

"We'll deal with that if or when it arises. Come on, how about an omelette?"

"I couldn't eat a whole one."

He smiled at her. "Then we'll share one. I know you probably think I'm talking out of my arse, but please, try and remain positive. It's not worth going down the negativity route, it won't do you any good. You need to keep your spirits up at all times, you hear me?"

"Yes, Doctor Wallender."

He grinned and kissed her temple. "Let's get the ingredients out."

They worked well together, after which Matthew instructed her to sit at the table while he prepared the meal.

"Does she have any family? Should you ring them?"

"No, I believe that's why we're so close. We're all alone in this world." Sadness draped itself around her aching shoulders, and her head dipped.

Matthew darted across the room, placed a finger under her chin and forced her to look at him. He kissed her and said, "Let's get one thing straight, sweetheart, you're not alone, you have me and my family." Then he darted back to check the omelette wasn't burning. He placed the frying pan under the grill to fluff it up and grinned at her.

"Thanks, I needed to hear that. I don't mean to sound so down all the time. It's not been the best of times lately, what with Shirley getting murdered."

"All since I came into your life. Do you think I'm a bad omen for you?"

He was smiling when he said the words, but it didn't stop her mind working overtime.

What if he's right? Is a member of his family behind this? Are they trying to drive a wedge between us? Am I next? What? Who? Why? So many questions which need to be answered. I really don't have a clue where to begin.

"Hello, Lucy? Where did you go? I was only joking, you know?"

"I know. It just made me think, that's all. I'm concerned right now."

He dished up the omelette, set the two plates on the table and sat next to her. "Understandable. Why don't you stop beating yourself up about things until you receive the full facts from the police?"

She sighed heavily. "I know you're right, but my brain has a mind of its own. Ouch, that was terrible, did I really say that?"

He laughed and tipped back his head. "Yep, I'm afraid you did. Eat. We'll try and figure out what to do after we've filled our bellies."

She stared at her plate. "Hardly enough to fill my belly, but I'll give it my best shot." She stood and wandered over to the high cupboard and removed a couple of glasses. Then she took a bottle of wine from the fridge. "Should we? What if the hospital rings and asks me to go back there to be with Trisha?"

"They won't, and yes, you should, if only one glass, it'll help settle your nerves."

They ate in silence and cleared away the dishes after they'd eaten, then they retired to the lounge.

"Do you want to talk things through? Will it make you feel better?"

"I'm not so sure now. Maybe we'll snuggle up instead."

"That's my girl. Do you want to take your mind off Trisha by discussing the wedding?"

That's the last thing I want to talk about.

"If you really want to."

"I don't, I just thought you might want to."

"Not really. I think your mother has it all in hand, don't you?"

He angled her head upwards, and their eyes met. "Are you all right with that?"

She shrugged. "It's too late to prevent it now, isn't it?"

"Meaning?"

"Meaning, that all I want is you and me there really. It's our day. Why does it have to be attended by people we don't know—sorry, I'll correct that—people *I* don't know?"

"We can call a halt to things, it's not too late, if that's what you truly want."

"Bloody hell, if we even suggested that at this late stage, I'm sure your mother would have a goddamn fit."

He sniggered. "I think you're right."

They fell into silence again. Her eyelids suddenly felt heavy, and she drifted off in the comfort and security of his arms.

16

ive years ago

"*Y*ou bitch! If you screw this up for me…" Patrick's threat lingered in the air.

"What did I do?" she bit back, regretting it the instant the words left her lips.

Whack! Whack! Whack! The blows came thick and fast. One minute she was standing in front of him, and the next the force of his hits sent her hurtling face-first across the room. He pounced on her and continued the beating for nearly five minutes, although the time elapsed seemed an eternity to her as she scrunched up into a ball against the wall, trying to protect herself.

"No, Patrick, please, stop this…"

An arm surrounded her, and a distant voice filled her fogged brain. "Lucy, wake up, you're having a nightmare."

Lucy sat upright, tears running down her cheeks, and stared at Matthew. "Oh shit! I'm sorry."

"You cried out the name Patrick. Who's he?"

Averting her gaze, she shook her head. "Did I? I don't know anyone by that name."

He pulled her close and held her tight. "I'm not surprised you had a nightmare after what you've encountered recently."

She shuddered. *What the hell is wrong with me? Why does Patrick's name keep resurfacing when things go wrong? Guilt. It's my subconscious sticking the boot in, that's what it is.*

17

Matthew held her tightly throughout the night, sensing her need to feel the security of being in his arms. The next morning, her appetite had returned, and she got up early to surprise him with breakfast.

He came downstairs, dressed, ready to start his day. He wrapped his arms around her and kissed her neck. She almost dropped the frying pan she was serving up from.

"Down boy, we need sustenance."

"I know. How are you today? Any more nightmares during the night?"

"No," she lied. There had been a few, nothing as tense as the one that had surfaced on the couch the evening before, but they were prominent, nonetheless.

"Good. Shit, is that the time? I need to shovel this down my neck and get back home to get changed."

"Sorry, maybe I should've woken you earlier."

He waved away her concerns. "It's not your fault. I have a board meeting this morning that I need to prepare for. I'll ring ahead and get my PA on the case. It'll be fine."

Over their hearty breakfast of a full English, she asked, "Will I see you tonight?"

"I don't know, it depends how the day goes."

"Shall we give each other a miss tonight? That way I can go visit Trisha at the hospital."

"I'd love to be there to support you but…"

"I know. Please, you don't have to do that. I'll give you an update when I get home, how's that?"

"I'll miss you," he said, dipping a piece of toast into his runny fried egg.

"Me, too."

He shot out the front door after Lucy insisted she had enough time to spare to clear up the breakfast things. Once he'd left the house, she sensed the loneliness of her confines. She shook off the feeling and jumped in the shower. The warm water did little to prevent her from shuddering.

She dressed and left the house. Kathy was waiting for her on the doorstep.

"Gosh, am I late?"

"No, don't fret, I'm early. You look dreadful, by the way. Probably not what you wanted to hear first thing, I know."

"Gee, thanks. Rough evening. I'll tell you about it once we're set up for the day. I'm going to need my coffee on tap today, just warning you."

"Bugger, now you've got me intrigued. Spill."

"All in good time."

That time came around once the door was open to the public. They had a small flurry of customers filter into the shop first thing, and once they'd left, Kathy turned her chair to face Lucy's and motioned for her to spill the beans.

Lucy told her about the call she'd received from Trisha on the way home and what the consequences were.

"Shitting hell! Seriously? I'm so bloody sorry, Lucy. Should you be here today? I'm not surprised you look terrible. I wouldn't have slept a wink if that had happened to my friend."

"Was that supposed to reassure me or make me feel guiltier than I already feel?"

"Sorry, ignore me. Have you rung the hospital this morning?"

"Not yet, I haven't had time. I'll do it now." She picked up the phone and dialled the ICU and was told that Trisha had had a comfortable night and appeared to be responding well. When she asked if Trisha was out of danger, the nurse told her that wouldn't be assessed until later that day.

She hung up and exhaled a huge sigh. "I think it sounded good. I'm going to continue to be cautious, though."

"I don't blame you."

The rest of the day appeared to be full-on with enquiries which kept the pair of them busy right up until they closed that evening. She secured the front door and then set off for the hospital. Once she left the car, she searched around her, keeping an eye out for the limping man from the previous day. Thankfully, he was nowhere to be seen. She made her way up to the ICU and sat close to Trisha, holding her hand and talking to her for the next couple of hours until she dozed off in the chair. A nurse woke her and urged her to go home for the night.

Over the next couple of weeks, that was how her life panned out. Going to work and then straight up to the hospital. Matthew was away most of the time on urgent business, so she hadn't been accused of neglecting him at all. His mother called her several times, insisting they should meet up to discuss a number of niggles in the wedding plan. Lucy had to be firm and tell her that she couldn't spare the time, which went down like a bloody lead balloon.

Things remained tense between Cynthia and herself, but she had other things to worry about, like Trisha and her possible road back to recovery. Trisha was transferred to another ward after two weeks; she hadn't come out of her coma yet, but her vital signs had improved significantly in the past few days to warrant the move. The nurses on the new ward welcomed Lucy's visits. They had placed Trisha in one of the side wards. She was the only patient, so she wasn't disturbed.

After work on the Wednesday evening, Lucy arrived and spoke to Trisha. She left her bag beside the bed and nipped out to use the toilet.

When she returned, there was a commotion inside the room. She glanced through the slats in the blind at the window and watched the doctor and nurses working on Trisha until one of the nurses closed the blinds.

She offered up a silent prayer. "Please, please let her be okay."

The nurses filed out of the room around fifteen minutes later. The last one to leave gestured for Lucy to enter. The doctor was still checking Trisha over.

"What happened? Did she have a relapse?" Lucy asked breathlessly.

"We're not sure. She was doing fine. I'm a little perplexed, if I'm honest with you."

"Is she likely to have another episode? Shouldn't she be transferred back to ICU?" Lucy went around the other side of the bed, and that was when she spotted the piece of paper sitting on the side table. She chose not to mention it to the doctor. Her gaze was drawn to it every time the doctor looked away from her. She was eager for him to leave.

"I'll pop in before my shift ends. I'm sure she'll be fine. Will you be staying long?"

"A few hours, the same as usual."

"If anything out of the ordinary happens with her breathing, just call the nurse. She can page me, and I'll come back straight away."

"Thank you, Doctor."

He left the room.

She reached for the slip of paper and opened it. What she read almost brought her heart crashing to a halt.

*S*HE'S NOT THE ONLY ONE WHO KNOWS THE TRUTH

*W*hat the fuck? Who left this here? What the hell are they *talking about? My past? What I did to Patrick? How would anyone know that?* Her legs gave way on her, and she sank into the nearby chair. She reread the note over and over, her hands shaking uncontrollably until she dropped it into her lap, her heart rate erratic and beating fiercely. What could she do? Nothing. She couldn't confide in Matthew. How could she do that and not expect him to hate her after she'd confessed to him that she'd killed her husband? No one would understand if the truth ever came out. Only Trisha understood the trauma she'd been forced to endure as Jill Maxwell. The thought of someone knowing her real name and the crime she'd committed sent shivers constantly rippling down her spine. A cold sweat developed and broke out on her forehead.

What can I do about this? I should tell the police. Shit! Was she deliberately targeted because of her connection to me?

A nurse entered the room with a welcome cup of tea. "I thought you could do with this."

"You're too kind, thank you. Before she relapsed, did anyone come in here?"

"No. Only you, although I did have a mini emergency with Mrs Cook to deal with. Why? You think she had another visitor?"

"I'm not sure, she doesn't have anyone else. Can you prevent people coming in here in the future, except me, of course?"

"I'll have a word with the ward sister. I'm sure that can be arranged."

"Thank you. It would put my mind at rest. Is it all right if I use my phone in here, I mean, it won't affect the machinery, will it?"

"Just to be on the safe side, maybe make your call from the hallway instead."

"Can you watch Trisha for me, just for a few minutes?"

"Go on then." The nurse smiled and went about making Trisha comfortable while Lucy left the room.

She fished a card out of her bag, rang the number and asked to be patched through to DI Terry Warren, who she'd contacted regarding Shirley's murder. She explained the situation about Trisha being in a car accident. He told her to hold the line while he enquired if they'd heard anything about the accident.

"Miss Brent, damn, are you telling me that no one has contacted you since the accident?"

"No, I'm so sorry, perhaps I'm to blame for not chasing it up. What can you tell me?"

He sighed. "We have proof that your friend's car had been tampered with. Her brake line was deliberately cut."

"What? No way. Shit, why didn't someone tell me? Fuck..." She then went on to inform the inspector that Trisha's life had been in danger moments earlier, although she omitted to tell him about the note she'd found.

"Okay, I think we need to have a serious chat, Miss Brent, the sooner, the better."

"I'll be here a little while. I'm worried that someone is trying to kill Trisha. Can't you put one of your officers outside her room?"

"I'll get that actioned right away. Are you free for a chat this evening?"

"Yes. Do you want to come to my house, or shall I call in at the station on the way home?"

"Whichever is easiest for you."

"I'll see you at the station in half an hour, would that be okay?" She relented, thinking it was better to see him sooner rather than delaying the inevitable any longer.

"I look forward to seeing you."

She ended the call and immediately rang Matthew to bring him up to date on things.

"What? Her brakes were cut? What are the police doing about that?"

"Apparently nothing. The inspector wants a chat with me tonight. He's as furious about this as we are. Why would anyone deliberately try to kill Trisha? Not only that, there's Shirley to consider in the equation, too."

"I'm at a loss what to say or suggest, love. I'm sorry I can't be there with you. Do you want me to get Jake to stay with you?"

"No!" she said, too sharply even for her own ears. "Sorry, no. I'll be fine. I don't want to get anyone else involved in this, Matthew. Please be careful."

"Hey, it should be me saying that to you."

"I'll be fine. I'm going to sit with Trisha for a while and then go to the station."

"Don't forget to eat tonight and let me know what the inspector has to say about all this."

"You have my word."

They said their farewells, and she returned to the ward to sit with Trisha. The nurse promised she would check in on her friend every fifteen minutes during her shift, time permitting, of course. Before Lucy left, a police officer stepped into the room and introduced himself. She told him not to let anyone in as she was the only family member Trisha had.

On the way home, she dropped into the station and spoke to the inspector. Again, he was apologetic about her not being informed of the results and tried to pin her down as to why she thought her friends were being targeted.

She had to dig deep into her reserves not to reveal the truth. How could she tell him? And yet, didn't she have a responsibility to do just that? Confused, she ran a hand over her face and denied everything. Someone out there knew the truth and was using it against her, but how could she tell the inspector that? The person was an unknown—yes, she had her suspicions who *might* be behind the actions, but she couldn't be definite, and she'd be buggered if she was going to start dragging Matthew's family members through the mud. *Can you imagine what would happen if I did that? There would be no wedding for a start.*

Not that a wedding should stand in the way of the truth being exposed. *Crap, I can't do this. I need Trisha by my side to get me through this, she'd know what to do and when to do it.*

The inspector saw her out of the station, appearing to be unhappy about her wasted trip. She was remorseful about that and went home. She made a cheese sandwich and nibbled on it while she sat on the sofa staring at the black TV screen for what seemed like hours. It wasn't until Matthew rang around nine that she shook herself out of her reverie.

"How are things? Trisha?"

She closed her eyes, wondering how much she should tell him. "She seems a little better. They've moved her to a private ward out of the ICU."

"Wow, that's excellent news. Why don't you sound happy about that, love?"

"I am. I suppose I'm tired. It's been a long week so far, you know, having to work all day and going to the hospital every night."

"I hear you. No time to chill out before you go to bed and have to rinse and repeat. I'll be back tomorrow. Shall we go out for a meal, give you a break from going to the hospital?"

"I'll have to pop in for a quick visit, I couldn't live with myself if I didn't show up."

"Okay, only a quick one, though. If you don't get your rest, you're not going to be much use to Trisha, are you?"

"Yes, boss. I know you're right. She needs me, though."

"Is she still unconscious?"

Lucy rolled her eyes, knowing what was coming next. "Yes."

"Then she won't miss you for one night, will she?"

"Okay, you've worn me down. Are you going to pick me up?"

"Yes, at seven-thirty, how's that?"

"Sounds perfect."

She worked out that she would have enough time to make a flying visit to the hospital before coming home to get ready for when he turned up at seven-thirty. They chatted for another ten minutes about what had happened at work that week, both of them steering clear of the topic of the wedding, which they agreed to speak about in person and never over the phone.

She ended the call, ran a bath and slipped into bed. Lucy drifted off to sleep not long after, but a noise woke her around midnight. Thinking she'd imagined it in her sleep, she tried to doze off again. Another noise sounded outside below her bedroom window. She hurried across the room and peered through a slit in the curtain. There was nothing there from what she could tell. All was quiet until she heard something downstairs. Her heart skipped several beats, and her stomach constricted.

Someone is in the bloody house. Her gaze darted around the room. *Damn, I've left my phone downstairs. Shit! Shit! Shit!*

Trisha didn't even have a house phone in her bedroom either. Lucy swallowed down the lump that had emerged in her throat and crept across the room, acting braver than she felt. She eased open the door and crept out onto the landing where she strained her ears to listen. Things were definitely being shifted downstairs, drawers being opened and closed. A door, probably the lounge, directly below her, opened. She retreated into the bedroom and locked the door, then she went over to the window and cursed Trisha for having small double-glazed units. There was no way she would be able to squeeze out through the small window at the top of the sealed unit. She peered over her shoulder.

The handle turned.

Tears of frustration burned her eyes, and she placed a hand over her mouth to prevent herself from screaming.

Shit! What if the person breaks down the door? There's no way I'm going to be able to get away from them.

She scanned her surroundings in search of some kind of weapon, but nothing sprang to mind. There was a bed, a wardrobe and a chest of drawers, not even a bloody chair that she could've ripped the leg off to use. She was doomed if the person managed to break down the door.

Maybe it's a burglar chancing his luck. Did I leave the back door open? I don't think I did. Shit! I need to check and double-check every door and window from now on. That thought process isn't going to help this situation, though, is it?

She expelled a breath when the person gave up and moved on to Trisha's room next door. Again, the sound of drawers being opened filled the house.

This has to be a burglar. If only I'd thought of bringing my phone up to bed with me. I'm stuck here, no way out until they leave.

Lucy remained glued to the spot, frozen in time, listening to what was going on next door. A floorboard on the landing squeaked. The person tried her door handle once more. Lucy sucked in a breath and didn't let it out until the stairs creaked, signifying that the person was going back downstairs. The question was, how long did she leave it before she opened the door and left the room?

In the end, when everything quietened down, she unlocked the door and gingerly made her way downstairs. Her hands out in front of her in the darkness, she went into the kitchen and found the back door ajar. She raced across the room and locked it. Then she switched on the light and hissed. "Crap, that was a close one."

"What was?" a voice sounded behind her.

She screamed and spun around to see Neil standing there. "Jesus, you scared the frigging shit out of me. What are you doing here?"

His eyes were glazed as if he'd been drinking. "I miss her. I wanted to come over and be amongst Trisha's things."

"Halfway through the damn night? Are you for real?"

He ran a hand through his already mussed-up blond hair. "I'm sorry. I forgot you were here."

"How could you forget that? Anyway, what were you searching for? I heard you rifling through the drawers down here and in Trisha's bedroom."

"Umm...I was searching for a decent photo of her. I told you, I miss her."

"If that's the case, why haven't you visited her at the hospital, Neil?"

"I can't bring myself to go there. I lost my grandfather a few years ago and find it difficult to visit those places."

"Really? Even though Trisha is in dire need of your support? How can you be so selfish at a time like this?"

"Don't start on me, Lucy. I need to go to bed."

"Not here. Go home, Neil."

"I need to be near her. I'm not going anywhere."

"Okay, I can't make you. Do you want a drink?"

"Yeah, a whisky would be nice."

"I was thinking more along the lines of a coffee. By the look of you, I think you've had enough alcohol for one evening."

"Don't nag. I get enough of that from Trisha."

"I wasn't aware that I was. Bloody hell, Neil, what's wrong with you? You haven't even asked me how she is."

"I haven't had the chance to ask."

She filled the kettle and switched it on, then turned to face him with her arms folded.

He lunged forward and tried to kiss her.

She managed to step to the side before he made contact. "What the fuck are you doing?"

"I've seen the way you look at me. As if that rich fiancé of yours isn't enough for you. Come on, with them both out of the way, what's stopping us from getting it on?"

"You're fucking sick! Get out of this house, now." Her anger erupted, and she pushed him towards the back door.

"I know your sort, you like to object, but given the opportunity, you'd bed any man going."

She thumped his back. "Get out, you sick frigging bastard. I don't know where you've got that idea from."

"Trisha keeps nothing from me. I know."

Her mouth dropped open. *Trisha would never betray my trust, would she?* "That's bollocks, and you know it."

"Is it? Dark secrets…secrets that could emerge when the timing is right. Are you truly willing to take the risk?"

"You're bluffing. You know nothing. You know how I know that?"

He frowned, as if her words had confused his addled mind.

"Because there's nothing to tell."

"Isn't there? The truth will out in the end, I'll make sure that happens."

She flew at him, her arms acting like the sails of a windmill in a turbulent storm. She caught him several times in the face. He cried out and tried to defend himself with his raised arms, but the blows continued to rain down on him. For once, she was the abuser and not the victim. She didn't enjoy the role reversal, but it appeared to do the trick. Neil ran out of the kitchen door and down the garden path. She closed the door, locked it, leaned back against it and panted, trying to recapture the breath she'd expelled. Then the tears came, fast and furious. Her skin crawled with imaginary insects. She had no idea Neil felt that way about her. Was his outlandish behaviour purely down to the drink? She didn't have a clue.

She checked all the doors again, made herself a drink and took her phone back upstairs with her, ensuring she locked herself into her bedroom on the way back to bed.

She shuddered and pulled the quilt over her head. The thought of Neil laying his hands on her the way Matthew did turned her stomach upside down. No matter how hard she tried, sleep evaded her the rest of the night.

*L*ucy showed up for work looking and feeling like a cast member from *The Walking Dead*. "Bloody hellfire, what the heck is wrong with you?" Kathy said the second she laid eyes on her.

"I'll tell you over a coffee. Fancy a cream cake or have you already eaten breakfast?"

"No, I'm fine. You stay here, I'll go fetch you one."

Kathy left her to set up the agency for the day and returned with the biggest coffee choux bun Lucy had ever seen. "There you go, that should fill a hole or two."

Lucy laughed. "I should say. What a night I've had." She went over what had happened at the hospital and at home with Neil, leaving out the part about the note she'd found.

Kathy sat there open-mouthed throughout. "Fuck, what a cheek! Did you know he had feelings for you?"

"No. To be honest, I think it was probably the drink making him braver than he is. It was totally unsettling nevertheless."

"I'm not surprised. The audacity of the man. You won't tell Trisha, will you?"

"If she ever comes out of her coma, you mean? I don't know. I feel like I have a duty to say something, but…"

"You can't. Well, let's just say, I could never do that to a friend."

"Seriously? Look at it from the other perspective. As her best friend, shouldn't I tell her what her boyfriend gets up to when she's not around, let alone bloody lying there unconscious in hospital?"

"Hey, okay, I never thought of it that way."

The first customer entered the front door, and from then on, their day turned out to be non-stop. They even worked through their lunch, only managing to find the odd ten minutes to shove a sandwich down their necks, even though the coffee was on tap during the day as usual.

Lucy closed up the business and drove to the hospital for a fleeting visit with Trisha. She found no change in her friend and left after fifteen minutes. She returned home and jumped in the shower and was all dressed and ready to go when Matthew showed up at seven-thirty. It had been a mad panic, but she'd made it.

They had a wonderful stress-free meal. He was buzzing about his week away and the deals he'd managed to secure that he predicted would bring in a lot of business to his firm. Lucy was delighted for him.

Once he'd shared his good news, he reached for her hand. "Tell me what sort of week you've had?"

"Hectic beyond bloody words, but you know what? I got through it, which is more than can be said for Trisha."

"I'm sorry, love. I know how hard this is for you. Didn't you say the nursing staff and doctor are happy with her progress?"

"Yes, it's not the same as having her sitting up in bed and holding a conversation with me, though."

He nodded. "I don't suppose you've had a chance to chat with Mother about the wedding in my absence, have you?"

"Sorry, I've been far too busy. I hope she isn't offended by my lack of input. It's just that what with everything going on at work and with Trisha, I really can't divide my attention more than that at present."

"She's fine. I'll have a word. Maybe we could go up to the house tomorrow, in the evening and discuss things then?"

Lucy smiled and sighed a little. "If we must."

"You're a star. I'll give her a ring and let her know."

Matthew dropped her home that evening but decided he needed to go back to his own place rather than stay with her for the night. At first, she was a little put out by that, until fatigue kicked in and she found herself grateful that he'd made the right choice.

After ensuring the doors were locked properly, Lucy went to bed, taking her mobile with her this time. Sleep overwhelmed her swiftly, and she dropped off soon after her head hit the pillow. However, just like the evening before, a strange noise woke her. This time she rang nine-nine-nine and made them aware of the situation. The woman on control instructed her to remain in the bedroom and told her that a patrol car had been dispatched to take a look. The blue light lit up her bedroom. She raced down the stairs and spoke to the uniformed officers who checked the back and front thoroughly but found nothing. She waved them off and returned to her bed.

In the morning, as she descended the stairs to put the kettle on, she found something lying on the doormat. It was a note. In capital letters it read:

*S*ECRETS ALWAYS COME OUT IN THE END

"*W*hat the fuck is going on? Who could be doing this?" She had her suspicions, and maybe it was time she acted upon them, even if it did cause trouble between her and Matthew. She couldn't deal with this any longer. It was beginning to weigh heavily on her shoulders, on top of everything else she was having to cope with.

Matthew was expecting her at six that evening. She worked until one at the agency and then spent a few hours sitting next to Trisha at the hospital. As she was leaving, a miracle happened and Trisha opened her eyes. The staff asked her to leave the room for a few minutes while they tended to Trisha. She watched her dear friend through the window. Trisha seemed dazed and confused. The nurse had a quick chat with Lucy, told her not to expect too much at this early stage and encouraged her to go back in and speak to her friend.

"Hello, stranger. How's it diddling?"

Trisha frowned and shifted in her bed. "Sorry, do I know you?"

She experienced a sucker punch to her stomach and tears moistened Lucy's eyes. Her best friend had woken up and hadn't even recognised her. She approached the bed and grasped Trisha's hand. Trisha tugged her hand free again.

"It's me, Lucy." She leaned in close and whispered, "It's me, Jill. Don't you recognise me, love?"

"No. I don't know you. Lucy or Jill, I don't know you. Leave me alone."

"But we're like sisters."

The door opened, and the nurse entered carrying a fresh jug of water which she placed by the bed. Trisha seemed agitated, and the nurse checked to see if she was okay.

Trisha shook her head. "No, get this woman out of here. I don't know her. I want to be alone."

"But, I'm…her best friend. She's all I've got."

The nurse nodded and ushered Lucy out of the room. "I'm sorry. These things happen. It's all going to take time for her to re-establish her identity."

"Oh, Christ! I thought she'd come round and everything would be like normal again. How long will it take?"

The nurse shrugged. "That's the sixty-four-million-dollar question. None of us know. Go home. Ring later, see how she's getting on then, eh?"

Disappointed, she went back in the room to fetch her bag. "Goodbye, Trisha, I'll see you soon."

Her friend cowered which deeply hurt her.

Lucy rushed off the ward and broke down once she was in the lift. "Why? She's all I've got, and now I have nothing."

Lucy drove home on autopilot and flopped onto the sofa in the lounge. Her thoughts remained with Trisha but also, selfishly, she recognised what this could mean to their friendship. What if the truth came to Trisha and she revealed her as being a murderer, what then? What was left of the afternoon, which wasn't much, slipped by in a daze, and by the time Matthew came to pick her up, she'd worked herself up into a frenzy.

"Are you all right? You look dreadful."

"It's Trisha, she's awake."

He hugged her and then pushed her away from him. His hands gripping the top of her arms, he tilted his head and asked, "What's the problem? You should be happy. Instead, you look as though she's just died."

"Maybe she has, to me," she mumbled.

"What? I don't understand, love."

"She woke up and didn't recognise me."

"Oh, no! But it's to be expected. Her face had a bad impact; it probably affected her brain. I'm sure it'll come back, eventually."

"How do you know that?" she snapped and wriggled out of his arms to pace the floor.

He shook his head. "She nearly lost her life. I don't understand your reaction to this."

"I'm sorry if you think I'm blowing everything out of proportion here, but she's all I've got left in this world."

He raised an eyebrow.

"Except you, of course."

"And my family," he added, causing her to wince.

"I want *her*. I want things to be the way they used to be. Her life as she knew it ended the day of the accident. I don't think she'll ever get her memory back again."

"You can't say that. It's an unknown quantity right now. Let's go, you need to get out of here."

"And spend the evening discussing a wedding with your over-bearing mother?"

He took a step back and stared at her. "Is that what you truly think?"

She waved a hand, dismissing her previous comment. "No, yes, oh, I don't know. Everything is so confusing to me."

He flung an arm around her shoulders. "Which is why you need to get away and be distracted by something else. What better than our nuptials?"

She sighed, unable to argue with his logic. Maybe it would be a good distraction after all.

Matthew fetched her coat and shoes from the hallway and handed them to her. She slipped them on and was ready for the off. Her heart rate fluctuated on the journey over, and a thousand butterflies took flight as she entered the main house. She was aware that her clothes weren't suitable for her surroundings and found it difficult to suppress the shame that had draped itself around her shoulders.

Matthew's mother eyed her warily as they entered the living room. "Hello, Lucy, it's lovely to see you again."

Lucy smiled. "You, too, Cynthia."

"We have good news. Trisha, Lucy's friend, has regained consciousness at the hospital."

"That's marvellous news. Will she be coming home soon?" Cynthia asked.

"I doubt it. She has no recollection of who I am, or who she is, for that matter."

"Oh, my dear, what a terrible situation. If there's anything I can do to help, you must let me know."

"Thank you. I will. I know we're here to discuss the wedding, but you'll have to forgive me if my mind isn't fully on the task in hand."

"Of course. We'll eat first and then get down to the nitty-gritty."

They gathered around the table, the five of them, Jake included. Lucy drifted off during the meal. No one seemed to mind and continued their conversations as if she wasn't there. If that had occurred at any other time, she probably would have been offended, but not tonight.

After the meal, they retired to the drawing room. The table was set up at the back of the room. Cynthia linked arms with Lucy and steered her towards it.

"Let me show you what I've managed to achieve so far. We're only a few weeks away now. The media interest is growing."

"It is?" Panic shot through her like a poisoned dart.

"Of course. It's to be expected. I may have had a hand in that, I might add. I have a few friends who own a couple of high-society magazines who have insisted on running articles regarding the wedding. You don't mind, do you?"

She shook her head. "No, ignore me. I never dreamed that type of thing would happen, that's all."

Cynthia laughed. "I think you're forgetting what family you're marrying into, Lucy."

"Probably, although, in my defence, I've had a lot on my mind lately."

"You have indeed. Here you go, what do you think? The only thing that has caused me minor problems is the lack of family on your side. It's traditional to have the bride's family on one side of the church and the groom's on the other."

"Sorry if that's been bothersome for you. Can't your family take up both sides?"

"I can't believe you have no one. Not even a distant uncle or aunt perhaps?"

"No. I only have Trisha. I doubt she'll make it now."

"That is a shame. Just to warn you, over the coming week, I'm going to need your input."

"For what? Haven't you got everything in place already?"

Matthew and his father left the room, leaving Cynthia and Jake with Lucy. Jake approached the table. Lucy found herself sandwiched between the mother and son, and an overpowering feeling of suffocation seeped through her veins.

"Now that Matt is out of the way, we wanted to have a wee chat with you," Jake said.

"Oh, about anything in particular?" She struggled to keep the anxiety showing in her voice.

"Mother and I have been doing a little digging into your past."

Here we go. Maybe I was right all along and they're both behind what's been going on. Would they go as far as killing Shirley, though?

She shuffled her feet a little and swivelled her head between them, undecided who to look at for the best. "And?"

"And, we discovered a Lucy Brent obituary from five years ago."

"How strange. In this area? What are you implying?"

Jake's chest inflated. "Yes, in this area. She was a different age, though, but it got us thinking, nevertheless. So, I dug deeper, and you know what, Lucy?"

She shook her head. "What?"

"You don't exist. Can you tell us why?" Jake sneered.

The door opened, and Matthew and his father entered the room. Jake and Cynthia took a few paces back, at least giving her room to breathe.

Shit! That was close. But they know the truth, or at least part of it, that I'm not who I say I am. They're bound to corner me again. I need to try and think up a plausible excuse. It's obvious they're gunning for me. The question is, how far are they prepared to go? They clammed up as soon as Matthew came back in the room. What about Shirley and Trisha? Are they both responsible for what's happened to them?

A sudden headache emerged. She stepped away from the wedding display and approached Matthew. Slipping an arm through his, she whispered, "I have a bad headache, would you mind if we go home now?"

He glanced down at her, his expression one of concern. "Have you covered everything Mother wanted to go through?"

"I think so, yes."

"Then we'll go. You've had a tiring week. I thought this might be too much for you. I'll make our excuses."

Outwardly, she smiled weakly, but inside she was jumping with joy. Their early departure was sure to piss Cynthia and Jake off, and she couldn't help but wonder what the consequences were likely to be.

Matthew insisted they stay at his place for the night. Lucy agreed, as long as she was still able to go to the hospital in the morning. She needed to keep up her visits with Trisha, in the hope that her friend's memory would soon return. She didn't have the foggiest idea what to do about the situation if it didn't. She was worried with a capital W.

18

The following week proved to be as anxiety-filled as the previous one. Trisha had started to remember tiny parts of her childhood memories, however, she was still very wary of Lucy every time she visited, which continued to be every day. She would never let her best friend down and cast her aside, not when she needed her the most.

So far, she'd avoided dealing with Cynthia and Jake personally, only answering Cynthia's calls regarding the wedding when she was forced to. Her responses were always clipped and brief.

The day before had been one of her hardest to date. Matthew had accompanied her to Shirley's funeral. There had been a large gathering, and everything had gone well until something had caused Lucy to shudder. Sensing someone was watching her, she scanned the crowd behind her and saw a man take flight, the man with a limp.

That encounter had petrified her enough for her to want to leave the wake early and to make her way home. Again, she blamed her early escape on a headache and insisted with Matthew that she wanted to spend time alone at the house.

She had come to regret that decision around midnight. She heard someone outside and peered out of the window. Standing close to the gate, staring up at her was the bearded man with the limp. Too scared to confront him, she climbed back into bed and wrapped her arms around her knees, pulling them tight into her chest.

Shit! Who is he? What the hell am I going to do? Trisha would know, but she's not here. I'm all alone in this now. I can't rely on Matthew to help me, not without revealing the truth to him. But why should I do that? Who is this man? Are Cynthia and Jake behind his sudden emergence? But why? Do they truly despise me that much?

The next day, she opened up the agency as normal, even though her lack of sleep was now hampering her way of thinking. At around eleven, after Kathy had made them both a coffee, the door opened, and Jake walked in.

"Whoa! Hunk alert..." Kathy joked.

Lucy rolled her eyes and whispered, "You'd steer clear if you had any sense." She left her seat to greet him. "Hello, Jake. Looking to book a holiday, are you?"

"No. I wanted a private chat with you."

"I'm busy."

He glanced around and back at her, his eyebrows raised. "Hmm... Dozens of invisible punters, I see."

"What do you want, Jake?" she asked, folding her arms defensively, her heart racing out of control the more his gaze seared through her.

"Is there somewhere private we can chat?"

"There is. Why should I want to be alone with you? Every time that happens, you make me feel uncomfortable with your threats."

He laughed. "Another objection. Do you have something to hide, Lucy?"

His words came out louder than his previous ones, and Lucy peered over her shoulder to see if Kathy had heard. She hadn't, at least, she wasn't giving the impression that she had. Her head was down as she studied some paperwork.

Lucy tugged on Jake's arm and steered him through the nearby door to their small staffroom. She gestured for him to take a seat and rested against the sink, her arms still folded. "What do you want? I don't have long."

"I wanted to pick up where Mother and I left off with you the other day. Tell me, what is it you're trying to hide from us, Lucy, if that's your real name?"

She swallowed, and the noise appeared to echo in the confined space, which put a smile on his face. "Who says I'm hiding anything?"

"We do. But most of all, every time we raise the subject, you look shifty."

"Wouldn't you, if the same two people kept hounding you about something you've denied over and over again? Why won't you take my word for it? What are you hoping to achieve, Jake?"

"I'm trying to safeguard my brother."

"Have you mentioned this to Matthew? Oh no, that's right, you and your bullying mother backed off when he returned to the room the other day. What the…?" She refrained from swearing, in spite of the temptation to do so.

"We're trying to protect him."

"From what? Me?"

"If we have to, yes. Mother and I have been digging into your past…"

"Yes, you already mentioned that, and you found nothing, right?"

"Nothing is correct, as in you, young lady, don't even exist. We want to know why."

She released her arms and clenched and unclenched her fists. "I have nothing to hide."

"You don't sound convincing, and the evidence proves otherwise."

She frowned. "What *evidence*?"

"Or lack of it, I should have said. I *will* get to the bottom of this, it's only a matter of time, Lucy." With that, he let out a frustrated growl and stormed out of the room.

When Lucy returned to the shop, he'd gone. She let the breath she'd been hanging on to seep through her lips.

Kathy frowned. "Everything all right, Lucy?"

"Yeah, I'll survive."

"Who was he?"

"My future brother-in-law."

"Oh, heck. The expression on his face when he left, well, he looked as though a bee had stung his backside."

In spite of her anger, Lucy roared with laughter. "You're too funny. Right, let's get on."

They had another successful day despite Jake's interruption. Lucy closed the front door and dropped in at the hospital for a brief visit. This time her heart skipped a beat when, instead of cowering away from her, Trisha smiled a little at her presence. Not wishing to overload her friend emotionally, Lucy kept her distance, even though she was eager to gather Trisha in her arms.

She stayed at the hospital for an hour and then drove home. Matthew was away again on another business trip. He assured her that once they were married he'd be delegating all the travel side of things to his right-hand man.

Lucy parked the car and gasped. Her bravery spurred her next actions. She left the car and flew across the road. The man with the limp started running, glancing over his shoulder as she got closer. Suddenly, it dawned on Lucy what she was doing, and she stopped chasing him.

What if he has a knife? What if he kidnaps me? What if, what if, what if?

Tears blurred her vision, and she made her way back to the house. She entered the front door and attached the chain. Now she felt like a prisoner in her own home.

Who the hell is he? He has to be keeping an eye on me and reporting back to Jake and Cynthia while Matthew is away.

During her meal preparations, she ran through the different scenarios in her head. Should she confront Jake and Cynthia? Try to tackle the man once again? Surely that would mean putting her life in danger, wouldn't it? Truthfully, she didn't know which way to turn for the best. All she sensed was things were about to come to a head. Would that be before the wedding or after?

---

19

*T*he next few weeks took place in a whirlwind. Trisha's memory had improved daily to the point of her calling her Jill when Lucy had visited her last. Luckily, they were alone in the room so no one else heard it.

Having Trisha back and on the road to recovery had lifted her spirits considerably. Matthew was the same caring man she'd fallen in love with. He made sure he rang her every day to tell her how much he was looking forward to the wedding. She had to admit, now that everything was in place and the ceremony was only a few days away, she couldn't wait to be called Lucy Wallender.

There was a negative to all of this, though. The man with the limp had become a constant part of her life. She should have called the police weeks before, but her past had prevented her from doing that. If only she could have laid her cards on the table with Matthew and his family. The truth was, she couldn't. Maybe it was Cynthia's and Jake's intention to try to drive her crazy, having the man with the limp follow her all the time. It hadn't worked. She'd been through so much in her young life already with her evil, dearly departed husband that anything anyone was likely to throw at her now could be classed as inconsequential by comparison.

Life was full-on. It consisted of going to work at the busiest time of the year for holiday bookings, visiting Trisha daily, being joyful of the significant improvement in her friend, to Cynthia arranging final fittings for the wedding dress. Everything happened in a haze right up to the last minute.

Trisha came home the night before the wedding. Although she was on a lot of medication, she raised a glass to Lucy all the same. They settled down on the couch for a long natter. It turned out to be an emotional evening for both of them. Trisha fell asleep on the sofa at around ten-thirty, exhausted by the emotion and the excitement to come. Lucy went upstairs to get Trisha's quilt and covered her over as she slept.

She kissed her forehead and whispered, "I'm glad you're with me. Tomorrow wouldn't have been the same without you there by my side."

Lucy locked the doors and windows and went to bed. The night whizzed by without incident and, when she came down the next morning, another note was awaiting her on the doormat. She tore it open and read it:

*I*N SICKNESS AND IN HEALTH UNTIL DEATH US DO PART

*W*hat the fuck is that supposed to mean? Lucy poked her head into the lounge. Trisha was snoring gently under the quilt. She went over to the window and eased back the curtain to find the man with the limp standing on the other side of the road, staring at the house.

Fuck! I've had enough of this jerk. She flew out of the house to confront him, but by the time she opened the front door, he'd vanished. She scanned the road—there was no sight of him.

For her own sanity, and the fact she was getting married in a few hours' time, she had to put the man out of her mind. She was still convinced Jake and Cynthia were behind the stranger's stalking behaviour.

She made toast and coffee and joined Trisha in the lounge.

Sleepily, her friend sat up and smiled at her. "Never thought I'd say I've had the best night's sleep in ages while sleeping on the sofa."

"Glad to hear it. You're looking well on it."

"Sod me. How are you feeling?"

"Nervous as hell. I have a confession."

"Uh-oh! Let's have it."

Lucy crossed the room and collected an envelope from the drawer in the dresser. She removed the contents and handed them to Trisha. "Read these and tell me what you think."

Trisha frowned as she devoured the information on the notes. "What the fuck are these?"

"Notes that have been left for me, mostly here, but that one"—she pointed at the one Trisha was holding in her left hand—"that one was found by your bed in the hospital."

"Bloody hell, don't say that, you're going to freak me out."

"It's true. The nurses and doctors had to resuscitate you."

"Why? No! Are you saying that someone tried to kill me?"

Lucy nodded. "There's something else I've kept from you."

"Which is?" Trisha's eyes widened.

"I hate telling you this, but I think you need to know. "The brakes on your car were cut."

"Deliberately cut?"

Lucy nodded and sighed. "So it would seem. There's also been a man stalking me."

"My God! Why didn't you tell me this sooner? No, don't answer that, you were trying to protect me. Bloody hell, Lucy, you have to go to the police."

"How can I? We've come so far. If I open my mouth now…I'll end up in prison."

"You won't. It was self-defence. That man abused you for years, and you never retaliated, not once."

"Not true, love. I killed him in the end. The greatest form of retaliation there is, for God's sake."

Trisha threw back her quilt and stood. She toppled forward.

Lucy caught her and eased her back onto the sofa. "Take it easy. I'm sorry, you're not yet strong enough to hear all of this."

"I am. You should've told me sooner. What's going on? Do you know?"

"Jake and Cynthia know I have a secret. They keep pushing me to reveal it. I think they're behind this man stalking me. Their aim, to unnerve me, possibly make me call off the wedding."

"Really? Surely if they had doubts about you, wouldn't they openly confront you?"

"Who knows what rich people get up to? I was mulling things over. Maybe this is why Matthew has never had a serious relationship in the past."

"The mother and brother scared them all off, is that what you're saying?"

"Yes." Lucy threw her arms out to the side then slapped them against her thighs. "Oh, I don't know. I suppose we'll find out today just how far the pair of them are prepared to go."

"No. Call it off if you suspect things are going to get worse. I don't want you putting your life at risk, nothing is worth that, love. Nothing and no one, no matter how much you love Matthew."

"I know you're right, however, wouldn't that only be letting them win? Why should I give up on the love of my life, merely because his family object to me? He loves me, shouldn't that be all that matters in this?"

Trisha fell quiet and sipped her coffee. "I appreciate you confiding in me. I don't have all the answers, though, lovely. My head's still a mess. I wish I could help you out, but I can't, I'm not capable at the moment."

Lucy rushed to sit beside her. "I'm sorry, I should never have burdened you with this. It's my problem, not yours. I'm such a selfish cow."

"You're not. Don't say that. My suggestion would be to tell Matthew, have it out with him before you tie the knot."

"What if he dumps me?"

Trisha shrugged. "My guess is he wouldn't do that. Is it a risk you're prepared to take?"

Lucy buried her face in her hands and mumbled, "I can't lose him. Not now."

"You have my blessing, either way, love. Time's marching on. You're going to have to consider getting ready soon."

"I know. I'll mull it over as I get ready. Hey, we need to get you washed and dressed, too. Do you want a bath?"

"I'd love one, will there be enough hot water?"

"Of course, I'll stick the boiler on."

*M*atthew called her at eleven to check how things were going. She was relieved to hear his voice. One hour later, and they would be walking down the aisle together. He told her the car was due to pick her up at eleven-forty-five. He'd also arranged for another car to transport Trisha to the ceremony. That had shocked her—she'd presumed Trisha would be going with her. Never mind, she'd enjoy the journey on her own. Maybe *enjoy* would turn out to be the wrong sentiment once her nerves kicked in.

The two lifelong friends stared at each other in the full-length mirror in Trisha's room.

"You look breathtaking. The most beautiful bride to ever grace this earth."

"You're so sweet. Ugh…I feel a bit of a fraud, you know, wearing white."

"It's your first true wedding. Ignore the other disaster, love. That's all it was. This one is forever and ever. Matthew is crazy about you."

A contented sigh escaped. "I hope so. I'd dread to think what I'd do without him by my side now. He's sending two cars for us. I presumed you'd travel with me; he had a different idea."

"That's a shame. Looks like he has it all in hand."

They hugged and left the bedroom. Lucy went over to the window in the lounge, half expecting the man with the limp to be there. He wasn't. *Maybe he's finally got the hint.*

"Oh God, the cars are here."

Trisha stood beside her at the window. "Not long now before you take your vows. I'm so thrilled for you. You promise you'll stay in touch, won't you?"

Lucy spun around to face her. "Are you kidding me? We'll never lose touch, ever. We've come so far together in this life."

"Oh shit! Don't start me off. My mascara is likely to run."

"It's waterproof and super-expensive, it'd better not. Are you ready?"

"Are you?"

"I think so. Let's do this."

They left the house, and the two drivers held open the respective back doors for them to enter.

"Good luck," Trisha shouted, getting into the car.

"Thanks. See you at the other end, lovely."

The driver dipped his head and closed the door.

Inside, the smell of new leather eased into her nostrils. She noticed the small window was open between the driver and herself. To calm her nerves, she struck up a conversation with him.

"Lovely day for it, little nip in the air, though, all the same."

"Aye, there is that."

"Do you drive for the Wallenders?"

"Aye, I do."

"For how long?"

"Several years now."

She noticed the man's eyes fix on her in the rear-view mirror. He seemed pleasant enough. The conversation died down between them. Lucy rotated her head from side to side to ease out the tension in her neck. The traffic ground to a halt ahead of them. *I hope we make it on time. I can't stand being late.*

The cars set off slowly. She watched out of the side window and smiled as they passed the cars next to them. Most of the drivers raised their thumbs at her. She smiled in return. The church close to the Wallenders' mansion was only a few streets away now.

"Do you think we're going to be late?" she asked the driver.

"Nope. Sit back and enjoy the ride, Miss Brent."

Something about the way he said her name made the hair on the back of her neck stand on end.

She tried to relax, but her stomach knotted when the car veered off in the wrong direction. "What are you doing? The church's that way. We're almost there, ignore the traffic."

"Leave things to me. I know a shortcut," he called over his shoulder.

Suddenly, the locks on the door clunked.

"What are you doing? I want to get out. Stop! I'll make my own way there."

She glanced over her shoulder, saw the other car, with Trisha inside, turn and stick to its original course. Fear rippled every nerve ending.

"Please, what are you doing?" The strain was now showing in her voice.

The driver put his foot down. Ten minutes later, he stopped at a clearing. He turned in his seat to face her and removed the contacts from his eyes and the thick-rimmed glasses. There was something familiar about him. *Shit! The man with a limp.*

"You. What do you want with me? I know Cynthia and Jake have put you up to this."

He laughed and tilted his head back, and then his hand went to his chin and he ripped off his beard.

Lucy thought her heart was going to stop there and then. *No! This can't be happening... It can't be him... It's impossible!*

"Recognise me now, Jill?"

She closed her eyes, in an effort to blank out his familiar features.

"Look at me, *bitch*."

Her eyes shot open. The past five years disappeared into obscurity. She was back there, with him. On that plane.

"How did you escape?" she whispered.

"How indeed. No thanks to you trying to kill me, Jill. Thought you'd start up a new life and I wouldn't be able to track you down, did you? You failed, bitch."

"I wanted to start over. I'm sorry for what I did," she murmured.

"Sorry for *murdering* me, you mean?"

"Yes, no. Shit! Let me go. I have another life now. I'm happy, leave me in peace."

"Even if I let you go today, you wouldn't be able to marry him. You're forgetting one thing: you're still married to me. You're still Mrs Patrick Maxwell."

She covered her mouth with her clenched fist, forcing back the scream threatening to break free. Her life as she knew it was now a figment of her imagination. Her whole being smashed to smithereens. A far-off pipedream, out of her grasp.

He would abduct her, keep her locked up somewhere for the rest of her life. Knowing what he was capable of, she had to escape, but how? The doors were locked, there was no way out.

"I need some fresh air."

"The windows still work."

She lowered the window and debated, for a split second, whether to jump out or not. She was slim enough, but her huge marshmallow of a dress could possibly hamper her progress. She decided it was a risk worth taking. Lucy darted through the window before he had a chance to stop her. She landed on the ground with a thud, her head hitting the concrete, leaving her dazed for a second or two. The car door slammed. *Shit! I have to get away! Get up and go!*

But it was too late. His hands dug into her arms, preventing her from taking flight. *Think, think, how do I get away? I have to get away, otherwise he's going to kill me.*

Her arms rotated, mimicking a windmill on the Norfolk Broads. She clobbered him a few times, enough to send him off balance. She took her opportunity to jump to her feet. Sinister thoughts ran through her mind. Her shoes, she'd use them as weapons, it was all she had. She stomped, driving her stiletto with force into his instep.

"You, fucking bitch. You're gonna pay for that."

During his cussing, she slipped off her shoes, grabbed one of them, hitched up her skirt and took off. Up ahead there was a small wooded area. Before long, she was under the canopy of the trees. Lucy hid behind a thick tree trunk and used the time to fill her lungs with oxygen and to mull over what to do next. Until she heard footsteps behind her. She peered around the trunk. There was no one there. *It was your imagination, idiot!*

She turned back, prepared to run again, only to find Patrick standing in front of her. She attempted to scream but his hand slapped over her mouth. He had her pinned to the tree with his knee and his other hand was up her skirt, searching for her panties. *No! No, I won't allow him to do this to me. Never again. If I die trying to fight him off, then so be it.*

Lucy bit down on his hand and shoved him back. She hit him numerous times with the heel of her shoe. "You, bastard. Get your filthy hands off me! Never again, you hear me?"

He cried out each time the heel punctured his body but his glare never faltered. "Bitch, you won't get away with this, not this time. I'll hunt you down until the dying breath leaves your scrawny body. I killed your friend. She died a pitiful death, just like your parents!"

She paused, her arm raised high above her head. "What? You did that? To Shirley? To Mum and Dad?"

"Yep, I did it all. Ran you off the road, cut the brakes on Trisha's car. Interfering busybody she is. I should have realised you would've counted on her for help. I should've come back and killed her years ago, except I thought you were dead then. I still wanted your parents to pay. They never did like me, did they?"

"They saw through you. They say love is blind—in my case that was true. Why I ever loved you I'll never know. You killed that over the years, with all your beatings, just like you killed our baby."

"You would never have coped with a kid."

"How would you know? Having a child would've helped me to cope living with a cruel, barbaric individual like you. Maybe it was better for my child to die. I couldn't have taken it if you'd started abusing it the way you abused me."

"I didn't *abuse* you. You enjoyed my rough treatment. You needed guidance. You weren't capable of thinking for yourself."

"You didn't *allow* me to think for myself. You, manipulative fucker. I wish you'd died in that crash…"

"But I didn't. Your attempt was thwarted. Did you really think I couldn't read what was going on in that pretty little head of yours? As if I would load the plane up with only one parachute. I jumped out not long after you, thankfully, before it started to descend. It was touch and go whether the plane would hit the mountain or not."

"Why didn't the authorities track you down? Your name was on the flight."

"You're not the only one who changed their identity. It was simple, as you proved."

"How…how did you find me?"

"I searched for you for days. All these years I believed you were dead. Until I saw the picture of you attending that charity function with your new beau. You were suddenly the talk of the town. You might've changed the colour of your hair but I instantly recognised you. I used to spend hours watching you sleep next to me. Every curve of your face was imprinted in my mind. You were, no, you are, the love of my life. Let's start over again."

To think this man perceived how he treated her all those years as love, absolutely floored her. She had to get away from him. She didn't want to know how he tracked her down or how he'd lived the past five years. All she wanted was to get away from him and begin her life anew, with Matthew. Anger surged through her core, ensuring she had the strength to end this, once and forever.

"You'll never lay another finger on me again, never, do you hear me?" She hit him with her heel, over and over, until he slumped to the ground, not moving. She inched closer and touched his neck with her fingers. There was a pulse.

His hand gripped hers. Lucy screamed and thrust her knee in his face then ran. Ran for her life.

Her dress was torn and nearly hanging off her. She didn't care what she looked like on what was supposed to be the happiest day of her life. All she was concerned about was getting as far away from him as possible.

She tripped on a branch buried in the undergrowth, lost her balance and fell flat on her face, but she got up immediately, finding the strength and stamina to continue her escape.

Nearing the edge of the woodland, a row of houses appeared. Lucy spotted someone in one of the gardens. She cried out, "Please, please you have to help me."

The woman's expression was that of a rabbit caught in the headlights and she backed up inside her house, slamming the door on Lucy, and any hope she had of being rescued. She wiped away the tears burning her eyes. *Please, won't someone help me?*

She glanced over her shoulder to see the limping Patrick, his face crimson with rage, coming towards her.

She screamed, hoping the noise would bring someone else out of their home. Nothing, no one offered to help her. There was nothing for it, she had to continue running. She had the upper-hand on him, at least, or she thought she did. He wasn't capable of sprinting—she was. She filled her lungs to capacity and bolted down the alleyway she spotted between the houses. It wasn't until she was halfway down the narrow passage that it occurred to her it could have been a dead end. Fortunately, it wasn't. Her breath was ragged as she struggled to synchronise her breathing and running.

Someone shouted behind her, "Oi, you, leave her alone. I've called the police, they're on their way."

Thank you, thank you, there must be a God up there, after all. Lucy emerged from the alley and found herself in the main road. Horns tooted and jeers rang out from some of the drivers. She ignored them and headed towards the church spire in the distance. All she wanted was to feel Matthew's arms around her.

A car drew up beside her and the passenger door flew open. "Lucy, bloody hell. Get in. Where have you been? I've been going frantic. What the hell happened to you?"

"Oh, Matthew…" She got in the car and melted into his arms. Horns blasted. The lights had changed and they were holding up the traffic. Nervously, she glanced over her shoulder to see Patrick standing at the end of the alley, glaring at her. "Please, go. Let's get out of here, Matthew. I'll explain everything, just go!"

"Who did this?"

"Go, please, listen to me. We need to get out of here. I can't marry you, Matthew. I need to talk to you. Once you've heard what I have to say, you'll probably want to dump me."

His eyes narrowed. "What are you wittering on about? Don't you love me any more? Is that why you want to call the wedding off?"

She looked back and then pleaded, "Just go!"

He put his foot down and an awkward silence descended between them. Twenty minutes later, he drew up outside a quaint thatched pub close to the river. "I'll get us a drink. I think we're going to need one."

In his absence, she contemplated how to tell him about her messed-up life and the lies she had told. *Let's face it, our whole relationship has been one big fat lie.*

He came out of the pub. "Come on, let's go and sit down by the river."

"As long as you promise you won't be tempted to drown me."

"What are you saying? Are you crazy? Nothing you could tell me would ever make me want to do that, Lucy." He shook his head.

They walked in sombre silence. Matthew carried the drinks over to the picnic table close to the riverbank. Lucy stared at the ripples in the water for a while and then turned to look him in the eye.

"What's going on, Lucy?" His face was pale as if all this had taken its toll on him.

She inhaled a breath and let it seep out slowly. "First of all, my name isn't Lucy, it's Jill. Up until today, I thought I was a murderer."

He leaned back and almost tipped off the seat. "What? I don't think I heard you right. Run that past me again."

"You did! Five years ago, I was married to Patrick Maxwell. Throughout my marriage he abused me. I suffered daily beatings at the hands of that man. He even killed the child I was carrying during one of his thrashings. And no, I'm not using that as an excuse, it's a fact. I couldn't take it any longer. He hired a plane; he had a private pilot's licence. I came up with a plan to attack him during the flight. I didn't care if I died with him at that point. But then I spotted a parachute on board and decided to escape instead. Once I'd landed and dusted myself off, I heard the plane crash on the other side of the mountain. I thought he had perished in the wreckage. Only Trisha knew the truth. She was aware how much I'd suffered at his monstrous hands. She helped protect me. She was the one who sourced a new identity for me."

"Holy shit! I don't get it. So what happened today? Wait, let me tell you one thing first. I found the driver of the car unconscious in the garage, that's why I came looking for you. Trisha told me the wedding car had gone in a different direction. I've been out of my mind with worry, and driving around, searching for you ever since."

"The driver turned out to be *Patrick*. He's still alive, Matthew. I didn't tell you, but for weeks, I've had a man with a limp stalking me."

"For Christ's sake! Why didn't you tell me, Lucy?"

She smiled and placed her hand over his. "I couldn't. I was dumb enough to think he was something to do with your mother and Jake. That they had paid him to scare me, enough for me to want to give up on our life together."

He snatched his hand away, ran it through his hair, loosened his tie and undid his top button. "What the hell are you talking about? What's my family got to do with your ex...er...your husband?"

"Your mother and Jake have been suspicious for weeks. They've been hounding me to tell them the truth about my past. They cottoned on a while back that I had something to hide, but they hid their suspicions from you. None of this was intentional. The last thing I anticipated was falling head over heels in love with you. You're my soulmate."

"What? Oh God, what the hell are you telling me? All this has been a lie, Lucy?"

"Yes and no. I had to shield the truth from you, but my love for you is real, I swear it is."

"Hang on, there's also the fact that you were prepared to become a bigamist in all of this."

"No, I wasn't. You're not listening to me. I thought, no, I presumed, he was *dead*."

He ran a hand over his face. "I can't get my head around this. You're not making sense. If you thought he was dead, why did you go to the bother of changing your name and your identity?"

"I was confused at the time. I thought if the authorities discovered his body and worked out that Patrick had been murdered, the police would come after me."

"Okay, I get that. I think. Bloody hell, this is all such a mess. What now? He's still out there, he won't let things lie, will he? I wouldn't if I was in his shoes."

"I don't know what to do."

"How did he know where to find you?"

"He told me he saw us together when the pictures of the charity ball were released and knew instantly it was me. Yes, I've changed the colour of my hair over the years, but my facial features are still the same."

"Jesus, you need to go to the police."

She bowed her head and stared at her glass. "I know I do. I know I have no right asking you this, but will you come with me?"

"Why should I?" he snapped.

She rose from the seat and headed back to the car. He caught up with her, spun her around to face him, and then hugged her.

"I'm sorry, I shouldn't have said that. Of course I'll come with you. I want this sorted out as much as you do."

Tears of relief spilled down her cheeks.

EPILOGUE

*S*ix months later

*L*ucy, who had now reverted back to Jill, had accompanied Matthew to the police station on the day of their wedding. After she had laid out the truth to DI Warren, he wasn't best pleased with her but, after he'd calmed down, he told her he understood why she had gone to the lengths she had to get away from Patrick.

Here they were now, she and Matthew, still hiding out at the family's holiday home in Scotland. Matthew had forgiven her and sworn that he would never leave her side until Patrick had been captured. He'd lived up to that promise.

They were walking hand in hand along the private beach when the news broke. Matthew answered his phone and smiled at her. She stood back, her hands clutched together, praying that Patrick had been caught. He had.

They danced around in a circle and tumbled to the sand, elated by the news. The past few months, which they had spent living on their nerves, were over now. He was no longer out there. They were free.

*T*hey packed up and returned to Bath, to their respective homes. She'd missed Trisha so much and regretted that she was absent during her reconstructive surgery on her face which had taken place three months before. Her skin was still showing signs of recovery, but all in all, the surgery had been a huge success.

The police spent two days questioning Patrick. He'd pointed the finger at Jill, told the officer in charge that she should be arrested for attempted murder. However, DI Warren refused to believe a word that came out of his mouth and arrested him for the murder of Shirley as well as the attempted murder of Trisha and Jill. Her parents' deaths were still being investigated but Warren told her Patrick would likely be charged for those too, soon. The counter charges Patrick tried to file against Jill were rejected. There was a new law which had recently come into force in the UK, protecting abused women and the lengths they were prepared to go to, to keep themselves safe.

The next step had been to face Matthew's family. She found it exceedingly tough explaining to them and apologising for the terrible lies she had told. Graciously, they had accepted her apology, and to her relief the wedding was back on and due to take place once the divorce from Patrick was finalised.

After that meeting, Cynthia had taken her to one side and given her a piece of her mind. Jill hadn't been perturbed by that, as she would've probably done the same thing in her shoes.

Once everyone's life reverted back to normal, Keith had welcomed her back as manager at the travel agent's after she'd revealed the truth. He told her Shirley would have wanted it that way. She was bowled over by his willingness to forgive all her sins. If it hadn't been for Shirley taking her on, her dear friend wouldn't have been killed. Keith assured her none of that mattered now.

A few weeks later, on her day off, while she was in the process of packing boxes ready to move into Matthew's gatehouse, she rushed to the bathroom and heaved. Trisha shoved a pregnancy test under her nose. "Use it."

"What? You think I'm *pregnant*?"

"Doh!"

After she did the test, Trisha linked arms with her, and together, they watched the blue line develop. Cheers rang out and they jumped up and down. All this proved to be too much for Jill and she ended up heaving down the loo again.

"Wow, what's Matthew going to say?" Trisha asked.

"I'm not sure. Bloody hell, it's not him I'm concerned about, it's Cynthia. Shit, she's going to hate me all over again when she hears about this."

"She won't. The fact you'll be carrying her first grandchild will make her think twice about going over the top, I'm sure."

"I hope you're right. I need to think of a way of telling Matthew. We've been through so much together in the last year. What if this news is too much for him and he decides to leave me?"

"Now you're talking out of your arse, girl. He loves you. Seriously, do you think he would've stuck around all this time, if he didn't?"

Jill sighed. "Fingers crossed."

"Think positive. Why don't you tell him you want to cook him dinner tonight, a special meal and tell him then?"

"Good idea." She called him at work. "Hello, it's me."

"I know it's you. Is everything all right?" She could sense the smile on his face.

"Of course. I wondered if I could come over this evening to cook for you."

"Now that's an offer I'm not likely to turn down. What's the special occasion?"

"Cheeky. I'll tell you later."

"I'll look forward to hearing it. I've got to go, I have a meeting planned. Love you."

"See you soon."

She and Trisha spent the rest of the morning sorting out a menu, not that she had much of an appetite as her morning consisted of visiting the toilet a few times.

Together, they finally decided on a menu of steak in a pepper and mushroom cream sauce with a sticky toffee pudding for dessert, reminiscent of their first meal together.

Matthew greeted her lovingly, the way he always did, admiring the dress she'd chosen to wear. "You look stunning, some might even say radiant. Have you had a good day?"

"The best. Trisha took a sickie and wagged some time off with me."

"That's unlike her. I'm glad you spent the day together. I know how much you've missed her lately. Have I got time to change?"

"Of course."

He made an effort, like she had, and put on a smart pair of trousers and contrasting cream jacket. She served up the steak and they chatted about general things all through the meal.

"Wow, that was amazing. Your cooking sure has improved lately."

"Cheeky sod. What are you saying? I was a crap cook before?"

He held out a hand and she took it. He drew her onto his lap and kissed her. "Nope, you've always been perfect to me."

She chewed her lip, hesitating.

"Something wrong?"

"I was just wondering how you would react…"

"React to what?" he frowned.

"To being called…daddy."

"What? Are you serious?"

She held his hand over her stomach and smiled. "Yes, we're with child."

He beamed and kissed her. "I do believe you've just made me the happiest man alive."

"What about the wedding? What will your mother say?"

"Who cares about the wedding? We'll elope. She might not be too thrilled about that but she'll be over the moon about the baby."

"Elope?"

"Yes, we'll go back up to Scotland at the weekend."

She laughed. "While I love your enthusiasm, I think it'll be too late to expect an opening at the weekend."

"If you don't ask, you don't get." He pushed her off his lap and reached for his mobile to place the call. Ten minutes later, after making several calls, he announced, "We're sorted. The registrar can fit us in Monday morning."

She laughed. "However did I cope without you being in my life?"

"I'm not sure. Happy?"

"That's the understatement of the century. I love you so much, Matthew."

"You're the reason I get up in the morning. The baby will only make me love you more than I do right now, if that's possible."

A note to you, the reader -

Dear Reader,

What a twisted read that was.
An intriguing tale nevertheless, I'm sure you'll agree.

If you enjoyed I KNOW THE TRUTH perhaps you'd be interested in reading one of my police procedural thrillers.
Pick up your copy of the first book in the DI Hero Nelson series here.
TORN APART

Thank you for your support as always. If you could find it in your heart to leave a review, I'd be eternally grateful, they're like nectar from the Gods to authors.

Happy reading
M A Comley

KEEP IN TOUCH WITH THE AUTHOR

Newsletter
http://smarturl.it/8jtcvv

BookBub
www.bookbub.com/authors/m-a-comley

Blog
http://melcomley.blogspot.com

Join my special Facebook group to take part in monthly giveaways.

Readers' Group

Printed in Great Britain
by Amazon

45921016R00147